Krysty lay ... gasping

Her vision smeared back into being—tripled, doubled and then finally was normal. She felt as if it had just rained hammers. Every cell of her body ached, and she tasted the copper of a nosebleed in the back of her throat. She reached out. "Ryan…"

Mildred moaned.

Krysty blinked at the afterimages behind her eyes and yawned at the ringing in her ears. "Ryan…"

Every muscle screamed as she shoved herself up to her knees. Krysty snapped her glance around the jump chamber in a panic. She, Mildred, Jak and J.B. were in the same gateway of the same redoubt.

Ryan and Doc were gone.

Other titles in the Deathlands saga:

Cold Asylum
Twilight Children
Rider, Reaper
Road Wars
Trader Redux
Genesis Echo
Shadowfall
Ground Zero
Emerald Fire
Bloodlines
Crossways
Keepers of the Sun
Circle Thrice
Eclipse at Noon
Stoneface
Bitter Fruit
Skydark
Demons of Eden
The Mars Arena
Watersleep
Nightmare Passage
Freedom Lost
Way of the Wolf
Dark Emblem
Crucible of Time
Starfall
Encounter:
Collector's Edition
Gemini Rising
Gaia's Demise
Dark Reckoning
Shadow World
Pandora's Redoubt
Rat King
Zero City
Savage Armada
Judas Strike
Shadow Fortress
Sunchild
Breakthrough
Salvation Road
Amazon Gate
Destiny's Truth
Skydark Spawn
Damnation Road Show
Devil Riders
Bloodfire
Hellbenders
Separation
Death Hunt
Shaking Earth
Black Harvest
Vengeance Trail
Ritual Chill
Labyrinth
Sky Raider
Remember Tomorrow
Sunspot
Desert Kings
Apocalypse Unborn
Thunder Road
Plague Lords
(Empire of Xibalba Book I)
Dark Resurrection
(Empire of Xibalba Book II)
Eden's Twilight
Desolation Crossing
Alpha Wave
Time Castaways
Prophecy

TORONTO • NEW YORK • LONDON
AMSTERDAM • PARIS • SYDNEY • HAMBURG
STOCKHOLM • ATHENS • TOKYO • MILAN
MADRID • WARSAW • BUDAPEST • AUCKLAND

First edition March 2010

ISBN-13: 978-0-373-62601-4

BLOOD HARVEST

Printed in U.S.A.

O miserable man, what a deformed monster has sin made you! God made you "little lower than the angels"; sin has made you little better than the devils.

—Joseph Alleine
1634–1668

THE DEATHLANDS SAGA

This world is their legacy, a world born in the violent nuclear spasm of 2001 that was the bitter outcome of a struggle for global dominance.

There is no real escape from this shockscape where life always hangs in the balance, vulnerable to newly demonic nature, barbarism, lawlessness.

But they are the warrior survivalists, and they endure—in the way of the lion, the hawk and the tiger, true to nature's heart despite its ruination.

Ryan Cawdor: The privileged son of an East Coast baron. Acquainted with betrayal from a tender age, he is a master of the hard realities.
Krysty Wroth: Harmony ville's own Titian-haired beauty, a woman with the strength of tempered steel. Her premonitions and Gaia powers have been fostered by her Mother Sonja.
J. B. Dix, the Armorer: Weapons master and Ryan's close ally, he, too, honed his skills traversing the Deathlands with the legendary Trader.
Doctor Theophilus Tanner: Torn from his family and a gentler life in 1896, Doc has been thrown into a future he couldn't have imagined.
Dr. Mildred Wyeth: Her father was killed by the Ku Klux Klan, but her fate is not much lighter. Restored from predark cryogenic suspension, she brings twentieth-century healing skills to a nightmare.
Jak Lauren: A true child of the wastelands, reared on adversity, loss and danger, the albino teenager is a fierce fighter and loyal friend.
Dean Cawdor: Ryan's young son by Sharona accepts the only world he knows, and yet he is the seedling bearing the promise of tomorrow.

In a world where all was lost, they are humanity's last hope....

Chapter One

"Move! Move! Move!"

Ryan Cawdor and his companions needed little urging as they ran for their lives through the empty corridors of the redoubt. The facility they found themselves in was nothing but an empty concrete bunker. Whoever had occupied it had bugged out long ago and taken everything of value with them. Dead campfires, graffiti and bones—human, animal and otherwise—showed there had been successive waves of habitation. At some point someone had managed to breach the main clamshell doors and then the interior ones. The spent shells of various makes littering the floors showed there had been many room-by-room firefights. It was odd that the victors hadn't bothered to retrieve the spent brass.

The companions' cautious venture outside the redoubt had drawn more stickies than the friends had shells to waste.

They raced for the mat-trans chamber. The pounding of their boots was counterpointed by the staccato slapping of scores of bare stickie feet behind them as the muties gazelled after them in rubbery, ground-eating bounds. "J.B.!" Ryan shouted. "Gren!"

The Armorer clawed into a pocket of his jacket as he ran and came out with his last grenade. "One!"

"Do it!" Ryan roared.

The party passed the corridor junction, and as they turned J.B. pulled the pin on the grenade. The cotter lever pinged away and he tossed the bomb behind them. The hollow crack of the detonation echoed in the halls. Stickies hooted and shrieked. They loved fire and explosions. Unless it ripped their heads off, even stickies directly caught in them didn't seem to mind so much.

The companions charged toward the corridor that led to the hexagonal mat-trans unit. Ryan stopped and shouldered his Steyr longblaster as his people went through the doorway that led to the control room. "J.B.! Close it!"

The door to the mat-trans was made of vanadium, and Ryan knew it would take powerful explosives to breach it. However, once it closed, the transportation cycle occurred, and Ryan wasn't quite ready to eliminate all other options. The chamber door didn't always lock. The outer door to the control room was ordinary steel. When the companions had arrived they had found the door jammed three inches ajar, and it had taken J.B. a good ten minutes of tinkering with the mechanism to get it to open. J.B. took a knee beside the inner control panel for the door and began fiddling with its guts.

"Hurry," Ryan advised.

J.B. twisted the exposed wires of the keypad together.

The stickies came around the bend in a fish-belly-white, boneless wave. Shrapnel scored some of the muties' bodies, but it wasn't slowing them. Doc stepped into the doorway and drew his LeMat revolver from beneath his frock coat. The weapon boomed as he fired the shotgun barrel, and the lead stickie's head was pulverized by the fist-size swarm of buckshot. Doc cocked the weapon again and pushed the hammer cone up to fire the pistol chambers of the weapon. For Doc Tanner the choices of being torn limb from limb by stickies or taking a mat-trans jump were equally revolting propositions. He took aim and shot a second stickie between its huge, shark-black eyes.

Ryan took aim with his blaster. "J.B...."

"Working on it!" J.B. snarled.

Ryan cut loose. The range was swiftly closing to spitting distance, and he fired in rapid semiauto and went for the head shots. Pale skulls popped like pumpkins but more muties kept piling forward from behind. Even at close range the bobbing and weaving heads of the stickies weren't easy targets. The corridor filled with the gray clouds of Doc's ancient black-powder weapon as he methodically cocked and fired. He fired his last shot and stepped back. "Empty!"

Jak Lauren instantly stepped in and his .357 Magnum Colt Python began detonating like dynamite in the echoing confines of the corridor.

Ryan slammed in a fresh mag. "J.B...."

Wires sparked between J.B.'s hands. "Got it!"

Ryan and Jak stepped back as the steel door squealed and ground against the floor. Ryan's lips split into a silent snarl as the door shrieked, then stopped, leaving the same three-inch gap they had first found. "Fire... Blast! J.B.!"

The Armorer threw up his hands. "The door's shot! No way will it shut."

Everyone jumped back as the stickies hit the door in a wave. The jammed portal rang and rattled as dozens of stickies slammed their rubbery bodies against it. Others shoved their suckered hands through the gap and began heaving at the steel with grotesque, elastic strength.

Jak sighed as he pushed fresh shells into his revolver and stowed his empty brass. "Jump."

Ryan eyed the door. He suspected it would hold, but Jak was right. They were low on food, water and ammo. The companions would have to come out sooner or later, and with low cunning the muties knew it, too. Ryan knew from hard experience that stickies could wait for days, days that his friends didn't have. Two jumps within an hour was as ugly as it got, but there was no way around it. "Yeah, we're jumping. We're jumping now."

Krysty stared steadily at the mat-trans chamber. "Lover, I got a bad feeling."

Ryan turned his single eye on his woman. Krysty Wroth was the most beautiful thing in his life. She was tuned in to Mother Earth, and he had learned long ago to trust her intuitions, but the fact was the mat-trans was the only way out. The one-eyed man ran a hand through the silken length of Krysty's scarlet tresses and her hair coiled around his fingers with a will of its own. Ryan smiled wearily. "Got no choice. We have to go."

Her titian tresses coiled tighter around his hand. "There's something bad hovering on the other side."

Ryan nodded. "Usually is." He looked at the other companions. "Let's do it, and hope the stickies aren't smart enough to open the chamber's door."

Krysty, Jak, J.B. and Mildred stepped within the glittering armaglass walls and selected a place to sit on the mat-trans's floor. Ryan turned a sympathetic eye on Doc as the old man stood at the doorway, staring at the mat-trans in trepidation. Dr. Theophilus Algernon Tanner had been ripped through time and space from the nineteenth century to the twentieth, where he had been mentally, physically and quantum mechanically experimented upon in brutal fashion until he had finally been flung forward a further century into the nuke-shattered America that had come to be known as Deathlands.

Doc had a low threshold for being dematerialized.

"Doc." Ryan often had to remind himself that the damaged, old-man body encased a man his same age. "We've got to go."

"I know." Doc stepped boldly into the mat-trans unit, but his hands shook as he did it. "By all means let us be on our way." Mildred held up her hand. He took it and sat on the floor beside her. Ryan stared in weary exasperation at the keypad in the wall. It did them no good. They had no destination codes for the matter-transfer device, so a jump in a mat-trans was a jump to anywhere. All they could do was activate the device by closing the door and hope for the best. Ryan depressed the lever. The door hissed shut and seconds later a mist began to coalesce as he strode across the chamber and sat beside Krysty. The disks in the floor and ceiling began to glow and flash. Doc groaned and buried his face in hands.

Krysty felt the pressure build up behind her eyes, and a roiling sensation began in the pit of her stomach. She brought a hand to her forehead as she felt the sucking darkness enveloping her. Ryan had once described the visual effect before the utter oblivion of dematerialization as patterns of red roses.

Krysty screamed as she saw lightning behind her eyes.

Something was terribly wrong. Her vision went black, but there was no momentary sense of oblivion. The lighting continued to crash inside her skull and she heard screams, some of which were her own. Her matter wasn't being transferred. Instead it felt as if a giant dog had picked her up in its jaws like a shoe and was savagely trying to shake her into her component atoms. The sensation ended with the abruptness and brutality of an ax stroke.

Krysty lay on her side gasping. Her vision smeared back into being, tripled, doubled and then finally a slightly skewed normal. She felt as if it had just rained hammers. Every cell of her body ached, and she tasted the copper of a nosebleed in the back of her throat. She reached out a palsied hand. "Ryan…"

Mildred Wyeth moaned.

Jak and J.B. were too busy puking to swear. Something in the female anatomy allowed a slight edge in withstanding the physical horror of a mat-trans jump but not by much. Krysty blinked at the afterimages behind her eyes and yawned at the ringing in her ears. "Ryan…"

Every muscle screamed as she shoved herself up to her knees. Krysty snapped her glance around the jump chamber in a panic. She, Mildred, Jak and J.B. were still in the same gateway of the same redoubt.

Ryan and Doc were gone.

Chapter Two

Ryan surfed into the terrestrial plane of existence on a wave of his own vomit. He groaned as he pushed himself to his hands and knees, shaking like a dog as he was wracked by heaves. Despite the nausea and disorientation, he knew something was very wrong. The armaglass walls were a veined chartreuse Ryan didn't recall from any past jumps. Ryan spit and wiped his chin. "Lover, are you all right—"

The one-eyed man shot to his feet, blaster in hand.

He and Doc were alone in the chamber. Ryan looked around wildly, lurched to the control panel and hit the Last Destination button. The display began to peep and ran a stream of letters, numbers and symbols that meant nothing to him. Ryan's shoulders sagged.

He punched the LD button twice more and got no further response. Ryan strode over to Doc, who was huddled in the corner, his knees folded into his chest, and rocking with his eyes squeezed shut as tight as fists. For most of the companions a mat-trans jump was like a surprise punch below the belt followed by an uppercut to the jaw. For the man time-trawled from the past, a jump was like a knife through an already damaged brain. At the moment there was no time for sympathy. "Doc, you've got to get up." Ryan shoved Doc's cane into his tremoring hand and hauled him to his feet.

The scholar put a hand on the glowing wall to steady himself. He shook his head and struggled to focus. Ryan stepped out of the chamber with his rifle leveled and didn't like what he saw. The redoubt, if it even qualified to be called that, was just a gutted and broken concrete blockhouse. A cold wind whistled through holes in the walls and through missing sections of roof. The sky above was gray, bruised and pregnant with rain. The wind was whipping up to storm conditions. There were only two things of interest in the cold, bare space. One was a great metal hatch in the floor. Whatever alloy it had been made of gleamed as bright as the day it had been forged and untouched by time. It was sunk in the floor almost seamlessly. Three raised panels in the center formed a triangle, but they were as seamless as the hatch and Ryan could see no way to access any of the controls inside them. Black blast streaks around one panel showed that someone had tried with explosives and failed. Ryan ran a finger over one of the blast patterns, and the streak in the residue showed gleaming metal that hadn't even been scratched.

The second item of interest was a corpse.

It was the body of a woman. Ryan eyed her desiccated flesh. Her black hair was cropped short around her skull like a helmet. Her skin was drawn tight against her bones, and her mummified corpse swam in the undyed homespun tunic clothing her. A leather sandal clung between two clawed toes. The other lay a few feet away. Incongruously a salt-corroded mechanical chron was hooped around one shrunken wrist. Ryan picked up the little blaster on the floor. It was a .32 revolver with foreign writing on it. He broke open the action. All six rounds had been fired. Ryan sniffed the cylinder and smelled black powder. Someone had been rolling their own rounds. Ryan tucked the little blaster in his pocket and turned his attention to the air-cured human body. It had been here for some time. No scavengers had been at it, which worried Ryan. Not even rad-blasted meat went to waste in the Deathlands. Ryan looked around as Doc stepped out of the mat-trans chamber. "You all right?"

Doc clearly wasn't, but he took a deep breath, straightened the front of his frock coat and squared his shoulders. "I have always found the ocean air bracing."

Ryan lifted his head and sniffed. Doc was right. The air moaning through the empty blockhouse smelled of the sea as well as rain. Doc took a wobbly knee beside the corpse and smoothed her blond hair. "Poor child."

"Child?" Ryan shrugged and kept his weapon on the open door. "She looks full grown to me."

"No more than sixteen or seventeen, I would say." Doc gazed sadly upon the dead girl's corpse. "It appears she starved to death." He suddenly bent and pressed his thumb against the inside of her elbow and then examined the other.

Ryan took a knee beside him. "What?"

"Wounds," Doc said.

The dead girl's flesh was paper-thin around her bones, but Ryan could see the puncture marks in her flesh. They had been fairly fresh when she died. "You think she was jolting up?"

"No." Doc shuddered at the term for the concoction of drugs that the most despairing in the Deathlands chose for oblivion. "The veins, in the arms, the legs, between the toes, are cratered like the moon above.

These wounds are surgical. She was either receiving or giving blood intravenously before she died."

Every once in a while Ryan had to remind himself that "Doc" stood for Dr. Theophilus Algernon Tanner, and that he was a doctor of both science and philosophy. Ryan had seen more bodies than most, and the Deathlands was full of them. They had bigger concerns at the moment. "We're alone and the mat-trans is fucked."

Doc rose and peered at the scrolling code on the control panel. "It means nothing to me." His snowy brows furrowed. "However, the device appears to be peeping." Doc pulled out his pocket chron and one eyebrow rose. "It appears to be peeping in ten-second intervals, and then the code repeats itself."

"It's on some kind of cycle." Ryan peered at the little comp screen. "But it's not telling us what the timing is. Mebbe it only lets two people through at a time, then cycles again. Some kind of sec measure."

"Given that theorem, then perhaps, given time, it will let the others through."

"Yeah." Ryan scowled at the screen. "But mebbe only two at a time." He looked toward the corpse. "Looks like mebbe she died waiting." Ryan looked at the rad counter pinned to his lapel. The place was clean. He jerked his head toward the open doorway. "Let's do a recce."

Doc drew his massive LeMat revolver from beneath his coat and rotated the hammer's nose to fire the central shotgun barrel. "By all means, let us go and take the airs."

Ryan recced the outside from both sides of the doorway, but all he could see was windswept rock.

"Doc, on my six." Ryan stepped out, blaster ready. There wasn't much to see. The howling wind plucked at his clothing and drew tears from his eye. There was no vegetation. They were literally on a rock, which was the size of a predark six-story building. The only distinguishing feature on the rock besides the blockhouse was a remarkable concentration of bird shit.

Of immediate concern was the fact that the barren rock they currently occupied was located in the middle of an ocean.

Doc was right. The dead girl had most likely starved to death, and Ryan had secretly put his remaining food in Krysty's pack back in the redoubt. All they had with them was two canteens of water. Ryan gazed about. The ocean around the rock was as gray as death and beginning to roil with the coming storm, and they couldn't LD button back. Doc sighed as he came to his own conclusions. "Oh, dear."

Ryan scanned the horizon and perceived a pair of smudges to the west. He took his collapsible brass telescope from his pack and snapped it up to his eye. "I make it two islands." The images were at the limit of the optics, but he could make out buildings and a port on the larger one. Smoke was definitely rising from chimneys. Smoke rose from the smaller island, but all he could make out was empty beach. "The bigger one has a ville."

Doc took another deep breath of the air. "You know? I believe we are in the North Atlantic."

Ryan regarded Doc. "And you know that how?"

"I do not know." Doc shrugged. "It is just an intuition. I do not mean to be obtuse, but back in my time I sailed the Atlantic, and this just…feels like the Atlantic.

The North Atlantic. With nightfall the stars will give us a better bearing, but I would say we are in the Azores, the Canaries or the Madeiras."

Ryan would never accuse Doc of being obtuse. Predark bastard obscure on the other hand… "Lantic or Cific, it doesn't matter. That girl got skinny waiting for the mat-trans to cycle. That's a ville across the water, and it'll have boats. They'll be watching the storm come in, looking this way. We need to build a signal fire and get off this rock."

"And if that poor girl died here fleeing the inhabitants of that island?" Doc queried.

"Doc, there's no food here. We can wait until we run out of water if you want." Ryan lifted his gaze toward the swollen, bruised storm clouds riding the howling winds behind them. "Course water's coming."

Doc nodded. "Then let us find the base of this island. With luck there should be driftwood." At the edge of the escarpment they found steps carved in the rock that led down to a tiny strip of beach and a concrete pier. Besides bird shit, driftwood seemed to be the second hottest commodity on the island. Ryan cut kindling with his panga and, with pages torn from a notebook Doc carried, they got a fire going. The old man fed in ropes of dry seaweed, and soon a significant plume of black smoke was billowing up into the sky.

Then there was nothing to do but wait.

Ryan spit on his whetstone and began putting a fresh edge on his panga. The blade was painted black against rust and glare, but the edge gleamed like quicksilver. Ryan watched as a rare smile crossed Doc's face. The man from another age walked over to a large rock, and he exchanged glances with a fat black-and-white bird with a rainbow beak. "Bless my heart, a puffin! We are definitely in the Atlantic!"

Ryan considered his blasters, but both his rifle and pistol would blast the meat right off the bird's bones. He quietly palmed an egg-size rock. "Don't scare it off. We might have to eat it."

"A most handsome fellow!" Doc took out his notebook and a stub of pencil. "I believe I shall sketch him."

Ryan dropped the rock and went back to honing. Doc calm and happy was such a rare occurrence that Ryan was willing to let his stomach rumble for a little while. A few strokes of the stone brought the panga back to shaving sharp. A few strokes of Doc's pencil created a remarkable likeness of the bird.

Ryan shot to his feet. "Boat."

Doc took a small pair of binoculars from his satchel. Ryan took his spyglass from his pack and snapped it open. It was a sailboat and heading in a straight line from the main island to their rock. Doc took in the steeply raked mast and the triangular sail. "A felucca, by the look of her." He nodded to himself. "By the lines and piled pots on the bow, I suspect they are fishing for octopus."

Ryan was more interested in the occupants than the catch of the day. He counted seven men. They were short and stocky in build and wore black, waxed canvas slickers, and wide-brimmed felt hats shaded their faces. Several wore round, dark-smoked glasses and gloves. Ryan didn't see any blasters on the boat but all the men carried knives on their belts, and gaffs and fishing spears stood in racks along the gunwales.

"Hmm." Doc lowered his binoculars and frowned.

"What?" Ryan asked.

"They seem a tad pale for fishermen. Men who work the sea tend to be well weathered. Those men look more like mortuary attendants."

They looked a lot like Jak to Ryan, except they had dark hair. He snapped his spyglass shut and loosened his handblaster in its holster. It didn't matter. They had to get off the rock, get fed, see if they could get back and work on the mat-trans. "What islands we in again?"

"The Canaries, the Azores and the Madeiras are just about the only island chains of note in the North Atlantic."

"They speak English?"

"Portuguese would be the lingua franca in the Azores and the Madeiras, Spanish in the Canaries. However, the presence of our puffin friend leads me to believe we are too far north for the Spanish possessions."

"You speak Portuguese?"

"My tutors insisted on Greek, French and Latin. However, Portuguese is a Latin-based language. It may suffice to convey basic concepts."

"Convey to them we want to get off this rock, but not much else."

"I believe I understand."

"Leave a note for our people. Put it on the body."

Doc scrawled a quick note on the back of his sketch and went back up the stairs. He returned just as the felucca thumped against the concrete pier. The pale, black-clad fishermen approached in a phalanx. Doc was half right. The men were chill-white, but up close their pale faces were seamed by lives led doing hard labor, and at least the ones not wearing gloves had thick calluses and whorls of scars both ancient and new from years of working knives, lines and nets. Their demeanor was neither hostile nor friendly. Doc doffed his hat and displayed what had to be the most gleaming white teeth in the Deathlands. He had a magnificent speaking voice when he was in control of himself, and he spoke in his most mellifluous tones in a type of English Ryan had never heard before.

The effect on the fishermen was galvanizing.

Ryan knew enough words in Mex or Spanish, as Doc called it, to do a deal or to insult someone south of the Grandee. What the fishermen were speaking sounded something like Mex by way of Mars. "What's going on?"

Doc smiled. "They think I am a baron. I assured them I am not."

Ryan resisted rolling his eye up to the stormy sky for strength. "Doc? The next time people we don't know think you're a baron, you let them think that until it's time not to let them think that."

Doc reddened and coughed into his fist. "Yes...I believe I take your point. These people do indeed speak Portuguese. The big island has a ville. I believe the baron there is a man named Xavier Barat." Doc gestured at a pale, powerfully built man wearing dark glasses, gloves and wide black hat. "This man is Roque. He is the fishing captain of the ville's fleet."

"Captain Roque." Ryan flexed his rusty Mex. *"Hola."*

Captain Roque regarded Ryan obliquely from behind the smoked lenses of his glasses. *"Olá."*

"They will take us to the big island," Doc continued. "I have revealed nothing about our companions."

"Good." Ryan's Steyr was slung, but his hand was never far from the blaster on his hip. "Let's go."

Captain Roque gestured toward the boat and they

boarded the felucca. The crew poled off, and the sail filled with the coming storm winds. The vessel began to cut swiftly through the sea. Roque reached into a pot and drew forth an octopus about the size of his hand. Its arms flailed, but he swiftly brought it up to his mouth and bit it between the eyes. The cephalopod shuddered and the captain swiftly cut off its eight arms. He dropped them into a clay pot, and when he pulled them back out they were sheened with oil and the red flecks of hot chilies. Roque offered one of the still vaguely squirming appendages to Ryan.

Short of his fellow human beings there was hardly anything that walked, flapped, flopped or crawled across the Deathlands that Ryan hadn't eaten. He nodded his thanks and shoved the tentacle into his mouth. It was on the chewy side, but the meat wasn't bad and the lime, hot pepper and olive oil made it genuinely tasty. The pepper oil blossomed down Ryan's throat and the heat was welcome. Ryan shoved another into his mouth and again nodded his thanks. Roque smiled and either his gums had receded or he had very long teeth. He turned and offered some to Doc.

The old man chewed his tentacle meditatively. "*Piri Piri* sauce, definitely Portuguese. The lime is an interesting addition."

A crewman wearing dark glasses approached and held up a leather wine bag. Ryan took it and poured a long squeeze of rough red wine down his burning throat.

He snapped his head aside as another crewman in shades behind him swung a belaying pin at his skull.

Ryan Cawdor had a prodigious reputation in the Deathlands. It was said that if you faced the one-eyed man in a fight and blinked, then you got chilled in the dark. The crewman in shades screamed and clutched at his eyes as Ryan slapped the bag across his face and the smoked glass lenses flew from his face. Ryan's blaster filled his other fist. A round from the SIG-Sauer punched out the lenses of the second fisher's dark glasses and dropped him to the deck. Ryan put two rounds through the back of the screaming man's hands and dropped him skull-chilled next to his friend.

The one-eyed man snarled as a three-inch iron hook ripped into the flesh between his thumb and forefinger. Roque yanked his gaff and the SIG-Sauer spun out of Ryan's hand as his flesh parted. The captain snapped the gaff around, and the needle-sharp steel hook pierced Ryan's jacket and sank between his ribs. Ryan grasped the shaft, but his adversary twisted the gaff with practiced ease and hooked his fifth rib. Ryan snarled in rage as Roque yanked the gaff and snapped the bone. The hook squirmed beneath Ryan's rib cage as the captain turned the gaff 180 degrees and went for the rib above. Roque was a powerful man, and with seven feet of shaft between them there was nowhere for the one-eyed man to go. Ryan unleathered his panga. The eighteen-inch blade rasped from its sheath and he chopped the blade once, twice, three times against the weathered shaft of the gaff before it splintered in two.

Roque stepped back with four feet of broken stick in his hands. Ryan's lips skinned back from his teeth as he unhooked his rib cage. He lashed out with the panga, and Roque desperately brought up his remaining wood to block. Ryan looped the gaff left-handed up between Roque's legs and hooked it through his scrotum. The captain screamed like an animal as Ryan hauled him forward for the kill by his lowest organs. Roque's torment ended in arterial spray as the panga painted a red smile beneath his chin.

Ryan ripped the gaff free of its reproductive moorings and turned toward what remained of the fight.

Doc had not deigned to draw his revolver. He had been a trained swordsman in his youth and fought duels at university. Fishers with belaying pins stood no chance against him whatsoever. Three crewmen lay chilled among the nets and octopus pots, each dispatched with a single thrust through the left breast. The last crewman came at Doc with a fishing spear, the tripod blade of barbed spikes shooting for his face. Ryan spun his longblaster on its sling, but there was no need. Doc effortlessly turned the spear thrust aside with his blade and lunged like a fencer. The fisher went as limp as the boneless octopi in the pots as Doc's steel chilled him through the heart. The old man recovered his blade and came on guard, but he had no more opponents.

Drawn up to his full height with his long silver hair and coat blowing about him and a bloody blade in hand, Doc looked as formidable as Ryan ever remembered. "Nice work, Doc."

The scholar drew his handkerchief, wiped his blade, slid it back inside his cane and locked it with a twist. "Thank you. I believe the sea air is doing me good."

Ryan glanced up at the clouds. There was a good chance the sea air was going to chill them right quick. There was a storm coming, and the island was still miles away. "You know we just chilled the entire crew."

Doc stared at the carnage strewing the deck and blinked up at the clouds, his shoulders sagging as he did the math. "Oh, bother."

"Yeah, but you've had a hand on a tiller, right?" Ryan

asked. He cut strips from the dead men's clothing and bound his ribs and wrapped his hand.

Doc helped him tie off the bandages. "Only the smallest of pleasure craft and then only on a lake upon a summer idyll." Doc swiftly moved toward the tiller. "I believe I can aim us at the larger island. After all, we have traveled on many a boat." Thunder rolled and the first wet drops of water began slapping the deck and diluting the blood it was awash in. Ryan snapped out his spyglass and examined the ocean between them and their destination. Rocks rose up in front of them like a field of tombstones in the water. "Doc, we got rocks ahead."

Doc tucked his cane beneath his belt. "Are you sure?"

Ryan put his spyglass away and grabbed a line. "Bastard sure."

Doc's knuckles went white on the tiller. "Oh, bother."

Chapter Three

"Gaia!" was the last decent thing that came out of Krysty's mouth for several minutes as she slapped, punched and berated the mat-trans control panel with ever more colorful bawdy house language. J.B. ran an ancient toothbrush around the bolt of his Uzi and enjoyed the show. The flame-haired woman wasn't exactly hard on the eyes, and when she was angry it was something to see. "Won't do any good," the Armorer opined. "It seems to be on some kind of timer."

Krysty's rage went glacial as she turned her jade gaze on him. J.B. prudently went back to cleaning his blaster. Krysty spoke low. "Try again."

J.B. sighed and went into the main control room for the tenth time. He had a well-deserved reputation as a man who knew his blasters. But a mat-trans was a challenge of a higher order, and he was totally at a loss. The control panel was a complete mystery. The situation was quite simple. The mat-trans had sent two of the companions somewhere, and now appeared to be on some sort of cycle. One of the comps had come online and was scrolling comp code that left J.B. baffled. No combination of button-pressing or typing in commands on Mildred's part had elicited any response. The cycle appeared to be locked in. It was clearly a situation of hurry up and wait. J.B. studied Mildred. Both she and the mat-trans were products of the twentieth century, but he knew from past experience that comp code had never been her thing, try as she might.

Mildred was more concerned at the moment on the stickie that was currently trying to extrude itself through the door. Mildred wasn't exactly the squeamish type. She was a medical doctor; and since her rude awakening in the Deathlands had seen some of the vilest crimes against man and nature imaginable. But somehow, like clockwork, when the very sickest shit came down…

There was always a stickie involved.

She watched in revolted fascination as through some form of stickie contortionism one individual had wormed a spindly arm through the gap between the wall and the jammed door. Mildred recoiled in disgust as the suckered, spatulate, fish-white hand opened and beckoned toward her as if in invitation. Suckers opened and closed in obscene, sphincterlike lust for her flesh. The huge, flat, black eye pressed to the opening never blinked or wavered as the stickie slowly squirmed itself against the gap. The stickie's shoulder suddenly popped like a gunshot. Mildred yelped and leaped back as six more inches of arm shot toward her face like a striking snake.

Mildred folded her arms across her chest and jerked her head at Jak. "Jak! I'm not going to waste brass on his pasty ass!"

Jak rose and quietly palmed one of his leaf-bladed throwing knives.

Mildred shook her head in disgust as the dislocated arm wormed around the inside of the door. The hand crawled about like a spider as it searched for some kind of egress. Suckered toes began curling around the bottom of the door like caterpillars dragging a flattened, distended foot and then a horribly turning ankle through the gap. Up higher the stickie's clavicle stood out like drumstick as it began to push its dislocated shoulder through the opening.

Jak's ruby eyes narrowed curiously at the tiny gap in door and the gourd-shaped skull pressing against it "Head?"

"I have no idea but—" Mildred's eyes flared as the stickie pushed its face against the gap in answer. "No…fucking…way."

The stickie's jaw unhinged with a pop. Needle teeth scraped against the steel door as the creature literally began dragging its distended lower jaw through by its tongue.

"Uh-uh." Mildred watched in mounting moral outrage. "No."

The stickie's cheek pressed against the door and the huge black eye began to bulge out of its socket through the gap. Mildred put her fists on her hips. "Oh, hell, no." Mildred pointed a condemning finger at the self-compressing mutation. "Jak?"

Jak's knife glittered through the air. The bulging black eye popped like a cyst as the blade passed through and sank into brain. The albino teen lunged and retrieved his blade as the mutie sagged. The stickies outside hooted and cooed. The dead stickie left far more violently than it had tried to enter. Its bones snapped and cracked as its brethren yanked its body back through the gap and fell upon it in a feeding frenzy.

Mildred whirled and waved her arms at no one in particular. "You see that? You see that? Little bastards are doing yoga now!"

No one in the room knew what yoga was. J.B. hadn't

liked what he'd seen, either. He'd never seen a stickie pull a circus stunt quite like that before. "Jak, keep an eye on the door. If one can do it, then mebbe another can, too. We don't want them oozing in while we're asleep."

Jak nodded and squatted on his heels in front of the portal. He began walking a throwing knife across his fingers like a coin trick as fresh, rubbery white hands began wiggling, pulling and probing at the door.

It was going to be a long night.

RYAN SLOGGED ASHORE, dragging Doc's limp, coughing body with him. The felucca had broken up on the rocks between the gateway crag and the islands. He had seized a piece of wreckage in one arm and held Doc in a death grip with the other as the wind and waves had had their way with them for an hour before depositing them on the beach. Ryan gazed at the empty rolling dunes. He and Doc were on the wrong island, and his snapped rib ached like fire. He hauled Doc a few feet above the tide line and dropped him exhaustedly to the sand. Ryan was cold down to the bone and soaked through, but his mouth was nothing but dry salt. He took out his canteen and took long slow gulps from it before bringing it down to Doc's lips. The old man sucked at the canteen in semiconscious greed. Ryan let him drink his fill. They'd seen campfire smoke. Where there was campfire smoke, there'd be water. "You all right?"

Doc flopped back to the sand like a fish. "A bit battered, but I must say battling the ocean was strangely invigorating."

Doc didn't look anything remotely invigorated. He looked more like a dog left out in the rain to— "Dog!"

Ryan's hand was numb with cold and ached with the hooking from Captain Roque's gaff, but his blaster was in his hand rattlesnake quick.

He blinked as a dog stood atop the dune and wagged its tail at him.

During the time of the skydark the family dog had become an immediate source of food. Packs of wild strays that had taken to eating their former human masters had been ruthlessly trapped, shot and eaten in return. Ryan had seen pictures of predark house pets, and the idea of people keeping animals that couldn't earn their keep, much less deliberately breeding so many useless mutations into an animal was beyond his comprehension. For the most part only dogs of the working, sporting and herding groups had survived into the age of the Deathlands. Whatever working specialty a dog might have, whether hunting, herding or hauling, their primary function was still guarding. They were both alarms and the first line of defense against mutant marauder and night-creeping norm alike. Most had been bred up in size and savagery, and all were trained to attack strangers on sight. This dog was a shaggy black color with a mop of hair falling over its eyes. At fifty pounds it was a bit runty by Deathlands standards but still had good lines. The strangest thing about the dog was its attitude. It gazed upon Ryan and Doc in tail-wagging, tongue-lolling, happy stupid expectancy.

Doc creakily pushed himself to his feet. "Cao da Serra de Aires."

Ryan kept his 9 mm blaster leveled. "What?"

"An Aires Mountain Dog. A shepherd dog from the Aires Mountains, north of the Tagus River." Doc nodded knowingly. "A Portuguese breed."

"So why isn't it trying to chill us?" Ryan shook his head in mild disgust at the happy dog. "It's not even barking."

"I suspect it does not regard humans as enemies."

Rustling was alive and well in the Deathlands, and a herd dog that didn't bark at strangers struck Ryan about as useful as bird shit on pump handle. He looked up at the sound of bells. The bleating sounds carried over the sound of the surf. A girl came over a dune being followed by a flock of snowy-white goats. The girl stopped at the sight of the two strangers, then shocked both Ryan and Doc by waving happily at them. Ryan observed her as she and her herd waded through the waist-high beach grass. She had long, unbound golden-brown hair, golden-brown tanned skin and golden-brown eyes. The effect was made more dramatic by the simple, chestnut-colored homespun shift she wore. Leather sandals shod her feet, and she wore a simple leather purse over one shoulder and a bota bag over the other. Ryan noted the corpse on the escarpment had been wearing the same outfit and kept his eye on the shepherd's crook she carried. Looks were deceiving and he had been on both ends of a skillfully wielded piece of wood.

The girl approached them guilelessly. Up close her slim arms and legs belied a chest that strained at the homespun enclosing it. She smiled with big white teeth and in every way was the healthiest specimen Ryan or Doc had seen in quite some time. Doc nodded in a friendly fashion at the dog. "Cao da Serra de Aires?"

"No..." The girl's nose wrinkled delightfully. "Boo."

Ryan regarded Doc dryly. "I think the dog's name is Boo, Doc."

"Hmm...yes." Doc scratched his chin. "Boo."

Boo thumped his tail in the sand at Doc. The girl beamed and pointed to herself. "Vava!"

"Vava!" Doc bowed. "Dr. Theophilus Algernon Tanner, at your..." Doc trailed off as the girl stared at him blankly. He sighed and smiled as he pointed at Ryan and himself. "Ryan...Doc."

The girl's smile spread across her face like the sun. "Rian...Doke."

"Doc?" Ryan shot the old man a look. "The dog doesn't bark and the girl likes strangers."

"I must admit it is unusual," Doc agreed. "Even in my time a lone shepherd girl and her dog would be wary of strange men. Clearly neither has been exposed to any sort of predation."

"Or it's some sort of trap. I'm thinking—" Ryan wasn't often shocked but even he was taken aback when the girl softly wrapped her hands around his. She ignored the blaster he held and raised the gaff wound to her lips and kissed it. The huge golden-brown eyes gazed upward at Ryan with an innocence that bordered on the erotic as she said something soothing in her own language.

Doc gave Ryan a wry look of his own. "All better?"

"Uh, yeah..." Ryan forced a smile onto his face. "Doc? You tell her to take her hand off my blaster or—"

The girl tossed her crook to the sand. "Boo!"

Boo picked up the stick and happily trotted off. The girl kept Ryan's hand in one of hers and took Doc's hand in her other. Ryan and Doc exchanged looks. "Doc?"

"Like lambs to the slaughter?" Doc suggested.

Vava gave their hands a slightly impatient tug. "Dunno," Ryan said. He had learned the hard way to read a trap. The girl gave off nothing but wide-eyed goodwill. Boo the dog was positively anomalous. Then again, in the very best traps the bait had no idea it was bait. Circumstances decided it. They couldn't stay here, and goats implied a hot meal. Ryan sighed and put his blaster in his other hand. He was almost equal with both. "Doc, give her your left."

"What?"

"Give her your left hand. Keep your right on your blaster."

"Ah, yes. I see." Vava smiled happily as the hand- and blaster-holding was arranged and led them into the dunes. The goats followed with their tin bells tinkling. Ryan surveyed the countryside. The dunes gave way to rolling grassland, rock formations and thin, windswept forest between the hills. The island wasn't a tropical paradise but everything was a healthy green and the needle on Ryan's rad counter never moved as they walked. Golden-brown fields waved in the sea breeze and he spied a few thatched huts on top of some of the hills. Several times people in the distance waved at them. They cut through a field and Doc ran his hand through the heavy sprays of grain.

"Pearl millet. Wheat, rice and corn overshadowed millet in the Americas except as feed for livestock, but in Africa, India and Asia millet has been a staple cereal grain since ancient times. It is a cereal grain well-adapted to soil low in fertility and high salinity."

"That's real interesting, Doc," Ryan said.

Doc frowned. "I assure you sarcasm is uncalled-for."

"It's not sarcasm." Ryan tracked his eye across the breadth of the horizon. "This rocky soil isn't bad, but it's workable. These people are making the most of it, but I noticed one thing."

"Good heavens, you are right!" Doc saw it. "They are not fishing."

"That's right. They're growing grain, raising goats and wearing homespun, but I haven't seen a boat, a pier or a net, and right across the water there's a ville where they got buildings, sailboats and they're eating octopus in sauce."

"It is a conundrum," Doc admitted. "And our Vava is wearing the same clothing as the poor girl by the mat-trans."

"But Vava isn't wearing a chron and I doubt she's carrying a blaster."

"Indeed."

They came to a little valley. Sheltered from the omnipresent ocean wind the oaks grew tall rather than twisted and among them sat a little cluster of thatched huts. Ryan stopped just short of drooling as the smell of a goat roasting on a spit wafted toward him on the breeze. They descended the steep goat path and three young men around the barbecue pit rose to meet them. All wore homespun tunics and crude leather sandals like Vava and had the same tanned, golden-brown good looks. Vava and the man in front talked for a few moments. He was tall enough to look Ryan in the eye, looked as healthy as a horse and about as strong.

Vava waved at him by way of introduction. "Ago."

Ryan remembered his meeting with Roque on the dock and spoke the only word of Portuguese he knew. "*Olá,* Ago." He motioned at Doc and himself. "Ryan, Doc."

Vava beamed.

If Ago had a tail he would have been wagging it with Boo. He grinned like an idiot instead and shoved out his hand. *"Olá!"* The other two men were introduced as

Marco and Nando. Everyone shook hands all around. The afternoon sun was fading, and the islanders led Ryan and Doc to the fire. Others began gathering. Ryan counted a score of men and women in equal number. Most of the women had babies in their arms or small children clinging to the hems of their tunics giving Ryan and Doc wide-eyed looks. Slabs of goat meat and heaping bowls of millet gruel were shoved in front of Ryan and Doc without ceremony. Doc began picking at his food and making pleased noises. Ryan shoveled it down. He had burned off his two octopus arms hours ago, and he was ravenous. Vava told an involved story that Ryan gleaned was about her and Boo finding the visitors on the beach.

Ago handed Ryan a large clay bowl with a grin.

Ryan brought the clay bowl to his lips. The sloshing contents were a foamy, unfiltered dirty blond and the smell of yeast was almost overpowering beneath his nose. Ryan tossed a swallow back. It was carbonated to the point of being fizzy and tasted like a train wreck between hard cider, ale and the gruel. The assembled islanders gazed on expectantly. Ryan tilted the mixing-bowl-size container of home brew and drained it.

The islanders clapped their hands happily.

Ryan wiped his mouth with the back of his hand. The bowl was refilled and Doc smacked his lips as he took a sip. "Millet beer."

People filled their bellies and talk roamed about the common circle. All the shy glances pretty much indicated Ryan and Doc were the hot topic for the night. Ryan spoke quietly. "Doc, what've you learned?"

"I believe these people live communally. I get the impression this is but one of a number of hamlets scattered across this island. These few here could not maintain the fields alone. The islanders probably all gather for group planting and harvest of the arable land. Everyone seems to have a knife. They are all crude and of a kind, but I have yet to see a forge."

"Trade knives."

"My thought exactly. I suspect any axes, plows or other ironworks will have come from across the strait."

It squared with everything Ryan had observed. "I haven't seen any old people."

"Dear Lord!" Doc stared around in shock. "I believe you are right!"

"Ask if they've seen any other strangers."

Doc spoke a few words and got blank looks. "I am afraid the Portuguese word for stranger has wandered far from the Latin."

"Talk around it," Ryan said. "Use your hands."

"Ah." Doc began speaking very slowly in Latin and gesturing at himself and Ryan and pointing out toward the sea and the island housing the mat-trans. Ago sat upright and for the first time lost his smile. The islanders around the fire began a rapid exchange.

"Tell them we found a girl."

Doc nodded. "Very well."

"Tell them we found her on the escarpment and she was dressed like they are, but had dark hair, short, had something on her wrist."

Doc made a show of touching his hair, Vava's clothes and circling his wrist with his hand as he spoke words in Latin. Vava suddenly got very excited.

Ryan knew they were hitting pay dirt. "Tell them she's dead."

Doc stopped. "Are you sure?"

"Do it."

Doc said a few words. Vava burst into tears and ran from the circle. Everyone else grew very quiet. "Doc, ask what her name was."

Ago sighed unhappily at the question but answered. "Galina."

"That Portuguese?" Ryan asked.

Doc shook his head. "No, it is a Russian corruption of the Greek name Helen."

Ryan wasn't surprised. "Ask if Galina had friends."

Doc asked and Ago held up a single finger as he spoke, and that confirmed Ryan's suspicions about the mat-trans. "I believe a man named Feydor, that's Russian for Theodore," Doc said.

"A Russian team tried to jump and the mat-trans here only let two through, just like us. Something happened and Galina and Feydor got separated. I'm thinking that something was the people on the other island."

"So deductive reasoning would dictate," Doc agreed.

"Ask them about the mat-trans."

Doc spent long moments doing some very elaborate pantomime. The islanders stared uncomprehendingly until he finally dropped his hands to his sides in defeat. "I cannot seem to communicate the concept, and frankly I do not believe these people know of mat-trans devices much less what they do."

Ryan agreed. "I think the folk in the ville do. They came quick as a bullet from a blaster when they saw our fire."

"Yes." Doc nodded. "And they were willing to sail straight into a storm to retrieve us."

Vava returned with tears in her eyes and a basket laden with bundles of homespun and a collection of sandals, and began pushing them at her guests. Doc sighed sadly as he surveyed the garments. "I believe these good people want us to put on these clothes and try to blend in. I believe they intend to hide us."

"Didn't keep that Russian girl from taking the last train west, and we can't hide here forever."

"So, we journey across the strait and confront this Baron Barat?"

"In our favor that felucca went down with all hands chilled in the storm. With luck he won't know we're coming. We'll do a recce to get the lay of things and then decide how to play it," Ryan decided.

"And how are we to negotiate the strait?"

Ryan glanced around. "I doubt these folk have much in the way of boats. We'll have to build a raft."

Doc looked at Ryan steadily. "My friend, you are wounded."

"Yeah." Ryan's hand went unconsciously to his side. Vava instantly leaped up and her breath sucked in as she noted the rent material of Ryan's coat. Ryan almost pushed her away but the hot fire, hot food and millet beer were beginning to have their way with his beaten, half-drowned exhausted body. Vava called to a girl named Eva and the two of them led Ryan to a hut. Doc followed as they sat Ryan on a straw pallet and began brewing things in a clay pot.

"Willow bark, chamomile and bee balm by the smell. Traditional herbals." Doc looked askance as Vava and Eva began chewing mouthfuls of herbs both fresh and dried and then packing the dripping green chaw against Ryan's hand and side. "I shudder to guess what that may be but I suspect it is the most effective treatment available until we can reacquire Mildred and Krysty."

The goo stung. Ryan gritted his teeth as Eva and

Vava pushed his broken rib into place and bound it with strips torn from their shifts. Eva shoved the steaming pot beneath Ryan's nose. It smelled like a swamp and tasted about the same. Ryan drained it and sat back on the pallet. Vava undid the stained bandage on his hand, then washed the wound and took an iron needle and sinew and began to sew it. The sting and tug felt far away, and Ryan knew there was something in the brew stronger than chamomile and bee balm. It was cozying up to the bucket of beer he'd drunk.

"Doc, keep watch. I'm gonna shut my eye for a while."

Doc laid his LeMat revolver in his lap. "You may rest assured."

Ryan was asleep as his head hit the straw.

Chapter Four

Ryan awoke with his blaster in his bandaged hand. Dawn was rising gray out the open door of the hut. Vava and Eva were gone. Doc sat snoring in his sentry position. The one-eyed man checked his pack and found none of his belongings had been messed with. He sat up and did a quick self-assessment. His side and hand ached but far less than he'd imagined, and no infection or fever had set in. His stomach was growling, and he took that as a good sign. Checking the loads in his blasters, Ryan warily stepped out into the morning.

Ago, Nando and another man were standing around the coals of the previous night's fire, passing around another huge bowl. They waved Ryan over and he took his turn slurping down leftover millet gruel that had been mixed with some kind of watery goat yogurt. Doc came out with a sheepish look on his face, painfully aware that he had fallen asleep on guard duty. Ryan simply handed him the bowl. "Tell Ago we need to get to the big island."

The old man took a few swallows and handed the bowl to Ago. He pointed toward the big island said some words. Ago started talking excitedly and pointing inland instead.

"What's he saying, Doc?" Ryan asked.

"I believe he wants to show us something."

Ryan nodded. "Tell him we're amenable."

Ago nodded. He whistled, and Vava and Boo came out of a hut across the way. They spoke for a moment. Vava looked unhappy but she nodded, and they began walking inland. Ryan and Doc followed. The wind blew strong across the rolling hills and whipped the grassland as they came out of the vale. They walked for a quarter of an hour through fields and vales and passed more villages. They stopped in a gully. Ago and Vava began pulling apart a deadfall of twisted branches to reveal a skiff. Ryan ran his hand across the graying wood. The little rowboat had been sitting there for some time. The oarlocks were rusted and the oars themselves were warping. "What do you think, Doc?"

"I believe we would be safer building a raft."

Ryan stood and shook his head at Ago and Vava. The two islanders looked crestfallen but Ago pointed farther inland. Doc rose from the rotting skiff. "I believe there is more they wish to show us."

Ryan and Doc followed the islanders through more rolling hills and came upon an overgrown gravel path and followed it through another little valley. As they came out, they stopped and stared at the structure at the top of the hill in front of them. It was taller than it was wide. Four slender, two-story spires encompassed a high, peaked roof. The central spire was three stories. It was made of ancient gray stone that was worn but intricately carved. Ryan noted the wrought-iron fence with spear tips was of more recent manufacture and unrusted. "What's that? A castle?"

"In a sense," Doc said. "It is a church. God's fortress on Earth. Sixteenth-century Gothic architecture, I would say."

"Haven't seen a church ever like that."

Doc smiled wryly. "Well, they do not build them like they used to."

Vava plucked at Ryan's sleeve and spoke rapidly, first pointing at the church and then pointing out to sea. Ago nodded and appeared to agree with everything she was saying.

Ryan sighed inwardly. "What's she saying, Doc?"

"I'm not sure. Something about Pai Joao and danger."

"Pai Gao?" Ryan scratched his chin. "That's a card game. They got a gambling house in the ville we need to avoid?"

Doc smiled tolerantly. "No, I believe *Pai* in Portuguese means 'Father,' as in Father Joao, a priest. I believe we are being warned against him."

Ryan stared at the forbidding structure of the church and what appeared to be statues of winged muties standing guard over the eaves. In the Deathlands everything was a survival situation, and most things were negotiable through barter, jack or the threat of violence. But Ryan had seen book pounders with motivated congregations who could convince themselves of anything, and once they made up their minds about right and wrong the only thing that got through their skulls was lead. "We'll keep an eye out for Father Joao." Ryan did a little sign language of his own. He pointed at Ago and Vava, pointed at the church and shrugged. Ago and Vava both nodded and pulled out little hand-carved wooden crosses from beneath their tunics. Ryan refrained from rolling his eye. "They're book pounders, Doc."

"I believe they are illiterate, but I take your meaning. However, I would point out that they seem to be book pounders who are afraid of their priest," Doc countered, "and willing to help strangers not of their faith."

"Yeah, there's that." Ryan unslung his longblaster and slowly began to circle the base of the hill. He found a little cottage nestled up against the back of the church. Unlike the villager huts, the cottage was of plank and beam construction with a shingled roof and glass windows. No smoke came from the chimney and the windows were dark. Ryan approached the cottage from the side and peered in one of the windows. It consisted of a single, sparsely furnished room. A cross hung over a simple rope bed in one corner and a small desk, an armoire and the fireplace filled the others. He beckoned, and Doc and the two islanders followed. Ryan rounded the cottage and came to a shed. There was no lock on it and inside were some axes, hatches, shovels, coils of rope, hand tools and several buckets of different size nails.

"Doc, ask them where Father Joao is."

Doc asked and Ago and Vava pointed toward the sea and the bigger island out in the distance. Doc pondered. "Well, by my reckoning today is Tuesday. If the priest ministers to these people but prefers to live on the main island, and they are on the same calendar as us, and still practicing Catholicism, then he may not be back until Friday for Mass."

Ryan nodded to himself. With Captain Roque's boat lost at sea with all hands and Father Joao not expected back until Friday, they had a little time. He looked at the Gothic building and the two islanders. "You think they're going to get angry at us if we go in?"

"I suspect not," Doc replied.

Ryan went to the front of the church and unlatched

the gate. He kept his eye on the stone muties over the lintel and pushed open the high, narrow double doors. The inside was dim and shot through with shafts of light coming from the high narrow windows. It smelled vaguely of incense and beeswax. Two rows of benches led to the altar. On the wall above it was a crucifix and below it the painting of a man. The man sat back in an ornate chair. He was as chill pale as Roque and his crew, with aristocratic features, his long black hair shot through with silver, and he was dressed all in black clothing. He had the same kind of black eyes as a shark or a stickie, and they seemed to follow you wherever you went in the room.

Doc pointed at the painting. Ago, Vava and Boo hovered in the doorway. Vava nodded and said, "Barat."

Doc grunted unhappily. "I believe I detect something of a theocracy going on in these islands."

Ryan swept the rest of the church. There were a couple of antechambers. One was full of barrels and sacks of supplies. The other led to an empty cell with iron bars and chains on the wall. Ryan came back and stepped past Ago and Vava. "Wait here."

Ryan went to the shed and ladened himself with axes, hatches, saws, rope and hammer and nails. He came back and handed a hatchet to Doc. Doc looked at the implement. "And what is this for?"

"The skiff is useless." Ryan surveyed the church. "But barrels and benches would make a decent raft."

Doc sighed as he glanced around the ancient Gothic architecture and the antique appurtenances. "Yes."

"We don't have time to go chopping down trees." Ryan's eye narrowed. "You got a problem with busting up a church, Doc?"

"Well, I was taught men's highest spiritual goal was to establish truth, righteousness and love in the world." Doc smiled wryly. "Nevertheless, I believe I can say without fear of contradiction that few things would have pleased several of my Oxford companions more than to observe their learned colleague taking an ax to a Papist establishment." Doc hefted his hatchet. "Lay on, Macduff."

"We need bench seats, four of them to make a square. We nail them together and then lash a barrel beneath each one. We'll take the oars from the skiff and chop them down to paddles."

"As sensible a plan as any," Doc agreed. "I will take the saw and try to carve us a rudder."

Ago and Vava gasped as Ryan's first ax stroke knee-capped the closest pew, but they made no move to stop them or to run away. Ryan and Doc worked throughout the day. They nailed together four lengths of pew and bound them with rope. One of the barrels in the storeroom was filled with water, one with wine and two with oil that Doc said came from a whale. The wine was thin and sour, but they emptied it last and Doc dosed himself liberally from it as they worked. The winc and the exertion brought color to his cheeks and he worked with a will. Vava left and came back with dried meat and an earthen pot of goat curds. Ago watched almost unblinkingly as the hours passed and the grand construction came together. Ryan and Doc lashed the last barrel in place and surveyed their handiwork. They had a four-foot by four-foot square supported by barrels at each corner and had nailed a pair of planks across the square to sit on while they paddled. Doc had sawn out a bench back into a rough fin that they roped in place to form a rudder.

Ryan wiped his brow on his forearm. "Doc, tell Vava to go get the oars from the skiff. Tell Ago we're going to sail for the big island at sunset and that we need four men to help us carry down the raft and launch it."

Doc went through some complicated hand signals.

Ago suddenly seized Ryan's wrist and shook his head as he spoke in rapid-fire Portuguese. Only the desperate earnestness in the young man's face kept Ryan from snapping Ago's arm at the elbow. "Doc?" Ryan said quietly. "Tell Ago to let go."

Doc spoke a few words and pointed at Ryan's wrist. Ago reddened in sudden shame and stepped back, looking at his feet. Ryan took pity on the young man and clapped him on the shoulder with his left hand. "Tell him it's all right. Ask him what's wrong."

Doc and Ago had a very long conversation that didn't seem to go anywhere fast. Ago was trying to get something complicated across, and hand gestures and common verb roots weren't enough. Ryan sighed. "Doc you get anything out of all that?"

"Only a few basic concepts," Doc admitted.

"Such as?"

"There is danger on the big island."

"Figured that." Ryan nodded. "Anything else?"

Doc frowned unhappily. "It is possible I am misinterpreting."

"Best guess, Doc."

"Ago wants us to go to the big island during the day."

Ryan shook his head. "They'll see us coming."

"I tried to explain that to him. But when he learned our plan was to make landfall at night? That was when he grabbed your arm."

Ryan was fairly sure Ago had their best interests at heart, but he was loathe to give up the element of surprise. "Can you figure out why?"

"He has been trying to tell me, but he is using words that have no classical Latin base to tell me." Doc shook his head in failure. "I am sorry to say that Latin is a dead language. Ago's Portuguese on the other hand is a living, breathing entity that has continued to grow and evolve to this day. The two languages were far apart in my time and have only grown further in the intervening centuries. There is danger on the big island, but the day is safer, of that I am fairly sure. The nature of this danger I cannot determine, though it is clear Baron Barat and Father Joao are to be feared regardless."

Ryan gave Doc a long hard look. The scholar had been more lucid for the past couple of days than Ryan could remember. Maybe the sea air was doing him good, or being more useful than usual was helping him focus, as well. "What do you think?"

Doc shrugged. "These people have shown us nothing but kindness and hospitality. They were also clearly willing to hide us, quite possibly at risk to themselves. Ago is adamant, we must not go to the island at night."

"Fireblast." Ryan wanted to go now. He had a very grim feeling that time wasn't on their side. But he could tell that Doc needed rest. Ryan felt the ache of his own wounds. If they left now there wouldn't be much left of them to meet whatever awaited on the big isle. "Fine, we leave at first light, but under one condition."

Doc blinked. "What would that be?"

The die was cast. "You're a baron until I tell you different."

J.B.'S HEAD SHOT UP as the comp in the control room chimed. He was sitting guard duty while the rest of the party slept and almost didn't hear it over the moans, coos and shrieks of the stickies as they pressed themselves against the door and reached for him. He'd chilled two of the muties with head shots as they had tried the contortionist routine; but luckily full-body dislocation didn't appear to be a universal stickie skill set, at least not yet. He perked an ear and realized the comp was no longer peeping. "Jak!" J.B. called. "Watch the door."

Jak was awake, on-station with Colt Python drawn in an eyeblink.

Krysty and Mildred roused themselves wearily as J.B. examined the comp screen. Mildred pushed at her face sleepily. "What's up?"

"The mat-trans." Data no longer scrolled down the screen. J.B. checked his chron and then the comp screen again. "It's been seventy-two hours. I'm pretty sure to the second. I'm thinking the mat-trans is enabled again."

Krysty leaped to her feet. "We're out of here." She shouted into the corridor "Jak! We're leaving!"

Jak trotted into the control room. Krysty surveyed her friends. "We leave the food and half the water we got here. There's a chance there'll be supplies on the other side. Here there's none, and if J.B.'s right on the timer, anyone left behind will have another three days before the mat-trans cycles again."

The party put down their canteens, water bottles and stacked their meager store of provisions on the main console of the control room. One by one they filed past and took their seats on the mat-trans floor. Krysty went and put her hand on the lever. Ryan was always the last man in. He was always the one to pull the lever and the first one to step out of the chamber. Watching him do it had always given Krysty confidence. She felt very nervous now but kept it off her face. "Everyone ready?"

J.B. nodded. "Let's go."

Krysty shut the door and quickly sat on the floor disk as a mist began to fill the chamber. The lights began to flicker and the sucking darkness started to pull her in into oblivion. Krysty screamed in rage rather than fear this time as the lightning suddenly sledgehammered behind her eyes. She wasn't going to meet Ryan. Krysty screamed on in agony as she felt the savage wrenching for the second time as the universe seemed to pull every last fiber of her being in a separate direction but stopped just short of ripping her apart.

Krysty collapsed face-first into a puddle of her own bile and lay shuddering for long moments. Locks of her mutant hair snapped and twisted like beheaded snakes. Her battered brain knew she had been left behind again and she was still in the same redoubt. Instinct curled her fingers around the grips of her snub-nosed blaster. She pushed herself to her hands and knees and another wave of nausea ran its course through her. A clinical part of her noted dark, internal blood mixed in with the mess that had nothing to do with her bleeding nose. J.B. lay a few feet away, clutching his Uzi like an anchor as he was racked by his own gastrointestinal fireworks. Krysty could have wept.

Jak and Mildred were gone.

Krysty reeled onto her knees and mentally bucked herself up as she stood. Her hand shook as she pressed the lever and the chamber door hissed open. The comp was peeping. Data was scrolling. The supplies were still there. The corridor outside echoed with the sounds of besieging stickies.

Three more days.

Chapter Five

Ryan's broken rib stabbed and sawed at his side with each stroke of the oar. The sea was calm and the current slight, but they were still pushing a craft shaped like a brick across several klicks of open ocean. Doc was clearly no longer invigorated by the call of the sea. Each dip of the paddle was a groan and each return was a wheeze of effort, and Ryan felt his injured and exhausted body falling into the rhythm. The only good news about the journey was the morning fog. The big island was a dark smudge in the distance, and it would take a keen eye to make out the little makeshift raft in the vastness.

"I was on the rowing team…when I attended university…you know," Doc gasped. "I fear…I have since… lost…my wind."

"Save your wind for the sea, Doc." Ryan dug his cut-down oar into the Lantic. "We're getting close."

Waves boomed and hissed ahead of them as the ocean met the land. Both men instinctively dug down and dug harder as the big island loomed ahead of them like Leviathan in the fog. Doc suddenly gave a little sigh, and Ryan felt the sea change beneath them, as well. They had passed some invisible barrier in the waters and now rather than fighting the ocean current they were being pulled in by the tide. Ryan had scanned the beachheads the previous late afternoon and seen little in the way of obstacles, but he worried about the rocks and reefs he couldn't see. "We're coming in."

"Indeed...I believe we are." Doc set his oar aside and took the crude tiller.

The raft slopped and dipped as the waves slapped it, but so far the surf wasn't bad and Doc began to guide them in. Four barrels set in a square were very difficult to capsize. Despite several stomach-dropping descents down wave faces and being soaked to the skin, they were heading straight for the beach. Rather than rising up and down in booming waves they were suddenly in surf that sizzled like bacon. They gathered speed and Ryan could see the dull yellow sand of the beach ahead of them. "Nice work, Doc. We—"

Both men went flying as one corner of the raft smashed into a sandbar and the little craft went vertical. Ryan's rib screamed at him as he took a shoulder roll in the surf and came up on his feet with a splash. Doc ate a mouthful of beach and rose spitting and blinking sand from his eyes. Water churned around them as the wave receded. Doc splashed seawater onto his face and spluttered as they slogged up past the water line. "We have made landfall."

Ryan began to haul the raft onto the beach. It took long minutes for the two exhausted men to get the raft past the waterline and against the cliff. They piled seaweed on top to camouflage it, but most things in nature weren't square and covered with weed.

"A most suspicious lump," Doc opined.

"Check your powder." Ryan unslung his Steyr longblaster.

Doc drew his LeMat revolver from the waxed canvas

pouch he kept inside his jacket and made sure his powder was still dry. "How shall we proceed?"

"Talking with this Barat is a gamble, but we need to find out the cycle on the mat-trans. He might know it. We bluff our way in and bluff our way out and make him think it's to his advantage to help us." Ryan gave Doc a measuring look. "You better be at your baronial best."

Doc gave Ryan a sweeping bow in return and doffed his nonexistent hat. "Baron Theophilus Algernon Tanner, shipwrecked royalty, at your service."

"You don't serve, Doc. You give orders."

"Ah." Doc snapped his fingers at Ryan imperiously. "You, knave! Attend me."

"Better."

They moved down the beach. The smaller island had been a rambling affair of hills and dunes. The land here was more rough-hewn. The beach was a thin strip of sand abutting tall and jagged cliffs. They followed the strand westward for several miles toward the ville. Twice they saw the gray shadows of masted ships in the fog. Buoys clanked to mark the path through the rock-strewed channel as they got close to the wharf. Ryan stopped. Doc started as his companion put a hand to his chest. "What? Is there—"

Ryan put a finger to his lips and then pointed. The black mouth of a cave gaped out of a jumble of rocks at the base of the cliff. Ryan examined the sand. Seaweed and barnacles on the rocks around the cave mouth indicated the water reached right up during high tide, and it had erased any footprints or signs of passage. Ryan stared at the cave and knew without a doubt he was being watched.

Doc shivered and Ryan knew the old man felt it, too. Doc took comfort in Shakespeare. "'By the pricking of my thumbs, something wicked this way comes.'"

"Something's in that cave, all right," Ryan agreed. "And it's got bastard bad intentions."

The click-click-clack of Doc's ancient single-action blaster seemed very loud even over the boom of the surf. It made a final click as he set the hammer to fire the shotgun barrel. "Hold fire, Doc," Ryan said. "You shoot, the whole ville will hear it." Ryan's eye narrowed. "And whatever's in there isn't raising a ruckus."

"You know?" Doc shivered again. "I almost wish it were."

Ryan and Doc were both getting the same vibe. They had both been to terrible places where terrible things had happened. There were places in the Deathlands imprinted with the horrors they had witnessed that almost had a palpable aura of their own. Almost a life of their own. The cave was a very bad place, and there was something very bad inside it. That something was watching them now with a very cold will to chill them.

"Shall we double back?" Doc asked quietly. "Perhaps there is another way inland, or perhaps we might find a scaleable spot along the cliffs."

Ryan felt the chiller in the dark, and he knew it was feeling him, too. He really didn't want to walk past that cave, but neither did he want to go swimming again. He was reminded of how insistent Ago had been about not coming to the island at night. He thought of Roque and his crew hiding from the sun beneath wide hats, long coats and smoked lenses. "I don't think it's coming out."

Ryan shook his head. "I don't think it can. At least not until nightfall."

"Then let us proceed as quickly as possible while the day is still ahead of us." Doc gave the cave another leery look. "One at a time, or together?"

Ryan hefted the Steyr. "I'll cover you. Don't shoot unless something actually comes out."

"Indeed." Doc drew his sword stick. Interminable moments passed as he crept warily down the little strip of sand. At this bend in the beach there was barely more than a scant ten yards between the cave mouth and the sea. Ryan kept his crosshairs on the cave but whatever lurked within was staying back. Doc almost sagged with relief as he crossed out of the cave's line of sight. He sheathed his sword and knelt behind a boulder, taking his LeMat in a firm, two-handed hold to cover the cave. "I am ready."

There was no point in creeping. Both Ryan and the lurker knew the other was there. Ryan strode down the beach as though he owned it, daring the chiller in the dark to do something about it.

"Ryan!" Doc shouted.

The rock was the size of Ryan's head. It flew out of the cave as if it had been thrown by a catapult. Ryan dived for the sand. The rock ruffled his hair in passing and smashed into the surf with a tremendous splash. The one-eyed tucked into a roll and his hand snaked out to snatch up a rock the size of a hen's egg. He rose and flung his stone dead center for the cave mouth like he was trying to hit the last train west. He was rewarded by the meaty thud of rock meeting flesh. He'd hoped to be rewarded with a cry of pain or at least an outraged roar. What he felt were eyes burning into his back as he ran out the line of fire. Ryan knew as long as he stayed on this island he had an enemy, and he knew if he was still here by nightfall that the cold-heart lurking in the dark was going to come looking.

Before it was over someone was going to take that train.

"THEY'RE IN THE VENTILATION ducts," J.B. said.

Krysty looked up. She had been dozing, but as she listened she could hear the muffled thumps and scrapes of stickies squirming their way through the ducts. "How come they didn't do that before?"

"Dunno," J.B. said. "Nobody's been here in a long while. Mebbe this generation never learned."

Krysty was reminded of the piles of bones, cracked for their marrow and scattered throughout the corridors. "They're learning now."

J.B. was reminded of the stickies trying to extrude themselves through the three-inch gap between the steel door and the wall. He glanced at the ventilation grills in the room, which had been punched out from the inside long ago. The redoubt was a predark military facility. It wouldn't have air ducts a spy or saboteur could crawl through. The openings were mere twelve-by-six-inch rectangles. The redoubts were wonders of engineering, but the twentieth-century architects hadn't built with assaulting stickies in mind. In his mind's eye J.B. could imagine the stickies in the ducts, dislocating their bones and pulling themselves along with sluglike muscular contractions anchored by their suction-cupped fingers.

It wasn't a good image.

Krysty filled her hands with blaster and blade. "What's the plan, J.B.?"

"Can't come through the ducts more than one at a time." J.B. pushed off his scattergun's safety. "Mebbe we chill the ones in front. Make a pile of them. That'll confuse them."

"They'll figure to just push them forward."

"Until they do, that's the plan." The Armorer nodded. "Go check the door."

Krysty walked out into the hall. "Gaia!"

A stickie was halfway through the opening. Pushing past the unyielding steel had turned its skull into a stepped-on melon. That didn't seem to be hindering its progress. The stickie's flattened chest snapped and crackled and popped back into place as its torso reinflated. Its hips were posing something of a problem, but the grotesque crunching and grinding noises as it pulled its pelvis against the gap implied it was making progress.

Krysty's blaster cracked once and chilled it through the skull. The crunching and grinding turned to snapping and tearing as its brethren devoured its lower half in a frenzy to get to the opening. "J.B.!" Krysty called. "They can get through the door!"

J.B. took a knee beside one of the ventilation ducts, removed his survival flashlight and gave the generator handle a few cranks before shining it down the shaft. He scowled. There it was, a stickie, one hell of a lot closer than he would have liked. Its squeezed-out-of-shape skull was impossibly jammed against its outstretched arm in the tiny space. Nonetheless, it splayed out its suckered fingers and its rubbery muscles squirmed beneath its flesh, conspiring to pull it forward a few more inches. J.B. spit in disgust. "Dark night."

He fired his M-4000 and filled the duct with buck.

J.B. racked a fresh round into his scattergun and peered down the shaft again. The stickie was mostly a gooey mess now. J.B. rose and walked over to the other duct. One peek showed him the same situation. The stickie worming its way up the other duct blinked into the glare of J.B.'s flashlight before resuming its creeping progress. J.B. let fly with another buckshot blast that obliterated the stickie's hand, arm and face. For the barest of seconds there was a moment of blessed silence.

The shattered stickie's jammed-up corpse jerked a little and J.B. heard the crunch of bones as the mutie behind began chewing its way toward him through its friend from the toes up.

Krysty walked in reloading the round she had spent in the hallway. "Given time, they can get through that door."

"Heard you." He glanced up as the thumping and bumping in the ceiling continued and pondered the unpleasant idea of the stickies ripping their way out of the ducts and falling upon him and Krysty through the light fixtures.

"How are we on chron, again?" Krysty asked wearily. She already knew, but she vainly hoped that somehow J.B. or maybe even Gaia herself would give her a happier answer.

J.B. looked at the mat-trans comp unhappily as she shucked fresh shells past the loading gate of his blaster. "Two more days."

Chapter Six

Ryan and Doc examined the ville through their optics. "This ville is old," Doc said. "Plainly it was already old in my time. The cobblestone streets are original." They scanned the steep streets and crowded narrow buildings. "Almost all the modern construction, buildings from Mildred's time, have rotted away. Like the church on the sister isle, it is the ancient and solid construction that has survived. It is Mediterranean in style, in keeping with their presumed Portuguese forebears. Everything fashioned post the apocalypse is plank-and-beam or dry-mortared stone. Clearly the present generation has not the skill to copy the ancient buildings."

Ryan ran his eye appraisingly over the ville. Far too many people in the Deathlands were still feasting on the bones of Mildred's predark time. This island appeared to have escaped skydark and transitioned fairly smoothly. Ryan grimaced and considered the chill-pale Roque and his crew. He noted the heavy iron-bound doors of all the houses. None that he saw had first-floor windows, the lower windows of those of older construction were either bricked up or barred, and that brought his thoughts back to whatever it was that awaited the night in the cave behind them. The island hadn't escaped skydark entirely.

Not by a long shot.

Men in long coats and wide hats moved about on the streets. Some few more were engaged in activities on the dock. Others Ryan assumed to be women wore equally dark-hooded robes and veils. A clutch of them were busy down on the beach harvesting buckets of shellfish from the rocks.

"And in what fashion should the Grand Turk and his illustrious vagabond enter upon the stage?" Doc asked.

Ryan simply stared.

"How shall we…make our play?" Doc tried.

Ryan had been giving that some thought. "What you said this morning. Shipwrecked royalty. It's not bad. We tell them we went down in the storm. Since they lost Roque, they might buy it. With your fancy talk and Latin you might convince them you're somebody to be reckoned with. Try to make some discreet inquiries about the mat-trans."

"And you?"

"I'm your right hand. I'll just stand around and look mean. We haven't seen much in the way of blasters or sec men. Tell them there were two more ships with us, and if they didn't go down they're looking for us, and tell them they're big. If they think you got a few dozen guys like me looking for you, that might keep them honest. You? Be charming. Be imperious. Be a baron. Don't bastard it up."

"*Decorus Imperiosus Rex,* so shall I be," Doc assured him.

"Let's get fed."

They emerged from their hide among the boulders. The strand opened up to a decent stretch of beach around the harbor. Doc drew himself up to his full height and spun his cane jauntily as he walked down the sand.

The women bolted erect from their labors to reveal veiled faces and smoked lenses. They made suitable sounds of alarm and then hiked up their robes with gloved hands as they scuttled toward the pier. Ryan kept his Steyr at port arms. Doc wasn't exactly acting like a baron, but to his credit he didn't appear to be afraid of anything. The men on the docks and boats drew knives and clutched at gaffs. Others ran full-tilt into the ville shouting. Ryan and Doc ignored them all and mounted the stone steps that descended between the ville and the sand. The area had a fountain and formed a bit of a ville square before the twisting streets wound up into the steep hillsides.

A church bell began ringing in alarm.

Doc stopped and struck a pose with one fist on his hip and the other on his cane. He made an imperious gesture with his hand. Ryan bellowed up at the ville. "Baron Theophilus Algernon Tanner seeks words with the baron of this island!" The cliffs on either side of the harbor gave his voice a nice echo. Doc whispered in Latin.

Ryan roared out, and punctuated it with a full auto burst from his blaster into the air. "Baron Theophilus Algernon Tanner *peto lacuna per Baron ilei Insula!*"

A phalanx of men in black came charging down the cobblestones. The man in the lead had some kind of assault blaster. The five men behind him had long double-barrel blasters, apparently homegrown, and probably black powder. The street behind them began to fill with men carrying single-barrel blasters, axes, shovels, sledges and anything else that was heavy or bladed.

Doc looked utterly unimpressed. Ryan took two steps forward to interpose himself between Doc and the mob and arranged his scarred features into their hardest look. His body language radiated that very little was keeping him in check from chilling them all. The leading man was tall and whip-thin. A sparse beard and mustache were visible beneath the shadow of his broad hat. He had a predark blaster in an open holster on his belt. As he halted, so did his men and the mob behind them. Clearly there was fear. Ryan detected the people here weren't used to being surprised. It seemed certain they were used to occasional visitors from the mat-trans and perhaps spying a sail upon the sea. They weren't expecting company dropping out of nowhere on their doorstep.

"I heard." The leader spoke. Ryan was reminded of the accents when he had been to Amazonia. "You…speak English?"

"You." Doc snapped his fingers. "Your name."

"Jorge-Teo." The man came an inch from snapping to attention. "Constable Jorge-Teo."

Doc waved a dismissing hand. "Show us to Baron Barat."

Ryan's stomach tightened. Doc was already blowing it.

Ryan could hear Jorge-Teo's eyes widening behind his dark glasses. "You…know the baron?"

Doc peered down his nose from his six-foot, four-inch height and recovered nicely. His voice dropped an intolerant octave. "We are aware of him."

"Will you join me in my office?"

"We will." Doc turned his eye upon the crowd and raised an eyebrow. The constable began shouting and the ville folk turned from mob to gawkers as they moved to either side of the street. Constable Jorge-Teo's men made a move to arrange themselves in escort around Doc. Ryan stopped that with an ugly smile. The island sec men backed down and led Ryan and Doc up the steep street. They came to a ledge of flat land that formed another square. The building they walked toward was old even before skydark but was recognizable as a sec station. A police station as they would have called it back in the day.

They went through the heavy wooden doors. Inside were some desks and holding cells. Ryan's arctic-blue eye slid over a rack of long blasters chained in place through the trigger guards. Two of the weapons were bolt-action predark hunting blasters and two more were double-barreled scatter-blasters of the same vintage. In other racks along the walls Ryan saw nets and traps. Still more held boar spears, catch poles and whaling lances. They seemed of recent manufacture, and well used and well maintained. The ville was rolling their own black powder but predark blasters and their ammunition were in short supply.

The constable pointed to a table and a pair of chairs. Doc ignored them and went straight to the back office. Doc flung the door open and took command of the constable's desk. Ryan stood behind like a tombstone. The constable and his posse shifted from foot to foot beneath Ryan's unrelenting gaze. Doc consulted his chron and rolled his eyes.

Ryan's head turned at the sound of a wag outside.

The constable and his men were visibly relieved. The station door swung open and two tall men wearing the universal island attire of black hats, caped coats and dark glasses entered, openly carrying long, predark blasters. Their plastic furniture had long ago been replaced with local wood stocks and grips and the original matte-black finish replaced with gray phosphate. J.B. probably could have identified them instantly. Ryan noted the hilts of swords protruding from out of their coats. Baron Barat followed. He was of medium height and wore the dark island garb; however, his was of finer cut and well tailored to his frame. The baron walked up to Jorge-Teo and their faces disappeared as they tilted their broad hats together. They consulted together in whispers for a few moments, and then the baron strode into the office and sat in front of Doc. He removed his gloves and handed them to one of his sec men. His skin was chalk-white and the nails on his fingers purplish. His long black hair had streaks of silver and fell loose to his shoulders. He removed his dark glasses and Ryan wasn't surprised to see the man from the portrait in the smaller island church gazing upon him with cool curiosity.

He turned his attention to Doc and gave him a cold, sharklike smile. His teeth were as gleaming white as Doc's, but the baron's purple gums had receded to make them appear entirely too long. It was the smile of a skull. "Baron…Tanner, is it?"

Ryan spoke low and threatening. "Baron Theophilus Algernon Tanner, Baron of Strafford and Baron of Maine."

"Americans," the baron said. The skeleton smile stayed painted on Barat's face. The black eyes remained cold. His English was heavily accented but predark educated and formal. "Forgive me, Baron Tanner, but I have spoken with my constable, and I do not remember making your acquaintance."

"Your constable exaggerates. I did not claim to have had the honor of your acquaintance, dear Baron. I merely informed your constable that I was aware of you."

"Aware of me?"

"Aware of your island," Doc corrected.

Ryan eyed the disposition of the sec men again and readied himself to start blasting. Doc sounded like he was about to drop the ball. Doc waved an impatient hand at Ryan and handed off. Ryan gave Baron Barat a withering look. "We've recced it."

The baron's face froze.

Ryan went with gut instinct. "It's not hard to move among you. Particularly during the day."

The baron flinched and Ryan knew he had given him a gut shot where it hurt. Barat raised a hand to Jorge-Teo and spoke a few words in Portuguese. The constable left and the baron returned to Doc. "Forgive me, Baron. I have neglected my duties as host." Jorge-Teo came in with a tray bearing a carafe of wine, cheese and smoked fish. The constable poured wine. Doc nodded at Ryan, who assumed the role of royal food taster and picked up the goblet.

Baron Barat sighed and took up his own cup. He toasted vaguely toward Ryan and drained the goblet. He set the empty glass down, smacked his lips with relish and smiled condescendingly. Ryan took a swig from the goblet. The wine was heavier and sweeter than the communion wine on the sister island. Ryan poured it back and set the goblet down in front of Doc. The constable refilled the glass.

Doc ignored it. "Baron, let me be blunt. My ship, the *Vermont,* went down in the other night's storm."

The baron kept his poker face, but Ryan could almost hear him considering his own lost boat and calculating.

"I believe my escort ships—"

The baron blinked. "Your escort ships?"

"Yes, my *Vermont* was a cargo ship and was heavily laden. The *Maine* and *Hampshire* are warships and faster. Last I saw of them from the *Vermont,* they were running ahead of the storm. We signaled them with lanterns before we went down. They will of course return in a few days' time."

Ryan sensed Baron Barat's discomfiture. Doc was playing his hand well. Now if he could just— Ryan's stomach reared within him like a striking cobra. He tried to bring up his blaster to bear but his stomach ejected its contents so violently it almost tore the lining of his throat. Ryan fell to his hands and knees as sickness that made a mat-trans jump feel like an after-dinner belch racked him. "Doc! I—"

Ryan went fetal as his bowels spasmed.

Doc's hand froze on the grips of his blaster as the baron's sec men leveled their weapons. One was pointed at Doc. The other at aimed at Ryan's retching form on the floor. Jorge-Teo relieved Doc of his LeMat, then knelt and relieved Ryan of his weapons. Doc struggled to maintain an imperious mien. "You disappoint me, Baron."

The baron ignored Doc and poured himself another glass of wine. He swirled it in his glass and admired its color before sipping it. He peered down at Ryan in mock sympathy. "Sadly, one's first few experiences with our native lotus are somewhat...purgative. For one who imbibes it for the first time, I must admit he was given a very powerful dose. I fear his dreams shall not be pleasant."

"Baron Barat, I must protest this—"

Barat turned to the constable. "It has been three days since we lost Roque." He held up his glass. "I feel the draft upon me, and must sleep until the effects have passed. You know what must be done."

"Yes, Baron." Jorge-Teo grinned unpleasantly at Ryan and Doc. "And what of these two?"

"Put the sec man in a cell. He will be of use to no one for at least a day."

They both looked at Doc. "And the baron?" the constable asked.

"Yes, the *baron.*" Barat gave Doc a very hard and measuring look. "Make him comfortable." The skull-face smile returned once more. "I will speak with this man again after I have slept. Bring him to the manor come sundown."

NIGHT HAD NEARLY fallen. Mildred stood and peered out into the drizzling rain and fog. They had spent the afternoon exploring the tiny island and found damn little. She shivered in the cold ocean breeze and stepped back inside the shattered blockhouse. Mildred took out Doc's note and read it again for lack of anything better to do. On one side was a picture of what looked to her like some kind of penguin. On the back Doc's spidery longhand read:

Dear friends,
If you are reading this missive then you have successfully journeyed through the mat-trans.
A boat approaches, time constrains me to brevity.
In summary:
-being picked up by fishing boat
-believe we are in an island chain upon the Atlantic
-disposition of natives unknown
-advise caution
-circumstances of corpse most curious (Mildred, please take note of marks on deceased's inner arms.)
-presume us to be upon the big island.
I remain,
Your faithful servant in all things,
"Doc"

Mildred turned the note over and looked at the date scratched beneath the bird sketch. "Doc wrote this three days ago."

Jak nodded. "Not been back."

Mildred shivered again. "Make a fire."

Jak frowned out at the rain. "Driftwood's wet." He dug into the pocket of his jacket and pulled out a handful of hexamine fuel tabs and bounced them once meaningfully in his hand. Each cube had a burn time of about fifteen minutes. "Two hours."

"I'm cold."

Jak nodded and took out flint and steel. He wrapped a fuel cube in a scrap of char cloth from his backpack. Sparks shot as he scraped the steel and magnesium rods together. It only took him two strikes and Mildred sighed as the tiny fire came to life. She warmed her hands over it and gave Jak her most winning smile across the fire. "You're the man, Jak."

Jak nodded at the wisdom of the statement.

"I'm hungry."

Jak sighed and stuck out his hand. "Note." Jak studied the words for a moment and handed it back. He drew one of his throwing knives as he rose and headed for the door. "Be back."

Mildred gave Jak a suspicious look. "You're not going to hunt down Doc's penguin, are you?"

"Puffin."

"What?"

Jak held up the sketch. "Puffin."

"How the hell do you know what a puffin is? Tell me you aren't going out there to kill Doc's puffin."

Jak gave one of his rare smiles. "Our puffin."

Mildred's stomach betrayed her and growled in

agreement. A part of her mind was already hoping it tasted like chicken. "Well, possession is nine-tenths of the law."

Jak blinked. Half the time he couldn't fathom her predark gibberish. He turned and stepped into the night with his blade glittering between his fingers.

"Might as well be talking to myself." Mildred sighed. She turned her attention to the body and began talking to herself out of habit as she went into medical doctor mode. "Deceased is a Caucasian female, mid to late teens. Body shows obvious signs of acute starvation. Final cause of death most likely dehydration once victim became nonambulatory." Mildred shook her head sadly as she examined the body. "Girl, you went the hard way." She peered at the puncture marks Doc had noted. The holes on her inner arms were large and the bruising was bad. Just looking at them told her the IV needle had to have been fourteen gauge or bigger. It looked like work from Doc's time rather than hers, and it was pretty clear to her that someone had been drawing blood rather than administering fluids.

Jak called out of the darkness so he wouldn't get shot by mistake. "Back!"

"That was quick!" Mildred called back. "Come ahead."

Jak came in holding Doc's bird by its webbed feet. Mildred mentally corrected herself. Their puffin. Her chicken dinner. Jak tossed down a bundle of branches of driftwood suitable for roasting sticks. Mildred took out her knife and began shaving points on the likeliest-looking pair. Jak got busy dressing the bird. He filleted the serving portions of meat off the bone and removed the giblets. He stuffed the guts and odds and ends back into the carcass for bait. At first light he would try his luck at rock fishing. Puffins were chubby birds, and he warmed some fat over the fire and rubbed the meat with it. He threaded cubed meat and giblets onto sticks and handed one to Mildred as he put two more hexamine tabs on the fire.

Mildred began salivating as the smell of roasting puffin kabobs began to fill the blockhouse. Mildred eyed Jak's jacket. It was like a superhero's utility belt. You could never tell what Jak was holding. "Don't suppose you have any marshmallows in there?"

Jak peered at her. "What?"

"Crackers?"

Jak stoically returned his attention to roasting his puffin.

Mildred didn't bother with the Hershey bars. Anyone who habitually dropped their prepositions and articles was too good a straight man for his own good, and hers. Baiting Doc was infinitely more fun. But Mildred was cold, tired and more than a little scared. She searched for a subject that might tempt Jak into blurting out a few more monosyllables than usual. Generally his favorite subjects were knives and food. "Doc mentioned a fishing boat. Maybe tomorrow we'll be eating—" Jak's head snapped up. His ruby gaze burned intently out into the darkness surrounding the broken blockhouse. Mildred had seen that look before. She had a terrible, sinking feeling she wasn't going to get to eat her barbecued puffin. She drew her blaster and spoke low. "Company?"

Jak rose and stepped on the fire. Night had fallen outside. The hexamine cubes were crushed and smothered beneath Jak's boot, and the blockhouse plunged into darkness. Mildred heard him thumb back the hammer on his Colt. "Trans," he said softly. Together they moved to the doorway of the mat-trans chamber. They knelt within and put the door of the blockhouse into a cross fire. Outside the wind moaned and the drizzling rain pattered. Collected water on the roof dripped through the shattered ceiling.

Mildred whispered, "What's our status?"

"Surrounded," Jak replied.

"Fuck."

Jak grunted agreement.

Mildred's eyes ached with effort as she tried to perceive anything in the inky blackness. She blinked as she caught site of something through one of the empty windows. "Jak, nine o'clock."

"See it."

Something was moving. Mildred squinted. It was like a few tiny orange fireflies moving up and down and winking in and out. They were coming toward the blockhouse. The fireflies suddenly multiplied and started acting crazy. Mildred did the math. Someone was carrying something covered and burning. Feet slapped on the wet rock of the escarpment outside. Someone had broken into a run. "Jak! They've got some kind of bomb—"

The interior of the blockhouse strobed with the muzzle-blasts from Jak's Magnum blaster. Mildred's .38 joined it. A big bundle of something flew through the window. Pottery shattered as it hit the floor of the blockhouse. A bucket load of red-hot coals spilled over the abandoned puffin kabobs. Something black and dirtlike mixed with the coals as the ceramic components of the bomb shattered. The coals flared brightly and then black fumes as thick as smoke began billowing out of the burning mess.

"Trans!" Jak shouted.

Mildred hit the lever to close the door and activate the mat-trans, but it failed just as it had done on the last hundred attempts. The mat-trans was still locked into its seventy-two-hour cycle. Jak's blaster boomed, but the enemy was making no attempt to assault. They were letting whatever filth they had thrown do their work for them. Mildred got her first whiff of the fumes and nearly gagged. It smelled like some rotting sweet combination of burned sugar and incense. The moaning wind blew through the empty windows and doorway of the blockhouse, and the foul smoke billowed straight into the mat-trans chamber like sentient barbecue smoke chasing its chosen victim at a cookout. Mildred covered her mouth and nose with her hands, but it did no good. She had to breathe.

"Jak!" Mildred hacked and choked. Jak didn't answer. She couldn't see anything through the smoke and darkness other than the smoldering coals on the floor and the dark fumes endlessly blossoming out of them. The light of the coals began spinning. Mildred closed her eyes and the entire planet spun. She opened her eyes again and squeezed off two more rounds at nothing in particular. Her eyes were burning. Her lungs were burning. She felt like she was violently drunk on tequila. Her hammer clicked on an empty chamber. Mildred fell to her knees and threw up. She tried to stand again and realized she had dropped her blaster. She knelt and fumbled for it in the darkness, but she couldn't find it. Mildred's eyelids felt like they were filled with hot sand and as heavy as a mountain. It was nice to close them. It was nicer down here. Someone had wrapped her brain in soft, fuzzy blanket. The smoke was rising, and the cold air at floor level was refreshing. Mildred blinked and when she opened her eyes she didn't remember lying down. The surface of the mat-trans floor was blissfully cool against the side of her face.

Mildred closed her eyes again.

Chapter Seven

The stickie erupted out of the duct in slow motion, like toothpaste out of a tube. J.B.'s shotgun blast had smeared away a great deal of its face and head. As the stickie was pushed outward, it dripped congealed goo from its cratered skull into the control room. Its narrow, dislocated shoulders crackled and popped as it was squeezed forth like sausage. J.B. slung the M-4000 and hefted his Uzi, pushing the selector lever to semiauto and dropped to one knee as he waited for the dead stickie to finish extruding.

The stickie's corpse popped like a cork.

J.B. got off one shot and then the mutie's cadaver flew into him like they were lovers who'd been separated for years. J.B. saw stars as they went skull-to-skull. Jellied blood and brain filled his eyes and mouth as he fell backward, gagging as he tried to disentangle himself. There was nothing left of the stickie below its rib cage. J.B. shouted as something grabbed his ankle.

Krysty snapped awake at the sound of the blaster shot and scooped up her weapon.

"J.B.!" The Armorer was flat on his back and covered with gore as he wrestled with approximately half of a dead stickie. Spindly arms dragged him by the ankle toward the duct. Krysty leaped forward and grabbed a rubbery wrist. She leaned in to get off a head shot down the duct. The stickie let go of J.B. with one hand and grabbed Krysty. She screamed as suckers bit into her flesh, and the stickie yanked her to her knees. She could see the mutie's head impossibly hunched between its arms in the duct. Krysty arm-wrestled with the creature and quickly began to lose. The rubbery, boa-constrictor-like strength of the stickie was sickening. Her blaster fell with a clatter as her hand went numb. Any progress she made helped pull the stickie out of the duct. Krysty spun in the mutie's suckered grip. She braced one boot against the wall and then drove the heel of the other again and again into the stickie's face. It hissed and cooed and bit at the stacked heel.

J.B. rolled the corpse away and did a sit-up. "Move!"

Krysty yanked her foot back and J.B. shoved the barrel of his Uzi down the duct and into the stickie's mouth. He pulled the trigger once and the stickie's arms went limp. J.B. ripped his boot out of its dead grip. He pulled a bandanna out of his pocket and began wiping the gore from his face.

"Gaia!" Krysty snarled as she pulled her wrist free. The stickie's hand suckers popped and made wet kissing noises as they very reluctantly loosened their hold on her flesh. Krysty flexed her hand as circulation returned and grimaced. Her forearm was a mass of circular lamprey-like wounds. There was hardly anything in the Deathlands more septic than any orifice in a stickie's body. J.B.'s eyes would bear washing out if they could spare the water.

Krysty jumped as the stickie twitched.

J.B. shook his head as he heaved himself to his feet. "It's just the one behind."

"J.B., we need to..." Krysty's shoulders sagged in exhaustion. She shook her head at the other duct. "J.B.!"

The Armorer looked across the room and saw a pale head bulging against the opening. Whatever body subluxation the stickies were capable of in life was being forced upon this dead one by the weight of numbers behind it. Its skull and shoulder filled every available bit of space. The jammed skull strained with the pressure being exerted behind it.

J.B. finished wiping down his weapon and tossed away his soiled bandanna.

"J.B., they're stuck in there. Worming around in pipes. Can't you just blow them up or something?"

"I blow the ducts then they really are in the ceilings and the walls." J.B. gave the light fixture panel above them another unhappy look. "Then they're in here." He had been considering some kind of shaped charge to go burning down the ducts but they were sheet metal and he couldn't risk weakening any section, much less ripping them open. J.B. walked over to the duct and this time stood back a prudent distance as the mutie corpse slowly squeezed through.

"So what do we do?" Krysty asked.

"Dunno." The Armorer took a deep breath and checked his chron. It had nothing good to tell him. He looked back and forth between the two ducts and out toward the hall where the assault on the door continued. The enemy had three access points, and it was only a matter of time before all that squeezing and squirming finally popped a duct. "But we can't afford to sleep anymore."

THE LONG BLACK WAG pulled to a halt. Doc peered out the tinted windows at the manse. The stone wall surrounding it was tall and topped with a wrought-iron fence with sharpened spikes. Night had fallen, and the driver and the two sec men had removed their glasses, hats and gloves. Doc noted the same long-toothed mouths, purplish gums and lavender tint beneath the fingernails. However, the men all had either black or brown eyes. The manse was well lit, just as the inside of the sec station had been. The inhabitants of the large isle weren't sensitive to light. They were very sensitive to the rays of the sun. Doc was starting to come to some conclusions.

The wag had come at sundown and despite Doc's protestations they had forced him to leave Ryan behind in the holding cell, naked and raving in fevered dreams. On the drive into the hillsides Doc saw farms and vineyards. He found that nearly every home and building was of fortlike construction, and he was interested to find that he saw nothing in the way of horses, oxen or farm animals.

Doc also found the wrinklies who had been conspicuously absent on the smaller isle.

They all wore the same simple homespun. However, unlike their young brethren on the smaller isle who glowed with health, these men and women were stooped from hard labor, and all over the age of twenty-five. Many were moving wagons and toting bales. All of them without exception walked with a very suspicious limp. Many bore signs of the lash. Others had fresh bandages covering their inner arms.

All of them moved swiftly and fearfully as the sun set.

Doc began coming to other unsavory conclusions, as well.

The sec man beside the old man motioned with a huge, double-barreled blaster that looked suitable for elephant hunting. "Out."

Doc exited the wag and was escorted into the manse. The interior was opulent by Deathlands standards and furnished in a hodge-podge of ancient, predark and cruder new manufactured items. Baron Barat stood in the foyer. He wore an elegant red-and-gold brocade robe for the occasion. A semiauto blaster was tucked into the belt for the occasion, as well. "Ah, good evening, Dr. Tanner, thank you for coming."

"Doctor? I am Baron Theophilus Algernon…" Doc trailed off under Barat's bemused gaze. Doc sighed defeatedly. When the drug had violated Ryan, he had called out to him, and called him Doc.

The baron smiled in satisfaction. The admission of the first lie was the key point in any interrogation. "Come, Doctor, will you join me in my study? Nero, you may accompany us." The baron turned without waiting for an answer. Doc considered the blade hidden within his cane but decided he wished to learn more. Nero prodded him with his blaster and Doc followed the baron into his parlor. The room was wall-to-wall books of every description and age. A cheery fire burned in the little fireplace.

Doc decided on flattery as his own opening gambit. "I see you and many of your citizens speak excellent English."

"Ah, well." The baron smiled and gestured at the chair in front of his desk. "We have maintained a tutorial-based education system here as best we can, though I must admit it trickles down somewhat slowly from the high to the low. In many ways it is the second language of our island."

Doc noticed his LeMat on the desk and noted it was unloaded. He took his seat and Barat gestured at the confiscated weapon. "I must say, Dr. Tanner, that is a grand old piece you have there. It is remarkable that it still functions."

"Yes." Doc gazed fondly upon the ancient blaster. "Nearly as old as I am."

The baron smiled, not knowing how true the statement was.

"Nero." Barat motioned his sec man and nodded to the sideboard by the fire. Nero brought a decanter and two glasses. "Will you join me in my evening constitutional, Doctor?"

Doc eyed the amber liquid warily.

Barat laughed. "Fear not, it is merely Madeira."

"Then I would be delighted," Doc replied.

Nero poured and Barat raised his glass. "To your health."

"And yours." Doc sipped the amber liquid. His closed eyes in near ecstasy. It had been over two hundred years since he had drunk Madeira. "Is this Sercial?" Doc took another sip. "No, Rainwater, bless my stars and garters, a real Rainwater Madeira."

The baron was plainly shocked. "You are the first man not of this island I have ever met who would know the difference. May I offer you a cigar?"

Doc leaned forward eagerly. "Oh, indeed!"

The baron removed a pair of thick, blunt cigars from a humidor on his desk and handed one to Doc. Nero approached with a candelabra and the baron and Doc both leaned across the desk to light their cigars. Nero refilled Doc's glass. Doc and Barat spent long moments silently smoking and sipping fortified wine. The baron smiled. "You approve?"

Doc leaned back with a sigh and blew heavy blue

smoke toward the still ceiling fan. "People in my time always touted Cuban tobacco, but I always felt it was too powerful. I preferred Jamaican shag, much as I preferred Jamaican Blue Mountain coffee."

The baron's black eyes starred at Doc unblinkingly.

Doc blinked. The wine, the tobacco and the antiquity of the surroundings were flooding him with memories and feelings he could barely suppress. Despite Barat's civility, this was an interrogation. They were playing chess, and Doc realized he had made some very bad moves. Doc tried to maintain his poker face. He waved the cigar casually. "Tell me, Baron, from where did you procure it?"

The baron smiled to reveal his too-long teeth but his black eyes were hard. "Fogo."

"Fogo Island?" Doc sat up straighter. "The Cape Verde Islands survived, then?"

"Some of them." The baron stared very long at Doc before answering. "The voyage is somewhat long and perilous, but we do occasional trade with them."

Doc drew himself up in his chair. "Let me speak plainly, Baron. Clearly, I am—"

The baron cut him off with an impatient wave of his hand. "Let us not bandy words, Doctor. Clearly you and your sec man are not the shipwrecked sailors you pretend."

Doc finished his Madeira and sighed. "I fear you have discovered our ruse."

"So then, you admit you came through the matter-transfer device on the escarpment."

"Indeed I do." He gestured at the decanter. "May I?"

The baron gestured at the cut crystal generously. "Please."

Doc refilled his glass.

Barat's black eyes went predatory. "Clearly, you are no baron. You are a fascinating conversationalist, I will admit, but you do not carry the weight of authority nor command across your shoulders like your sec man does. Indeed I believe he is the true leader here. You are a historian of some kind, using your knowledge to fool your way from ville to ville, from jump to jump, hoping to get a meal and perhaps supplies before moving on."

Doc sighed inwardly. He was living history rather than a historian, but the baron was close to the mark on their intentions. Ryan had told him to be a baron until told otherwise, but Doc knew all too well he was a terrible liar and Barat was seeing through him all too well. "I am a doctor of natural sciences and philosophy."

"I see."

"I am prepared to render you all services I am capable of in return for the safety of my friend," Doc offered.

"I believe I am in a position to make you to do whatever I wish, regardless of the final disposition of your companion."

"Hmm." Things were going from bad to worse. Doc stalled for time. "I gather you realize the mat-trans device has been set to transfer only two people at a time and is set upon a timer. I have never encountered such a preset and have jumped many times. Would you be so kind as to tell me what the timing and the purpose of the cycle is?"

Baron Barat ignored the question. "I pray you, Dr. Tanner, tell me, how many more are there in your party?"

Doc ignored the question in turn and glanced around. "You have quite an impressive library, Baron. May I?"

"Please." The baron gestured about the room. "Avail yourself. We have time."

So, Doc thought, he feels no haste about the timer. Doc walked among the bookshelves with Nero as his hulking, somber shadow. Doc found many volumes he was familiar with as well as many predark books well after his time. Just looking at the books and tomes and touching them gave him great pleasure. The baron watched with benevolent malice, like a cat watching a mouse move around a closed room. Doc stalled. He wasn't particularly afraid of dying, indeed being slaughtered in a well-stocked library while drinking Madeira, smoking a cigar and having an educated conversation was a far better fate than anything the Deathlands was likely to offer him. Most important, Doc had seen Ryan Cawdor escape from worse dungeons than Jorge-Teo's well-buttressed but primitive establishment, and Doc was prepared to buy Ryan every second of the baron's attention he could, whatever the cost. Doc suddenly smiled and stopped by a volume for several long moments.

The baron raised a mocking eyebrow. "Something intrigues you, Doctor?"

Doc pulled forth an ancient copy of *The Time Machine.*

Barat smiled at the choice. "Ah, H. G. Wells…a true classic. I whiled away many happy hours in my youth reading his works."

Doc absently ran his finger down the spine of the book. Despite its advanced age it had been lovingly preserved, far more lovingly than he had. He sighed in memory. "Yes, Herbert was an interesting man. I met him when he was studying biology at the Royal College of Science under T. H. Huxley."

Baron Barat stared. "You...met him?"

"Yes, well, we all thought young Herbert had quite a bright future ahead of him in either the natural sciences or philosophy. You might well imagine my surprise when I learned in later years that he had bent his talents to writing scientific romances."

Barat had begun to suspect his guest might be mad, but now he was sure of it.

Doc shrugged guiltily. "Nevertheless, I must admit I had never before been able to claim the privilege of having known a successful novelist, and curiosity compelled me to peruse a few volumes of his speculative fiction." Doc turned and tossed the book to the desk between them. "The Eloi, innocent and childlike, living in bucolic idyll beneath the sun, while the technologically advanced, cannibalistic Morlock dwell in their dark catacombs beneath, rising up at night to shear them like sheep." Doc gazed coldly upon the baron. "The longer I live in these dark times the more truly amazing, and may I say regretful, it is to learn how many things poor Herbert succeeded in predicting correctly."

One of the greatest ironies of Doc's life was that it had been a twentieth-century man by the name of Wells who had torn him from his time, ripped him from the bosom of his family, experimented upon him, and then flung him like garbage into a future horrible beyond his imagining. Doc was a man always walking the thin edge of madness, but sometimes he became calmer before he snapped rather than the other way around; and sometimes rather than leaving him gibbering, hallucinating and dwelling in the past his madness was a glorious relaxation of all safeguards. Doc felt the wine relaxing him and bringing color to his cheeks. The strong tobacco stimulated him. He knew that he would very likely die in the next few moments. He decided to give himself over to violence, enjoy it, and take the baron with him.

The baron laughed. All he saw was an old man, possibly mad, disarmed, separated from his sec man and leaning upon a cane. Barat was blissfully unaware of the danger he was in. He leaned back in his chair shaking his head. "Come now, Doctor. You accuse me of being a Morlock? Surely as a man of science you realize that cannibalism is a woefully inefficient method of food production." The baron waved expansively toward the window. "You have seen our fishing boats, our fields of grain, our laden vines."

Doc found himself in a more lucid state than he could remember. He was relishing the educated discourse even as bloodlust welled within him. "But of course, Baron. The reproductive and maturation cycle of man is far too long and complicated for our poor species to make any decent sort of livestock. Though I must say that all too often in these intervening years I have seen the practice of cannibalism used quite successfully as a dietary supplement. However, I do not accuse you of being a cannibal. On the contrary, Baron, from what I have observed, I would name you hematophage, and blood, unlike human flesh, is a rapidly renewable resource given a large enough source of human stock. Say, an entire island of people in your thrall?"

"Hematophage?" Baron Barat gave Doc a very thin, cold smile at the scientific name for blood eater. "You name me vampire?"

"The accusation is metaphoric, Baron. Though I suspect the blood in you and your people's veins is purple from the effects of the disease porphyria in some mutated form, and that the light of the sun would ravage your flesh as any revenant of legend, I still strongly believe that you walk among the living rather than the undead. Black with sin as it may be, your heart still beats within your breast, and it would take no wooden stake driven through that heart to slay you. Indeed!" Doc's sword cane suddenly hissed from its ebon sheath as he lunged. "Cold steel should suffice!"

Nero gasped and fell transfixed through the heart as proof of Doc's theory.

Doc rounded upon the baron. Barat drew his blaster with remarkable alacrity, but he gasped in turn as Doc transfixed his blaster hand before he could present it. The weapon clattered to the desktop. The desk was still between them, and Barat pushed himself back abruptly and out of range of the sword. Doc deftly slid the point of his rapier through the trigger guard of the baron's blaster and flipped the weapon far out of reach. He jerked his head at the sword hanging over the fireplace. "Come, my good Baron! I see a blade hanging above your mantel! Let us contend like men of honor!" Doc tossed the silver hilt of his sword stick into his left hand. "Having pierced your hand, I will handicap myself appropriately!"

"Contend? As men of honor? With you?" The baron sneered as he retreated. "In the first, you are no baron. In the second, you are clearly insane. And in the third?" Barat spit in contempt. "You are an American."

"Upon my soul!" Doc grinned savagely as he advanced around the desk. "Guilty upon all counts!"

Barat continued his retreat. "I will admit to you, Dr. Tanner, I am not the swordsman I should be. I recognize the need for steel in the world we live in but I was always more of a marksman. My son, on the other hand?" The baron reached out his unwounded hand and pulled a silken rope that hung from the ceiling. "He will be more than happy to give you the match you crave."

A bell rang out in the hall.

Doc stopped as the door to the study swung open.

A figure filled the doorway from top to bottom. The man was draped in a caped long coat that reached his boots. A wide-brimmed black hat left his face in shadow.

Barat's smile was sickening. "Sylvano, you are late."

The big man's voice sounded like well-educated slate breaking. "Forgive me, Father. I thought the situation was in hand."

"It appears the good doctor is something of an adept with a blade, and you, dear one, have languished far too long for lack of a challenge. I thought perhaps you might contend with him."

"Thank you, Father." Sylvano shrugged off his long coat. He wore no shirt beneath it. His skin was as chalk white as Jak Lauren's and muscled like a circus strong man with purple veins crawling beneath his skin in twisted road maps of strength. He doffed his hat and black hair fell lank and straight to his shoulders. His eyes were as black as his father's. He unbuckled his blaster belt and hung a pair of revolvers next to his hat. He took a moment to tie back his hair and then his black-hilted rapier rasped slowly from the sheath. The giant grinned to show horse-size teeth with the gums purple and receded. "You know something of fencing, Dr. Tanner?"

"I've gone out," Doc admitted modestly.

"Gone out." Sylvano savored the anachronism. "You

have dueled. I myself have not yet had the honor of a formal duel." For such a huge man he held his weapon almost daintily. Despite that Doc was a tall man, Sylvano adopted a low guard position *en tierce.*

Doc matched him. The tips of their blades hovered scant inches away from each other. "I see you have studied, *Maestre* Sylvano."

The pale giant's eyes never wavered as he nodded. "It is what I do during the day."

"Come then." Doc took a last drag on his cigar and tossed it into the fire. "Show me what you have learned."

Sylvano lunged.

Doc parried and retreated. Their blades rang as Doc was forced to parry and retreat twice more. He flung a wild cut at Sylvano's arm that turned into a thrust straight for the heart. Sylvano narrowly avoided being impaled. The giant retreated a step and beat back Doc's following attacks. Doc found he was enjoying himself. He had spent far too long skewering brutes and savages without skill. Doc smiled slyly as Sylvano turned away two more rapid attacks. "You use the Bonetti defense."

Sylvano exposed his mulelike teeth as their blades rang between them. "Yes, I await your response with Capoferro."

"Such would be a logical expectation." Doc surged forward with a flurry of feints and thrusts. "Unless one's opponent knew his Agrippa!"

Sylvano came within an inch of losing his left eye. He jerked his head back as Doc knew he would, and Doc's blade arrowed for Sylvano's heart at the opening. Only shear athleticism allowed Sylvano to turn the thrust aside. The attack failed, but Doc was never one to forget his blade's edge and Sylvano's desperate defense left another opening. Doc lashed his blade across Sylvano's forearm in retreat.

Purple blood spilled upon the antique Persian carpet that served as their fencing lane. Barat shouted out in alarm. "My son!" He moved toward the door, and Doc leaped back and flung a warning cut at the baron. Barat cringed back in the corner, clutching his hands.

Doc resumed his attack on Sylvano. The wound upon the big man's massive forearm was long and deep. "Porphyria, as I suspected. The ancient blood disease, though undoubtedly mutated into some obscene form brought about by this new age. I fear it will take Herculean measures to stem your hemorrhaging, Sylvano. Come now! Let us cease this! I have a friend who is a healer of some skill. Release my friend in jail and I will prevail upon my other companions to assist you!"

Sylvano roared like a lion and charged. His blood flew in purple ribbons as he attacked. Doc suddenly found he could do nothing but parry and retreat. After he had divined the islanders' illness, Doc had hoped Sylvano would falter once wounded. Instead Sylvano charged like a bull. Doc found his lungs burning in his chest. He had seen far too much exertion in the past two days, and the liquor and strong tobacco he had imbibed were no longer his friends. Grim reality reasserted itself. In strict chronology he was a man no older than Ryan, but biologically, being time-trawled had left him with the body of a sixty-year-old man. Temporally he had seen three centuries' worth of the worst behavior humanity had to offer, and had the mental and physical scars to prove it.

Doc gasped for breath. Sylvano was larger, faster, stronger and younger than him. His rapier's blade was a full foot longer than Doc's. The old man had the superior skill, but as his wind began to fail he felt like he was fencing with a freight train unconstrained by tracks. Doc heard the baron moving behind him but he could pay no attention to it. Sylvano's attacks fell like rain. Doc parried, retreated and parried again. His arm began to feel leaden. It was only a matter of time before the behemoth in front of him beat down his blade and butchered him.

Doc had but one last ace up his sleeve.

"Sylvano? For a man with the bleeding disease, taking up the sword must have taken great courage. I honor you for it."

Sylvano ignored Doc's compliment and concentrated on destroying him.

"And for a self-taught swordsman?" Doc's praise was sincere. "You are magnificent. In this configuration I am finished."

The giant's sword flashed and flashed again. He didn't commit himself. He left no more openings. Every time they crossed swords his thrusts and parries were hammer blows intent on slamming the last bit of speed and strength out of the old man's failing arm. Despite his blood spilling in a river upon the floor, Sylvano knew he had his opponent. With two more steps Doc's back would be against the wall and he would be done for. Still, something in Doc's demeanor troubled the giant. "Why do you smile?"

Doc gasped. "It is just…that I know something…you do not."

Sylvano rose to his full seven feet as Doc sagged back against the wall. The point of the old man's sword drooped like a reed bereft of water. Sylvano moved in for the kill. "And what would that be, Dr. Tanner?"

"I am not left-handed."

Sylvano displayed his status as a gifted amateur rather than a true swordsman. He should have run Doc through, but instead he gaped as Doc passed his blade from left hand to right. Doc summoned his last strength and attacked. There was very little left to draw upon, but he was proud of his bravado, determined to die well, and Sylvano had allowed himself to be awed. The giant gasped as Doc transfixed his sword hand just as Doc had transfixed his father's. The heavy rapier fell from Sylvano's pierced hand and he staggered backward, clutching his wounds, and shouted in genuine terror, "No!"

Doc lunged. Twice he had sought Sylvano's heart and failed. On his third attempt his timing and his target were in perfect accordance. He thrust his point straight and true for the purple, beating fist of the giant's life.

Baron Barat's blaster sounded like a cannon going off in the small study.

Doc's thrust missed as a huge, invisible fist slammed him sideways. His legs no longer obeyed him and he buckled. Doc sighed wearily as he fell. "Oh, bother."

Chapter Eight

Ryan rose from his drug-induced dreams like Orpheus ascending from Hades. Every horror he had seen, every atrocity he had witnessed, every terrible act he himself had been forced to commit or had visited against him in this fire-blasted world had come to him, come back assisted, exaggerated and multiplied tenfold by his imagination and the hallucinogenic vileness Baron Barat had poured forth into his cup. The world spun as Ryan became aware of his surroundings. He tried to rise and put his feet beneath him, but fell. Constable Jorge-Teo and his sec men laughed as Ryan fell from his bunk and knocked over the slop bucket.

Ryan lay naked in filth. A shuddering smile passed across his crusted lips. Naked except for his eye patch. That was the second and last mistake these chill-pale, rad-blasted sec muties were ever going to make. The men stopped laughing as someone pounded on the door. Ryan lay where he was and spent time gathering himself.

The door opened. Jorge-Teo called out in greeting. "Father Joao! I see your fishing trip went well!" He laughed again and called back to the holding cells. "Hey! Prisoner! Your friends are here!"

Ryan ignored the imperative to look and just lay on the concrete. Ryan recognized Mildred Wyeth's voice as she made an outraged snarl. The constable wasn't pleased with Ryan's recalcitrance. "Mateus! Get him up."

Mateus was a lanky man as tall as Doc but with black hair and bad teeth. He walked up to the cell and drew another of the home-rolled, double-barrel blasters the sec men in these parts seemed to favor. "Hey, this one is loaded with salt." He jerked the barrels upward, indicating Ryan should stand. "But you still won't like it."

Ryan still felt as weak as a kitten, and being blasted with rock salt wasn't going to improve matters. He crawled across the floor and used the bars of the cell to haul himself up to a swaying, standing position. Jak and Mildred were bound by the hands. Neither one looked injured. The sec man behind Mildred couldn't seem to keep his chalk-white hand off her behind. The muzzles of the blaster pressed against the back of her head were telling her to shut up and love it. Another man was putting Jak's and Mildred's weapons and packs in a locker. Ryan's blasters weren't among them, and he suspected the baron had confiscated them for himself. Ryan met the eyes of a chalk-faced man in a hooded black robe with red piping. His black hair was tonsured rather than long, and he had a short mustache and beard. He wore a golden crucifix around his neck.

Father Joao.

"Prisoner." The priest gestured at his captives. "You know these?"

Ryan looked back and forth between Jak and Mildred. He spit as he surveyed Jak. "He's one of you." Ryan's eye slid across Mildred in disgust. "I don't know what kind of rad-burned mutie that is." Ryan turned and shuffled back to his bunk. He waited for the double blast of rock salt in his back, but it didn't come.

The constable was amused once more. "Well, either our friend is a very uneducated man or he is lying." He examined his two new detainees. His eyes lingered long on Mildred's shapely form. "An African and an albino. I must say I am intrigued."

Mildred was in no mood to be contrite. "Why don't you start singing *Ebony and Ivory* and watch what happens."

Constable Jorge-Teo stared for a few uncomprehending heartbeats and then jerked his head at the sec man behind her. "Valter!" Mildred crumpled as Valter drove the butt of his blaster into her kidney. The men all laughed. Father Joao tsked in unconvincing disapproval. Valter stared down at Mildred in open cupidity.

"I want this one."

Jorge-Teo scowled and his hand went to his semiauto blaster. Father Joao raised a warning hand. "It is the baron who decides who is to breed with who and when outside of marriage."

Tension filled the sec station.

Valter broke the tension with a leer. "Who said breed?" He stared down knowingly at Mildred as she pushed herself up to hands and knees. "She has other holes."

Jorge-Teo grinned and called back, "Prisoner! What do you think?"

Ryan stayed in the shadows of his bunk. The slop bucket scraped as he pulled it to him. He had nothing left in his stomach, but he stuck his finger down his throat and retched. The sec men all laughed once more.

"I don't think he cares," Valter stated.

Jorge-Teo nodded at Father Joao. "Perhaps you should go outside and keep watch."

"Constable!" Father Joao lapsed into Portuguese as he protested.

Jorge-Teo returned the conversation to English for the benefit of the captives. "Come now, Father, we all know what you do in your cottage with that little island girl the baron gave you."

Father Joao's alabaster skin flushed pink.

All the sec men laughed once more. Jorge-Teo shrugged. "You can do the same to the African when we are finished. As long as her womb is not damaged, the baron will not mind so much. I believe we would all like to see it." The men laughed again, but cruelty replaced shame in the priest's eyes as he moved to the door. Jorge-Teo raised a cautioning hand. "You see the baron's wag or his personal guard, you knock three times. Best we apologize later than be caught now."

"Yes, Constable, I understand."

"And, Father?"

"Yes, Constable?"

"I know you are distracted, and we are in town, and you pray for us, but remember our duty. Keep an eye out for the nightwalkers."

All lust and cruelty drained from Joao's face. Valter and Mateus both handed him a blaster and the priest took them. "Yes, Constable." Joao stepped out in the night.

Nightwalkers. Ryan filed that away. He rose as the sec men began unbuckling their swords and blaster belts. They shucked off long coats and shirts to expose worm-pale flesh. Valter and several others dropped their trousers to reveal the purple, engorged flesh rising between their legs. Ryan flipped up his eye patch. A pair of curved spring-steel slivers made a frame around its edges. They had keylike flanges and cuts on both ends.

The picks popped into Ryan's hand with a squeeze of the patch. He pulled the eye patch back into place and stalked to the bars of his cage. The constable's sec men had no attention to spare for a vomiting prisoner.

They had fresh meat in front of them.

Mildred suddenly rolled over and snapped her boot up between Valter's legs. Most of the men laughed and roared as Valter keened and dropped. They liked a victim with a little life in her. But not too much. Mateus stomped on Mildred's stomach, and she gasped and curled.

Ryan silently slipped his picks into the tumblers and began working the lock.

Jak struggled violently, but he got a flurry of fists and boots for his trouble.

Ryan felt the ancient lock responding to his seduction. The lock was old but oiled and well maintained. He suspected the holding cells had frequent guests. The constable was just stupid enough to keep the hinges of the cell doors well oiled, as well. He should have known that nothing should open silently in a jail.

The would-be rapists heard nothing as Ryan stepped from his cell.

The sec station blasters were all chained, and the sec men had piled their weapons on the other side of the room. Constable Jorge-Teo and his men stood in a circle, pants down, as Valter stood over his victim. Mildred feebly tried to kick him and he stomped on her ankle in reprisal when she failed. Valter grabbed Mildred by the legs and savagely flipped her onto her stomach.

Ryan draped a sword belt over his shoulder.

Valter took out a knife and began cutting his way down

the back seam of Mildred's khaki cargo pants. "Christiano! Hold her!" Christiano helpfully grabbed Mildred by her beaded plaits and rammed her face into the floor. Jorge-Teo dropped his pants. "Muisa!" He pointed to the man holding Jak. "That one does not move."

Muisa's paper-pale fist fell into the side of Jak's neck three times and left him twitching on the floor.

Ryan silently removed a whaling lance from the rack. Long ago Ryan had been upon the waters of the Lantic and chased Leviathan. He took up the seven-and-a-half-foot killing spear, and it felt familiar in his calloused hands. Half of the length was a wooden haft as thick as his arm. The rest was an iron shaft tipped with a fist-size lozenge of sharpened spearhead. Ryan took the lance in the underhanded hold. He took three short, sharp steps forward and let fly. It was a heave rather than a throw. Like many implements designed for killing rather than fighting, it was the weight of this weapon that did the work. The whaling lance was made to sink through half a fathom of whale flesh to seek its life.

Valter's spine proved little barrier to the twenty-pound pike.

He proved so unresistant to whale spears that the blade punched all the way through his middle and sank into Christiano's face where he knelt holding Mildred's head against the floor. Ryan's stolen sword hissed from its sheath as he stalked forward among the suddenly screaming blood-spattered sec men. He was only a middling sword-fighter. Nevertheless Doc had tried to teach him a few things in his more lucid moments. Ryan rammed his blade through Mateus's heart with an authority that would have done Doc proud.

The constable's blaster rose.

Jak jumped up from the floor and put both boots into Jorge-Teo's chest. The constable went flying over a desk, and his blaster sailed across the room. Jak couldn't break his fall with his hands tied, and his breath blasted out of his lungs as he hit the concrete hard. The remaining sec man grabbed for the pants puddled around his ankles and screamed for mercy. "No! No! No!" Ryan rammed his blade through the man's vitals and the sec man fell vomiting blood the color of wine.

Father Joao flung open the door. *"Que inferno..."* His already fish-belly complexion paled at the carnage in the sec station. Ryan darted his sword across the distance between them but it clanged off the door as Joao slammed it shut again.

Jorge-Teo was up and running for his office.

Ryan sprinted after him.

The constable slammed the door to his office shut behind him and flung the bolt home. Ryan dived through the frosted window. Jorge-Teo screamed as Ryan tackled him in a shower of glass. The two men rolled across the floor and Ryan came up on top. His fist pistonned into his opponent's face like a jackhammer. Jorge-Teo's lips split apart and his parrotlike teeth shattered beneath Ryan's knuckles. He checked his bloody hand midblow as Jorge-Teo's eyes rolled and he went limp. The one-eyed man rose and dragged the half-conscious constable back into the main jail.

Jak was free of his bonds and he rose from putting the wounded sec man out of his misery. As Mildred stared at the ruins of her pants, Ryan dropped Jorge-Teo. He walked over to the locker and pulled on his clothes and boots. He wished for his blasters; his blades were there. He tossed Mildred her pack and she quickly stepped into her spare pair of pants. Ryan strapped on his panga and then slid his slim-bladed combat knife into the top of his boot. He stalked across the room and picked up the constable's fallen blaster. It had a long barrel and said MAUSER on the slide. Ryan checked the load and found a spare mag in the constable's coat.

Mildred checked the loads in her blaster. "Where's Doc?"

"Baron had him brought up to the manor."

"Where that?" Jak asked.

"Dunno." Ryan looked down at Jorge-Teo. "He'll tell us. Where're Krysty and J.B.?"

"The mat-trans only lets two people through at a time, and it looks like it's set on a seventy-two-hour schedule," Mildred said. "Jak and I came through, so I'm thinking J.B. and Krysty got denied and are still back at the redoubt. The stickie situation was getting pretty ugly when we left and can't be getting any better. They'll be running out of food and water soon."

Ryan checked his chron. Two more days till Krysty and J.B. could jump, and the baron would have a welcoming party waiting. Ryan quickly filled his people in on the situation on the other island and what had happened after the crossing as the church bells began to ring the alarm out in the square. "I don't like it but we're going to have to split up. Mildred and I are going after Doc. Jak, I want you to get yourself a black hat and blend in."

Without a word Jak rummaged through the caped long coats of the fallen sec men. They were all too large, so it came down to the least bloodstained. Mildred tucked his snow-white hair up into the broad-brimmed hat while he pulled on gloves. Jak tucked his blaster away and picked up a pair of the local weapons. He put on a pair of the local smoked lenses and gave Ryan a shrug.

"At first glance," Ryan said, "you'll do."

"Job?" Jak asked.

"Father Joao. Get him. Get his boat. We need off this island and access to the sister isle and the mat-trans escarpment."

"Got it," Jak said. "Meet where?"

"Doc and I made landfall a couple miles north of the ville. Be there at dawn. We'll meet you." Ryan thought of the cave. "Don't come within sight of land until sunup. If we aren't there, then try again at noon, then dawn tomorrow. If we still aren't there, then getting Krysty and J.B. is your priority."

Jak moved to the back door of the sec station without another word.

Ryan turned his eye upon his former jailer. Ryan had beaten him senseless and Jorge-Teo's eyes were still rolling. Ryan yanked him up by the hair and slapped him back to lucidity. "Where's the baron?"

"Stop…I bleed! Please."

Ryan cracked his hand across the constable's jaw. "Where?"

"In…his manse."

"Where's that?"

"The biggest house! On the highest hill!" The constable sobbed and clutched at his mangled face. "You cannot miss it!"

Ryan closed his fist and sent the constable back to sleep. He wiped violet blood from his hands on the unconscious man's coat. "Let's get Doc."

DOC WAS SURPRISED and somewhat displeased to find himself alive and in a great deal of pain. His left side and his back were on fire. Doc was in a bed piled with pillows and had a stack of quilts atop him. A fire flickered in the fireplace. Doc discovered his hands and feet were bound to the bedposts.

Barat spoke from a chair beside the bed. "You are awake."

"I am surprised to be alive."

The baron held up Nero's massive double-barreled blaster. "The weapon was loaded with rock salt. Nevertheless, it is of .75 caliber, and I am afraid I gave you both barrels."

"Nevertheless, I am still surprised you have let me live. I admit I had every intent of slaying both you and your son."

"Well, that is understandable given the circumstances," the baron conceded.

"I am forgiven?" Doc asked warily.

"Most assuredly not." The baron smiled like a shark. "And not to unduly alarm you, Doctor, but the reason you remain alive is that our conversation is not yet finished."

Doc *was* duly alarmed.

Barat leaned over Doc, his black eyes examining him as if he were an insect. "And given your past resistance, I fear the remainder of our conversation shall not take place in my library over cordials."

Doc unconsciously pressed himself back into the pillows as far as he could.

The baron raised a calming hand and leaned back once more. "I believe you have more companions coming through the mat-trans, Dr. Tanner. Depending upon their affection for you, there is a chance you may prove of use as a bargaining chip."

Doc wasn't sure how much affection Ryan had for him, but the man's loyalty to his friends was iron. Doc's greatest concern was that Ryan would get himself slaughtered trying to effect his escape. He knew if Ryan were alive he would try, and so would the rest.

Barat gave Doc an inscrutable smile. "And..."

Doc regarded Barat warily. "And?"

"And Sylvano has spoken in your favor."

Doc went from alarm to surprise. "Oh?"

"Yes, he is prevailing upon me to make you his tutor and fencing master. I am of two minds about this. I will tell you honestly, Doctor, your cooperation from this point on will have a great deal of influence on your prospects for survival, the survival of your friends and your own possible employment. No matter what the final outcome, you will tell me what I wish to know, willingly or unwillingly."

Doc shivered despite the warmth of the fire and the covers. He would be damned if he gave Baron Barat one thing more, but nonetheless he shook. This was not the first time he had been brought down despite his best efforts and been taken captive. Bile rose in Doc's throat. Terror racked his brain. Nor would it be the first time he had been humiliated, tortured and broken. Cold sweat burst upon his brow, and the spiders of madness began spinning their webs around his consciousness. Memories he strove to suppress rose. The damaged dikes of lucidity he struggled to shore every waking moment began to crumble once more.

Alarm bells in the ville cut Doc's downward spiral and began ringing like hope.

Doc knew without a doubt his friends were coming for him.

"You think your friends come for you?" Barat inquired.

Doc was sure of it but shook his head. He searched through his tattered psyche for the courage he had found when he had faced down the baron and his son in the study. Doc was insufferably pleased that though he was bound and helpless and facing torture and death, a small, mostly hidden reservoir still remained. With the flickering candle of hope that his friends lived Doc found that he was still prepared to die. "No, but you have given them great offense, and they will make murder among your people until you see the error of your ways."

Barat sighed wearily. "Pray that you are wrong, Dr. Tanner."

"Forgive my impertinence, but if I may ask, by what reason should I devoutly desire such a consummation?"

The baron shook his head. "Because if your companions do not fall into the hands of myself and my men this night, they will most assuredly fall into the hands of my brother."

Doc was not entirely sure what Barat meant, but he felt his guts turn to ice at the remark. "I fear I am not entirely sure I understand you, Baron Barat."

"I fear I am not entirely in control of this island, Dr. Tanner." The baron stared out inscrutably through the heavy iron bars that secured the window and into the night. "And I fear your friends are in terrible peril."

Chapter Nine

Jak moved among his enemies. A crowd was gathering in front of the church, and he walked up and joined it. Father Joao was waving his arms, exhorting the mob in whatever speak he spoke. Ryan said it was Portuguese, whatever that meant. To Jak it did sound like the talk he'd heard in Amazonia. The islanders began moving off in heavily armed detachments. Father Joao turned and stalked into his church. Jak followed silently. Joao wasn't even aware he had a shadow until he was halfway down the pews. The priest jumped in alarm and whirled. His pale face flushed crimson with anger, and he began spouting off and pointing toward the door. Joao's jaw dropped in shock as Jak raised the double blaster he carried in each hand. One he leveled at Joao's guts. He used the muzzles of the other to push up the brim of his hat. Jak's blood-red gaze regarded Father Joao rather critically over the rims of the smoked lenses and his smile rearranged the scars on his face.

The priest went white again.

"Boat," Jak said. "Now."

Father Joao's eyes flew wide and he launched back into his outraged arm waving. He switched back to English for Jak's benefit. "Listen, fool! Your life and those of your friends are in my hands! Drop your weapons now and—"

Jak rammed the twin-muzzled blaster into Father Joao's solar plexus. "Shut it."

The priest's pale face fisted in agony as he shut it and dropped to his knees.

Jak replaced the blaster in his right hand with the .357 Magnum Colt Python from under his coat to let Joao know they were dealing in lead rather than rock salt. "You. Me." Jak tipped the black hat back down and jerked his head to snap the dark glasses back in place. "Wharf. Your boat."

Father Joao sucked wind but managed a disparaging look. "And just where…do you think…to go?"

"Beach." Jak glanced to the north. "Two miles. North."

Father Joao became so scared he lost his English, and Jak was pretty sure it wasn't him he was scared of. Joao was babbling a mile a minute but he kept repeating *"O Baron da Noite! O Baron da Noite!"* and kept waving his hands.

Jak was reminded of Ryan's tale of the cave chiller down on the beach, and he didn't like the sound of *Baron da Noite* at all. "Night baron?"

"*Sim!* I mean, yes!"

"Who's night baron?" Jak asked.

Father Joao's eyes got very wide. He spoke a name as if he were afraid its owner might hear. "Raul…"

"Raul's night baron?"

"Yes!"

"Xavier's day baron?"

"Yes!"

"Raul's out?"

"I am sure he has heard the alarms!"

Jak raised one speculative, snow-white eyebrow. "Raul swim?"

Father Joao blinked in confusion. Jak could tell the question had never occurred to him. In the end it didn't matter. Jak had a job to do. He jerked his blaster toward the harbor. "Move."

Father Joao cringed in dread. "We will die."

Jak cocked his blaster. "Chill you now."

Father Joao's shoulders sagged in resignation. "It might be preferable." Nevertheless the priest moved toward the door.

"Blast spine if you trick me," Jak cautioned.

"We will reach the harbor. Beyond that it will be up to you to keep us alive."

Jak silently slid his Magnum blaster back under his coat. He was already pushing it, and the weapon was completely out of place on this island. He palmed a throwing blade and kept the local blaster ready. "Go."

Jak saw people rushing this way and that. It looked as though the ville was girding itself for siege. Father Joao walked across the square with a purpose. Jak hustled along slightly behind him and kept his face in the shadow of his hat. So far Ryan's plan was working. A few islanders tipped their hats to the priest in passing, but other than that no one gave Jak a second look. Father Joao hesitated as they reached the wharf, and Jak gave him a prod to keep him moving. There were a score of armed men down on the beach. They had set up barricades with wags and barrels, and guarded the steps up the seawall where Ryan and Doc had entered the ville. The docks themselves were mostly abandoned. The islanders were defending the docks from outside attack and not expecting the enemy to be operating from within. Sailed fishing boats of generally small size and various descriptions were tied up at dock. Most did not have engines.

"Boat," Jak said. "Which?"

Father Joao pointed. "That is the one I use."

It was a whaleboat. Jak surveyed the craft. He had spent a great deal of his young life maneuvering canoes, pirogues and rafts through the bayous and could run a skiff, but open ocean sailing was a stretch. The boat was about twenty-eight feet long and the mast was stepped. Jak was relieved to see the boat had a small cobbled-together outboard motor and a jerrican of whatever it was using for fuel. Assuming another storm didn't hit, he could maneuver the craft from island to island. Jak glanced at the tiny iron cannon mounted on a swivel in the prow. A small keg of powder and short iron harpoons were racked next to it.

The albino teen's head snapped around at the sound of footsteps on the dock. One of the islanders was walking toward them. "Who?" Jak muttered.

Father Joao raised a hand in greeting as he spoke low. "That is Thiago, Captain Roque's brother. He is captain of the night-fishing fleet. What shall I tell him?"

"Baron business," Jak suggested.

"That should suffice," the priest agreed sourly.

Thiago raised the fishing spear he carried in greeting as he approached. "*Pai,* Joao." He was stocky and broad-shouldered and in the night wore a knit cap rather than the broad hat. A weighted hand net was wound over one shoulder, and he carried a long, single blaster crooked in his elbow. He didn't look happy. The fishing captain and the priest exchanged a few terse words. Thiago scowled at the priest in parting and turned away.

"You said?" Jak whispered.

"I said—"

Thiago spun and let fly with his fishing spear. Jak

dodged, and his throwing blade sang through the air. The range was so short the knife had no time to revolve. The trident-tined spear ripped the hat from Jak's head. The point of Jak's blade punched like a dart into the hollow between Captain Thiago's collarbones. A second blade instantly filled Jak's hand, but there was no need. The night captain dropped with his throat stoppered by steel. Joao's jaw hung open. It had happened so fast he'd had no time to react. Now he found himself staring down the double barrels of Jak's blaster. He raised trembling hands. "Listen…I…"

"Stupe." Jak snapped the blaster across Joao's mouth and the priest dropped to the dock spitting teeth. Jak rolled Thiago's corpse into the whaleboat and tossed his longblaster and the spear beside him. He gave Father Joao a few swift kicks to get him in motion. "Boat."

Father Joao moaned and held his face in his hand as he crawled into the vessel. Jak hopped in and cast off. He took up an oar and pushed them away from the dock. The tide was going out. The albino teen shoved a pair of oars into Joao's hands and took the tiller. "Row."

Father Joao very reluctantly began bending his oars. The whaleboat slowly slipped from the little harbor and out of range of the lights of the ville. Jak waited until they were in the channel and felt the pull of the current before he kicked the motor into life and began heading north. Ryan and Mildred would be heading inland.

Jak wondered how Doc was doing.

THE RUNNER STAGGERED into Doc's holding room breathlessly accompanied by two grim-faced guards of Baron Barat's personal retinue. The baron sat up in his chair and gave Doc a weary look. The runner began to gasp out his news, but the baron held up a calming hand and gestured to the bottles on the sideboard. One of the sec men took a decanter and poured. Doc watched as red wine splashed into the glass. He raised an eyebrow as the man splashed in a brown liquid from another decanter. Doc suspected this was the "Lotus" he kept hearing about. Doc's stomach turned as the concoction was finished off with the contents of a large corked test tube. The bright red blood hit the glass and hung billowy and suspended in the amber broth of wine and hallucinogenic drugs. The sec man stirred the contents into a blood-streaked cloud and held it forth. The runner took the offered glass eagerly and gulped the contents. Almost instantly he stood taller and his breathing slowed. He straightened his coat and stood at attention. The baron nodded for him to continue his report.

It seemed to be short and to the point; however Doc could make out almost none of it except names like Christiano, Mateus, Jorge-Teo and Joao. Baron Barat leaned back in his chair when the report was finished. The sec men glared at Doc and clearly wanted to kill him. Barat stared at his bandaged hand and then into the flames of the fireplace. The firelight reflected in his black eyes and his face was even grimmer than that of his sec men if that were possible. Whatever thoughts the Baron Xavier Barat was thinking did not please him.

To his shame Doc jerked back as Baron Barat gave him his full attention. "I am told, Dr. Tanner, that your one-eyed friend, an albino and a black woman are loose upon my island. I am further informed that they assaulted my constable and killed four of his men."

Doc tried to keep his voice cold. "I warned you they would make murder among your people, Baron."

Barat scoffed. "If they are so ruthless, then why would they keep a damaged wretch like you among them?"

Doc flinched. He knew that far too often he wasn't the asset to his companions that he should be.

"No, Doctor." The baron waved his wounded hand in dismissal of the rhetorical question. "I believe we both know they will try to rescue you and then steal a boat."

Doc unhappily admitted to himself that was most likely exactly was going on.

"It matters not if you have an army of murdering friends. They can only come through the mat-trans two at a time. They will have no way off the escarpment other than swimming, and there are things far more dangerous than the currents and the rocks in these waters."

Doc searched for a rejoinder and failed.

"The albino and the black fell easily to my men. The smoke of the Lotus is quite effective in this regard, and it is a performance I am prepared to repeat as often as I must. Further, I now have a fairly accurate grasp of their arrival time. Try my patience, Doctor, and rather than capture your remaining party members I shall simply have them blasted down while they are fresh from the mat-trans and still about their regurgitations."

Doc had no answer for that, either.

The baron sighed. "Dr. Tanner, tell me how many people you have in your party in total. I want their names, descriptions and how they are armed and equipped. Do this and perhaps there shall be some leeway in determining their final fate."

Doc rummaged among his dwindling courage. "And what will you do should I refuse, Baron? Break me upon the wheel?"

The baron smiled with genuine amusement. "Why, yes, Dr. Tanner! That is exactly what I shall do! I have things I must do this night, but we shall speak again at dawn, and if you do not tell me everything I wish to know, I will have my men overturn one of our largest wags and tie you to the wheel, whereupon you shall be stripped, crucified, emasculated and broken upon it." Barat shrugged carelessly. "It is our common punishment for rebellious slaves and invaders of our island. Afterward, when I am convinced you have told me everything of relevance, you shall be bled dry and the meager meat of your bones given to the nightwalkers."

Doc found he was shaking. There was only one consolation left. Ryan had outwitted and outfought barons with far more manpower and firepower than Barat. "My friends will come."

"I know, Doctor, and just three of them decimated the sec station. I am afraid I cannot have them marauding upon my island, or crossing back to the other island and causing trouble." The baron rose from his chair. The look on his face was terrible. "The fact of the matter is that you and your friends are forcing me to do something I do not wish to do, Dr. Tanner. Something I have not done in years, something I had sworn never to do again."

Doc wasn't entirely sure what that meant, but it didn't matter. He had seen both craft and cruelty on his ghost-faced host. What Doc saw now on the face of Baron Xavier Barat was a terrible resolve, and it scared him witless. "I—"

"In the meantime..." Barat snapped his fingers and pointed at Doc. The larger of the two sec men prepared two more drafts of wine, blood and drug. Doc recoiled in the ropes that bound him as the baron took one glass and the sec man brought the second one toward the bed.

"No!" Doc shouted. He desperately clamped his teeth together as the sec man's hand clamped onto his jaw.

"Dr. Tanner," the baron said. "Surely you know I cannot have you lying abed plotting, much less in any condition to assist in your own escape."

Doc thrashed helplessly.

The baron gave Doc his skull-face grin. "Dr. Tanner? The Blood of the Lotus can be introduced through other bodily orifices if you are uncooperative, and the only difference it will make is that you will not enjoy the taste of the wine."

Doc sagged in defeat. His sanity, strength and courage were at their limits. The glass was pushed against his mouth. Doc didn't resist, but the sec man still cruelly vised his mouth open and held it open as he steadily upended the glass. Doc gagged and choked as the sourness of wine, the coppery slickness of blood and the sickening sweetness of nightmare slid down his throat.

Barat raised his glass in mocking toast. "Pleasant dreams, Dr. Tanner."

RYAN RAN HIS EYE over the baron's manse. He examined the stone walls and spear-tipped iron fence along the top. The first-story windows were bricked over except for firing slits. The second- and third-floor windows were barred. Barbed wire and razor-sharp spikes ringed the roof. Ryan stared long and hard at the brass dome of the observatory that rose among the multiple chimneys. Movement returned his gaze earthward. Sec men with auto-blasters patrolled the grounds. The mansion had fairly extensive grounds, but the sec men all stayed behind the fence. Ryan was pretty sure he and Mildred could take them, but he had no idea how many people might be inside nor did he know where Doc was. Best to go in quiet. He frowned at the manse once more. It was the only house in the hills that was lit, and Ryan didn't like it.

He liked the almost total lack of pursuit even less.

The ville men had taken their sweet time organizing the posse. Rather than assaulting the sec station, the first thing they had done was secure the wharf. By the time they'd gotten around to the sec station and the constable, Ryan and Mildred were long gone. Ryan had paused for a while on the first hill outside out of the ville proper and watched the enemy's movements. They had posted a cordon of heavily armed men down on the beach and used carts to make a roadblock across the street that ran out of the ville into the hills. No attempt had been made to organize a sweep into the hills. Ryan didn't like it.

"Could be worse," Mildred opined. "Could be raining."

Lightning cracked out of the ink-black sky to the east and thunder rumbled off shore. Fat, cold drops began to spatter down through the trees.

Ryan stared at the manse with the patience of a stone.

Mildred shivered as the rain started to soak her through. "So, what do you think?"

Ryan shook his head at Baron Barat's manse. The windows were either bricked over or barred. He looked out into the rain. "I think we're safer in there."

"And warmer," Mildred agreed.

Ryan glanced up. "Let's climb."

Mildred shook her head. "Here we go..."

The forest was thick, but the stumps surrounding the manse proved that any tree closer than forty meters had been chopped down to provide a killing zone. Everything Ryan saw said the people on this island were used to sieges. Ryan scrambled up a spreading hardwood pausing every few feet to haul Mildred up behind him. He stopped in a crotch of branches that let him look in the second-story windows and froze. Doc was lying tied to a bed in one of the rooms. Ryan heaved Mildred up beside him. He flicked his eye from room to room, but the rest were either shuttered or had blinds or curtains drawn behind the bars.

Mildred gasped as she looked through the window. "Doc!"

Ryan nodded.

Mildred made an unhappy noise. "Tell me this doesn't stink like a trap."

It completely stank like a trap. Ryan gave Mildred a measuring look. "You can take anyone who comes into that room?"

By Mildred's own admission with a properly set up handblaster she could hit an ant in the ass at fifty yards and human reliably at a hundred. "I'm your woman."

"You cover me on the way in. When I'm in, you cover Doc. You cover us both on the way out."

Mildred took out her ZKR target revolver and checked the loads. "Okay, but how are you getting in?"

Ryan ran his gaze back up the manse and gazed fixedly at the observatory. "Top down."

"Okay." Ryan was the scariest son of a bitch Mildred had ever met, and if anyone could do it, he could. "How are you extracting?"

"Doc can't make it out the top unless I throw him."

Mildred had heard worse ideas. "So…?"

"I may have to carry him. So with luck, out the front. You cover. I'm thinking of taking the baron's wag if possible. Get us mobile and get us some distance. If I crash the gate, you've got to be ready to move." Ryan took a length of rope out of his pack. He tied it around the branch they sat on and let the rest fall to the weeds and mud below. He gave her a final look before he slid down the rope. "Be ready."

Mildred laid herself out along the bough and took her ZKR in both hands. "Born ready."

Chapter Ten

Baron Xavier Barat entered his cellar alone. In the light of his candle, barrels of wine and wheels of cheese aged in the cool, musty, cavelike vault. He crossed the cellar and went to heavy door. Three hooded, whale-oil lamps sat on a shelf, and he lit all three of them and snuffed out his taper. He examined the door and found that the iron bolt was still locked. The two heavy crossbeams were still in their brackets and unmolested. He shot the iron shutter of the peephole and prudently stepped back. No violence occurred, and he shone the light through. The iron grille was still in place, so he peered down the flight of steps that led deeper into the earth. The door at the bottom was closed and the bolts and trip wires were in place. The baron unlocked the door and hung a lantern on a hook outside of it. He took up the other two and descended the short, slimed stair to the catacombs.

It had been years since he had come down these steps, but he insisted his servants keep the lamps ready and the doors maintained. This night he was glad that he had. The door at the bottom was of very heavy oaken timbers, bound with black iron and studded with short spikes on the outside. The baron set down the lamps and took a deep breath. He flexed his bandaged hand and then loosened his sword in its sheath. He cocked both of the double blasters shoved through his belt. Rock salt wouldn't drive off what he feared this night. The pair was loaded with .75-caliber lead slugs that had a heavy nail down the middle, been filled with mercury and then sealed once more with lead. Barat eased the trip wires off tension and opened the peephole. The grille was still in place. He shone the light into the chamber. It was very low, of medieval origin and lined with the moldering bones of Barats from time out of mind. Xavier looked across the mausoleum chamber and stifled his sigh of relief. Iron bars blocked the dark passageway down into the cave system that riddled the islands' roots. The bars were as heavy as a castle's portcullis except that these were set in stone and were never meant to be raised.

Two of the bars were slightly bent where something had tested its strength against them and failed.

Barat unlocked the door and despite his fear strode across the chamber with purpose. The second security feature in the room was a short, triple-thick length of brick wall set perpendicularly just beyond the bars like a privacy screen. Behind the wall sat a simple chair. Barat stepped behind the barrier. He adjusted one lamp to its brightest and set it atop the wall. The other he set at his feet. The baron drew his two blasters, took a seat and waited. He could feel cold sweat trickle down his collar. His interview with Dr. Tanner had intrigued him so he took the copy of *The Time Machine* from a pocket in his cloak and opened to a page. He spent several minutes trying to read, but he couldn't concentrate on any passage. Barat was being outwaited and he knew it. He replaced the book and filled his hands with his blasters once more. They offered him no more patience but the cold steel did give him more resolve.

The baron finally spoke quietly. "Raul? Are you there?"

A voice far deeper than even Sylvano's answered. The voice was almost below human register. "You know I am, brother."

Barat shuddered as he always did. He knew it was a trick of the cavern's acoustics and his own mind, but it sounded like his brother was just on the other side of the bricks, rather than behind the bars and back where the lamplight didn't reach. Then again perhaps he was crouched but inches away. The baron had never dared to try to chart the catacombs and the caves they led to. There had always been talk of secret passageways from the ancient days. He wasn't about to step around the wall to find out, and if there were a hidden way into the chamber, Raul had never seen fit to come around the wall and face his brother, either. "I thought perhaps you might be…out and about."

"I smell blood upon you, brother."

Barat's eyes flicked his bandaged hand. "Do you?"

"Yes, just as I smell the fear sweating through your skin, and the mercury you so lovingly loaded into your pistols."

Barat grimaced but kept his voice neutral. He knew his brother lived to intimidate him during these interviews. "You heard the alarm bells?"

"I did."

"There are strangers upon the isle."

Barat was surprised as Raul paused before answering. "I know."

"You have seen them?"

"I have. The Cyclops is dangerous and wants killing. The other was an old man who smelled of madness."

"It was the old man who bloodied me. He carries a sword within his cane."

"You never practiced your swordsmanship as assiduously as you should have."

Barat cringed at the remark, and his hand almost went to very old scars upon his body. The baron kept his tone light. "He is a fascinating man. He speaks fluent Latin and claims the acquaintance of H. G. Wells. You might enjoy meeting him."

"Well, that is fascinating. Though I believe I might enjoy making him speak in tongues and acquainting him with God as I break his bones for their marrow more."

"He put similar marks upon Sylvano. Would you like me to arrange a match?" Barat remembered the old man's startling alacrity and skill. He almost hoped Raul might sneer and accept.

Barat's brother didn't rise to the bait. "Ah, my dear nephew. Does he send his love?"

"Nearly every day he bids me give him a hundred men with blasters and pikes that he might come down into these passages and drive you and yours forth into the light."

"Such a sweet boy." Raul's voice went reptilian.

Barat felt the old bitterness within him. "He misses his mother." He was surprised to find a cold reservoir of compassion within him, even for his brother. "I believe we all do."

Raul's roar shook the very walls of the catacombs. "She was mine!"

Answering roars boomed upward from the bowels of Raul's kingdom. The baron waited until the echoes faded. "Yes, Raul. She was your betrothed, but the marriage was arranged when all of us were children.

Just as you were firstborn, and the barony was to be yours." Barat kept malice and vengeance out of his voice and spoke the simple truth. "Then you reached the age of maturity, my brother, and you became what you became."

The words lay between them as solid as any brick wall or iron bar.

Raul's voice went back to being cold as his catacombs. "And how is my dear niece Zorime? I hear she is quite beautiful. As beautiful as her mother?"

Barat clenched his teeth but didn't rise to the bait as his brother had.

"You have many nieces and nephews down here, brother." Raul's demonic voice dripped with malice. "Some day you really must come down for a visit."

"The day I come down into those caves, Raul, will be at dawn, with every man of the ville, with blasters, pikes, the smoke of the Lotus and blasting powder."

Raul's voice dropped dangerously. "It would take you more than a day, your losses would be horrific, and with the night would come my counterattack upon the ville."

"I would annihilate you, Raul. The only card you have is that I am indeed unwilling to accept the losses such an endeavor would require, just as you keep your predations to a minimum and mostly among the slaves so as not to provoke it."

Silence hung heavy between them once more.

It was Raul who spoke first. "More strangers have come from the escarpment? At the usual interval?"

"Yes, the next two were an albino youth and a black woman."

"An albino?" Raul laughed. It was a horrible thing

to hear echoing through the chamber of stone and bones. "Coming to this island? Now there is irony. And a black, you say?"

"They were well-armed and equipped, but with the coming of the one-eyed man and the doctor we were prepared for them. You might find it of interest to know that the one-eyed man and Dr. Tanner were not taken on the escarpment. They appeared on the wharf claiming to have been shipwrecked in the storm."

Raul spent a few moments digesting this. "You believe they slew Roque and his crew?"

"And took his boat. The only truth in the matter is that I believe the two of them could not manage the boat and they were indeed shipwrecked upon the rocks in the channel. From things Dr. Tanner said I believe they washed up on Sister Isle and made contact with the slaves. Though where they found a boat to make the passage here is beyond me."

"They fashioned a raft."

"How do you know?"

"I found it."

The baron paused. "The one-eyed man was injured and Tanner old. They could not have felled enough trees to make a raft in the space of a day. The slaves must have helped them." Anger kindled in Barat's cold heart. "It has been some time since the last punishing. Perhaps the slaves are due."

"Oh, they are due, brother."

Barat didn't like the tone in his brother's inhuman voice. "Oh?"

"Yes, I told you, I have seen the raft, and it was not rudely fashioned of logs."

"What do you mean?"

"Let us say that good Father Joao will not be pleased at the modifications to his church."

"Damn them!" Barat's fist clenched so hard purple blood oozed through his bandages.

Raul shifted the subject. "Tell me, brother, what is the disposition of your charges?"

Barat saw no reason to withhold anything. It was that which had brought him down into this graveyard. "I have the doctor. The other three are at large."

"Then they will be coming here," Raul surmised.

"So I believe. I have the impression they are intensely loyal to one another."

"Brother…" Raul's voice registered mild surprise. "Are you giving me free rein to hunt them?"

Barat left off fencing with his brother. He knew that literally or figuratively he was bound to lose. What he could do was to be so openly honest that it took his brother off guard. "I suggest more. I suggest an alliance."

The baron was pleased with the silence that greeted that. His brother offered no vile personal inference, intimidation or taunt. The baron believed he had another card to play. Despite the horror Raul had become and the terrible crimes that lay between them, Xavier Barat believed his brother was still loyal to the family and to the island in his own twisted way. "I know we have not spoken in some time, and the last time we did, it ended in…acrimony."

"You told me when next you laid eyes upon me you would slay me."

"I meant it."

"I know you did, brother, and yet I have laid eyes upon you many times since that night, and only wished to embrace you as my sweet sibling."

Barat shuddered once more.

"I remember reading that men of power have troubled dreams, but you sleep so soundly, brother. You look like an angel."

The baron shoved the terror of the idea aside. If Raul had access to the manse he would have taken his vengeance long ago, nor would he have asked of Zorime. He would have taken her. Xavier believed he had another card to play. He sometimes thought of his brother languishing in his dark world. Huddled in these filthy dank passages during the day, coming out only at night, and then rarely, to raid the slaves' quarters for blood, flesh and women. The roars and screams one sometimes heard coming out the known cave mouths or out on the fringes of the ville or in the hills when Raul and his brethren hunted left Xavier with the impression that Raul hadn't played chess with anyone but himself in a very long time.

Raul Barat was a monster, but he was a classically educated monster.

Sometimes during these infrequent parleys, Xavier had the feeling that Raul was similarly starved for conversation. "We cannot have these outlanders trying to infect the slaves with dissent as the Russians attempted to do."

"As I recall, you ruthlessly crushed them."

"Yes, but they were cartographers and self-taught scientists, descendants of a predark research station in the Arctic and the local aboriginal people. They were suicidally idealistic about making contact and rebuilding the world. We were their third jump and they had encountered nothing hostile in the previous two. The only thing they had fought in a hundred years were polar bears. They were sec men, if they could even be called that. Hunters, not warriors. The few who escaped led us a merry chase, but they made the mistake of running into the caves. I believe you may have captured several of them."

Raul neither confirmed nor denied, but Xavier could almost hear the wheels of his brother's monstrous mind turning.

"These newcomers are different," the baron continued. "They are warriors, born of the Deathlands across the sea. Also, the Russians had no way to communicate with the slaves beyond hand signals. They engendered sympathy but could not illuminate the sister island population to their true disposition in our islands. This Dr. Tanner can make himself understood, and he seems quite sympathetic toward their plight, and we do not know yet how many more may be coming through. Even counting your people, Raul, the slaves upon this island outnumber us. Add the population of Sister Isle and—"

"The Sister Islanders are idiot children," Raul scoffed.

"They are not idiots, Raul. They are ignorant. Remember your Latin lessons. Ignorant, from the root *ignoramus,* which literally means 'we do not know.'"

"Yes, and we cannot have the sheep of Sister Isle realizing they are being sheared. They might take it badly when they find out that they do not come to our island and live in paradise but instead become your slaves, whores and unwilling blood donors."

"Despite everything that has transpired, I leave oil, wine, Blood of the Lotus and part of our catch by the cave mouths. It is the slaves who produce the Lotus on the hot plain that eases the pain of all of us. Their unceasing toil beneath the sun brings you these benefits. Their bodies produce the blood that eases our affliction, as well, and come fall of night, during your nocturnal raids, their bodies provide you with blood beyond that which I provide, as well as meat and brood mares. Is it true you no longer care for this arrangement?"

"I deny nothing you say," Raul rumbled. "What is it you propose?"

"The outlanders cannot be allowed to foment rebellion in the ville, much less be allowed to return to Sister Isle and apprise them of their reality and turn them against us."

"It has been a long time since we have fought together."

"Many years," the baron agreed.

"I will require a token of your good faith."

The baron had suspected as much. He reached down beside the chair and took up an old brass bell. Dust billowed from it as he raised it and clanged it three times. The baron waited as he heard the cellar door open above. Wood-soled boots clacked on the stone steps. The baron's two most faithful sec men, Breno and Nilton entered the catacombs. Other than Sylvano, they were the two largest men on the island. Breno raised his auto-blaster and pointed it at the darkness behind the bars. Nilton brought in a moaning woman wearing the homespun of Sister Isle with a hood of sackcloth over her head.

"Ahhh." Raul sighed happily.

The woman heard the sound and screamed.

The baron rose from his chair. The girl's name was Pretinha. Like all the others, Father Joao had anointed her head with oil in the church and told her she had been chosen. Undoubtedly she had wept with happiness. Xavier Barat could well imagine her falling to her knees and raising her hands and voice in supplication to his portrait. There would had been a great celebration for the chosen, feasting, dancing, the rare treat of wine and the sacrament of the sweeter dreams the Lotus could offer. In the morning the chosen ones were gone. Those left behind thought they had crossed the waters to a golden life of wonder in God and Baron Xavier Barat's bosom.

What they came to was a life of slavery beneath the sun, nights of terror when Raul and his brethren could no longer contain their bloodlust and assaulted their quarters, and the twice a month "donation" of their blood. The men of the ville would use the women's bodies, and though it was considered a dishonor, some women would be used to sire children in families where the women couldn't produce heirs. The men were hobbled and gelded. The most they could expect if they lived long enough was life as a house servant in their old age. When they began to fail at that, their end would be a final culling of their blood.

Pretinha was escaping that path.

Now, as in the past, sometimes sacrifices had to be madc.

Pretinha wept and begged beneath her hood as Nilton tied her wrists and ankles wide apart, face-first across the bars. Barat could hear his brother's breathing becoming ragged. Breno kept his auto-blaster leveled.

Raul's voice lost all semblance of humanity. "Remove her hood."

Pretinha howled at the situation she found herself in. She flung her head around and caught sight of Barat. "Baron! Oh, Baron!"

Barat jerked his head at Breno and Nilton, and the two sec men went back up the stairs and closed the door behind them. Pretinha howled in despair as Barat sat down again behind the wall. "Baron, please!"

Raul let loose a roar as the monster within him reasserted itself.

Barat couldn't bear to watch but he sat and listened to it all. It was a long time before the roaring and screaming stopped. The screaming finally devolved to mewling and moaning. The moaning soared to shrieks of inhuman torment as the sound of tearing of flesh and the snapping of bones joined the cacophony of the damned. For a long time there was nothing but the sound of feeding, and finally nothing but Raul's ragged, sated breathing.

Raul's voice glowed. "Did you enjoy it, brother?"

Barat spoke quietly. "Sometimes sacrifices are required, brother, and sometimes I need to remind myself of what you truly are."

"And these meetings of ours always serve to remind me, little brother, of the kind of baron you have become."

Barat's knuckles purpled around the grips of his blasters. He restrained himself from coming around the wall and finally finishing it once and for all, but if he killed Raul he would have to come down and invade these catacombs and the cave system below them. He couldn't justify such a sacrifice.

And there were invaders upon the island.

Barat spoke through clenched teeth. "Then we are allied?"

"We are." Raul's voice betrayed his excitement at the prospect. "As in the past, once we are victorious I will require a culling from the slaves here and upon Sister Isle. Blood and fresh wombs for my brethren."

"You will contain your depredations?"

"I will do my best. However, I suggest you keep the ville well guarded and those in the farm manors keep their doors barred and their bonfires banked high."

"Of course."

"You really believe they will come to the manse to rescue this Dr. Tanner?"

The baron nodded. "I am sure of it."

Chapter Eleven

"J.B., you've got to do something," Krysty said. She sat against the wall opposite a duct with her blaster in her lap. Where it wasn't smeared with blood, her face was nearly pale as Jak's. There had been no rest for the past twelve hours. A gnawed-upon, dead stickie duct-popped like a cork almost every fifteen minutes. You could set your chron to it. Then the one behind had to be killed and the process started again. Several times they had punched out from both ducts in tandem and it had turned into a very close call. J.B.'s and Krysty's arms looked like hamburger meat from wrestling with the stickies filthy, suckered hands as they went for the head shot. Despite Krysty's best ministrations between battles, both felt the beginning heat of infection in their wounds. There was no water left to wash with. The environment wasn't helping, either.

Dead stickies were stacked like cordwood around the control room. Their guts and bowels were everywhere, and the floor was a stickie soup of congealed blood. The control room looked like an abattoir. With the stickies in the ducts air had stopped circulating and the heat, cesspit stench and fetid humidity was reaching toxic levels.

"J.B.?" Krysty watched as the corpse in the duct began to uncork from the pressure behind. "Do something."

J.B. stood. "Keep watch." He went over to his satchel and examined the contents yet again. Explosives would do them no good, and J.B. was saving them for when the stickies got in the control room, and he and Krysty made their last stand in the mat-trans chamber. He eyed his pyrotechnics. Tactically fire would only burn one stickie at a time and the siege would continue as before. J.B. smiled wearily as inspiration burned through the fugue of fatigue.

Fire.

J.B. was an inveterate friend of fire. Mildred openly accused him of being a degenerate pyromaniac. Wherever the truth lay, the fact was J.B. knew a few things about burning things, and in his experience, where there was fire, smoke was known to follow.

Krysty read his expression. A flicker of hope kindled in her green eyes. "J.B.!"

The Armorer picked up a canister of white phosphorus. It ran counter to his normal desire to send things sky-high, but what he required now was a nice ugly smolder. He set down the tin of powdered metal and began ripping apart the control-room chairs. He needed a nice tight seal to keep his plan from backfiring.

The ancient plastic seats would do the job. J.B. set the seats down and shucked fresh shells into his shotgun. "Gotta make some room." A dead, buckshot-raddled arm stuck forth from one of the ducts and the rest of stickie was slowly following. He nodded at the arm. "Yank it."

"What?"

"Yank it!"

Krysty heaved, and three-quarters of a dead stickie flopped forth. J.B. instantly took a knee and sent a blast of buckshot down the duct. "Grab that one! Before the one in back starts eating!"

Krysty made a disgusted noise, but she reached in and grabbed a pair of rubbery wrists and pulled. She got it out past the hips, and then the stickie behind turned it into a tug of war. J.B. shoved his shotgun past the dead one's legs and shot the one pulling from behind in the face. Krysty dragged her grisly prize the rest of the way out. More of the control room was covered with dead stickie than wasn't. "So now we…?"

"Work fast." J.B. had a three stickie-length lead on the next one pushing through. He fired four more times and hoped some of the buckshot had smashed all the way back to the next one in line. He ran back to the pile around his satchel and brought a couple of canisters, a jar and a chair seat. He shoved the chair seat into Krysty's hands and opened a jar of homemade adhesive he used for setting charges in place. He painted the plastic seat liberally with the flat of his knife. "Hold that."

J.B. crouched in front of the duct and made a thick pile of white phosphorus inside the duct. The shaft was covered with blood, goop and gore but not even water would smother phosphorus once it caught. He cracked open a shotgun shell and poured a puddle of gun powder on top of the phosphorus as an igniter.

"You baking a cake?" Krysty inquired. A faint smile crossed the red-headed beauty's face.

The corner of J.B.'s mouth quirked. "Bakin' stickies." J.B. took out his flint and steel, then rasped the steel across the magnesium and shaved white-hot sparks into the pile of smokeless powder. He snatched his hands back as he was instantly rewarded by a hissing eruption of orange fire. "Now!"

Krysty slammed the seat against the duct just as the orange burn flared white with the phosphorus ignition. J.B. leaned his weight into the seat and waited for the adhesive and melting plastic to make the seal. Krysty gave J.B. a wry look. "This butt pad won't stop the stickies long."

"No."

"So?"

"So smoke rises. Smoke expands."

"Stickies like fire and smoke," Krysty chided. "Almost as much as they like Mildred."

"Stickies like fire and explosions," J.B. corrected her. "Smoke rises. Smoke expands. That's white phosphorus burning in the duct. The air in there is already bad. The smoke is going to fill it. Every move the stickies make, every shift, every squirm, that smoke is gonna seep, and the only way to go is backward. Figure the next ten stickies in line smother and die? It'll be too much weight to push forward."

"And failing that it's got to slow them down," Krysty finished.

"Mebbe," J.B. agreed. "Still leaves the door, but it's slower, and I'd rather fight on one front instead of three."

"J.B., you're a genius."

J.B. nodded. Blasters, fires and explosions—his area of expertise. He took his hands away from the seat. Krysty followed suit and for the moment the seat stayed in place and no smoke seeped out. J.B. looked at his chron and ran his tongue across his cracked lips. The only way he was going to get a drink was to live long enough to see the mat-trans cycle. He glanced across the room as another mutant corpse started to extrude. "Let's smoke some more stickies."

MILDRED STARED DOWN her sights. Despite the rain, the thick bough was a steady rest and the light spilling from the second-story room threw the sights of her target revolver into high relief. She felt as if she had been lying here for hours. She scanned the grounds and wondered for the thousandth time what the hell was taking Ryan so long. She had covered him until he had gone around back and he hadn't shown up since. He was either still running his recon or he was in. If he had been discovered, she figured she would have heard the fireworks. Mildred shivered in the rain. Why didn't he just start the bloodbath and give her a few clean shots so they could get the hell off this island? She knew the answer and looked at it as she returned her attention to the window. Doc just lay there in that goddamn feather bed snoring. Ryan hadn't reached him yet. Mildred was intensely jealous of the quilts covering Doc and the glow of the fireplace. She was fairly certain he had been drugged, but then again it would be just like the old scarecrow to—

"Good evening."

Mildred nearly dropped her blaster. It sounded like Darth Vader's even bigger brother who had taken up opera had just whispered in her ear. She yipped, flopped, flailed and tried not to fall. Mildred scissored her legs around the bough and started to snap her blaster around. She froze as something tapped her lightly on the shoulder of her gun arm.

The blade was half again as large as a human head. It looked like someone had pounded a square shovel flat and asymmetrical and then sharpened it on three sides. The blade was blackened and pitted with age. The sharp edges gleamed in the night like quicksilver. The impossible basso profundo voice seemed to read her mind. "It is called a flensing blade. In olden times they were known as head spades. Their primary use is in breaking down the carcasses of whales."

Mildred grimaced as the blade rested feather-light on her shoulder and inches from her face. She knew she would get "head spaded" before she could ever bring her target revolver to bear. She had come inches from being raped this night, she was soaked to the bone and now she was being intimidated by some extra out of *Moby Dick.* "That's pretty fucked up," she managed.

The laugh that greeted this sent shivers down her spine. "Well, I cannot convince the blacksmith to make me a sword properly fitted to my requirements, and sad to say, my brother simply doesn't trust me with firearms."

"That's fucked up, too," Mildred muttered.

"Yes, speaking of which, I fear I must ask you to drop your weapon, as fine as it is. The sward below is lush and it should withstand it."

Mildred's jaws flexed in fear and anger. It occurred to her that the only people who she'd ever heard use the word *sward* were Doc and her English Lit professor in college. The gigantic deblubbering blade prompted her with an ever-so-light tap. Mildred shivered as she let her most prized possession fall out into the darkness and rain. It made no sound when it hit and she couldn't see it in the gloom.

The giant blade withdrew from her shoulder. "You may turn about at your leisure."

Mildred considered her knife, but she wasn't quite ready to try to throw down on a tree branch two stories up with some guy wielding a whale-filleting shovel. She pushed herself up to a sitting position and carefully turned.

She nearly fell from the branch for the second time that night as she beheld the devil.

Satan's massive form squatted in the bole of the tree, naked other than his breechclout. His lion's mane of blond hair hung lank and tangled around his shoulders from the rain. Incredibly pale blue eyes regarded her unblinkingly even as the rain rolled down into them. Meeting that gaze for one gut-wrenching second wrote the word *sociopath* in Mildred's mind.

She gaped at her opponent.

Medically the satanic bulging brow, shelflike cheekbones and anvil jaw were clearly signs of acromegaly. However, in her medical experience, anyone whose excess production of human growth hormone had forced their bodies to this extreme of size was nearly crippled by it. This son of a bitch was huge and had sneaked up behind her thirty feet off the ground in a tree. There had to be some sort of abnormal steroidal hormone secretion balancing the damage that kind of gigantism caused as well as producing the grotesque muscular hypertrophy that allowed a body that big to move. The chances of so many major mutations producing anything viable was astronomical, but once in a while the Deathlands knocked one right out of the ballpark.

Mildred's medical diagnosis went right out the window as the son of a bitch smiled at her from beneath his blond beard. He had the same receded gums as the other islanders, but Mildred had seen mules with smaller dentition. He looked like he could bite holes out of a beer keg. The flensing blade's haft had been cut down to make it a one-handed weapon. It looked like a flyswatter in his horrific hands.

Horns and a tail would have been frivolous excess.

He also had a large, black suspicious-looking bruise on his shoulder and Mildred thought she had a good idea where he had gotten it.

The giant eyed her with far too much familiarity for comfort. "Truly, a black person. My brother did not lie. What shall I call you?"

"Dr. Wyeth will do just fine." All the islanders were paper pale, but this man had milk-white skin that had never seen a single rad of solar radiation. The porcelain flawlessness was ruined by a train station's worth of raised purple, keloid scars. "And you?"

The horror made a mocking bow from his perch. "Raul Barat, at your service."

"The baron's brother."

Raul's amused pretense fell from his face like an avalanche and Mildred knew she had a made a mistake. The mutant's voice went as a threatening rumble. "Xavier Barat is my brother. The barony is in dispute."

"Well, I wouldn't want to get involved in family politics."

"But, my dear Dr. Wyeth—" Raul's blue eyes roved her body "—you are already intimately involved."

Mildred couldn't suppress her shudder. She knew without doubt she had been better off back at the sec station with Constable Jorge-Teo and his sec men pulling a train on her than in the tender embrace of the demon in front of her. Mildred decided she wasn't having either. She was twenty feet up, but as the ghost-faced son of a bitch had said, the sward was soft and her ZKR was down there somewhere. Failing that, and assuming she didn't break her ankles, then fine. It was a foot race, and Mildred couldn't help but wonder how fast a human being that big could really run or how much endurance he could have. All she needed was a head start.

Mildred tipped over the bough and ejected.

Raul lunged with grotesque speed. His hand closed around her throat and reeled her back in. His thumb and fingers pressed into her flesh like cold chisels. Mildred's vision darkened as her carotid arteries squeezed shut. She fumbled for her knife, but her body refused to obey her as her brain starved for blood. Mildred scrabbled at Raul's arm, but it was nearly as thick as the tree branch supporting her. Her vision went long and dark along the sides as she took that trip into oblivion.

Raul eased his grip as Mildred went limp. He spent a few moments examining his catch. He had seen such dark skin only in a few books in his father's library. Raul ran one huge paw experimentally through the beaded plaits of her hair and felt himself stirring in his breechclout. Had he not slaked his lust, thirst and hunger earlier, Dr. Wyeth might well be hanging in bloody gobbets strung in the tree branches like Christmas decorations. Raul smiled in the darkness and rain.

There would be time for that later.

Right now she was a valuable commodity, and two more remained to be caught. Raul slung Mildred over his shoulder, swung down on the rope like a great ape and loped off into the night with his prize.

Chapter Twelve

Ryan climbed up the back of the manse. He would have preferred to climb up the front where Mildred could cover him but it was darker back here. A lot of effort had been spent to prevent people from climbing up the side of the manse. It seemed like everyone on this isle had a predisposed fear of cuts and bleeding, and the spikes and razor wire were strung in thick boundaries on the second and third stories. Bells like those strung around the necks of the goats of the little island were strung throughout the wire to alert those inside of anyone trying to penetrate the defenses. Ryan had climbed some of the worst crags in the Deathlands free-hand out of sheer necessity. A patient man who didn't mind a few cuts could creep his way through this.

Ryan could outwait a rock, which was useful because in the rad-blasted wastes of Deathlands sometimes even the rocks weren't what they appeared to be. Ryan had wrapped his hands in the long, weighted silk scarf that sometimes served him as a weapon, to grasp spikes. Wherever barbed wire bit into him or his clothing and gear, he had to stop with one hand on a spike or a bar and his feet jammed on a sill or wire strand, and reach back to slowly disentangle himself. Ryan crept through the vertical fortifications one handhold, one foothold and one sharpened obstacle at a time. The sec men passed beneath him but they kept their eyes and their blasters pointed out into the darkness beyond rather than up. It wasn't a terribly technical climb if one didn't mind getting a little shredded. His main enemies were rain, darkness and exhaustion.

Ryan finally pulled himself over the rain gutter and crawled up the shingles. He moved to a smoking chimney and hugged the bricks for long moments, letting heat seep back into his body and feeling back into his bleeding fingers. Then he moved in a crouch to the observatory.

The brass dome was like the top of a grain silo. A tiny, railed balcony let astronomers step out into the night. The French doors between them were no obstacle at all. Ryan picked the lock and stepped into the observatory. It was a converted loft. A cannonlike Dobsonian reflector telescope stood on a rotating platform. Astronomical charts covered the walls. A rack held various lenses and accessories. A table held notebooks and sketches. The bookcase was loaded with books on cosmology. He felt a need to follow the charts and steer his eye across the heavens through the telescope. The Deathlands could warp and change almost before a man's eyes. The stars were one of the few comforting constants in Ryan's world. Doc would love such a journey. He—

Ryan slid his panga silently from its sheath as he moved toward the door. He spent long moments listening but heard no sounds without. Peering through the keyhole, he saw a hallway lit by candlelight. Ryan turned the handle slowly and silently opened the door. The wood paneling was fairly new and in good repair. He stepped onto the rug to quiet the sound of his boots and moved down the hall. He stopped at a door where he heard voices. One of them was the baron's.

The one-eyed man knelt and peered through the keyhole.

Baron Barat and three other men stood around a table. One of them was huge and bore a strong resemblance to the baron. Two more big men stood with slung auto-blasters. The baron gestured at a map on his desk and pointed in various directions. The men nodded, then spoke their agreement. They all spoke Portuguese, but it was pretty clear to Ryan they were making battle plans. He smiled coldly. They were a day late and some jack short.

Ryan silently opened the door and stepped in. The men were so intent on their strategy and tactics they didn't notice the invader for several heartbeats. The big man suddenly jerked upright. His hands went for the huge revolvers strapped to his thighs. They froze as Ryan snapped his blaster out at arm's length. The stunned sec men looked to their leader. Ryan could read the islanders' minds. They were playing the numbers game in their heads. Their blasters were all slung or holstered and their swords sheathed, but they were all thinking one of them would get him if they all drew down. Ryan kept his eye on the big man but pointed his blaster at the baron's face. "Chill your pa."

The big man's black eyes flared wide. His hands hovered but he didn't draw. He flicked his gaze toward his father. The baron stared down Ryan's blaster with an admirable lack of fear. He slowly raised his left hand. "Wait, my son."

Ryan noted the matching bandages on both the baron and his son's right hands and smiled without an ounce of warmth. "See you met Doc." Ryan was rewarded with a snarl from both Barats. "Give him to me."

"Dr. Tanner is on the second floor, in the second guest room facing eastward," the baron said.

"I know where he is. I said give him to me, and our blasters."

"I do not negotiate with plebes."

Ryan pulled out a very old piece of swank. "I am Ryan Cawdor, son of Baron Titus Cawdor, uncle to Nathan Cawdor, current baron of Front Royal, installed by my hand."

"You know?" the baron said. "I believe you."

"Doc, and the blasters, now."

The baron regarded Ryan dryly. "And should I refuse?"

"I chill you. Then I chill your son. Neither of you will clear leather. Mebbe your sec men take me, but you better ask yourself what happens to the succession after that."

A strange look passed across the baron's face that Ryan didn't like. "Why, then, I suppose my brother will renew his bid for the barony."

Ryan wasn't interested in Barat family politics at the moment. "You're going to give me Doc. Now."

Conversation stopped as a bell clanked dully from somewhere within the manse. Irony filled Barat's voice. "Speak of the devil."

"What?"

The baron smiled.

Ryan snapped his blaster toward Sylvano's face. "You tell me in two seconds or I shoot your son."

The baron raised his left hand again. "I do not doubt you."

"Then get to it."

"That bell has not rung in years," the baron replied.

"What does that mean?"

"That would require my explaining a great deal of our island's history to you. Let it suffice to say that on this island, despite familial acrimony, certain channels of communication have been left open due to necessity. The last time that bell rang was late in the night, years ago, when pirates came raiding. They styled themselves as Vikings. They had found old ocean charts and decided there was a good chance the Atlantic island chains might have lain fallow after skydark and make easy pickings. As you can imagine they made significant inroads during the day." The baron's bleak expression was again disturbing. "They were not prepared for what befell them come nightfall."

"And it's ringing now because…?"

The baron exposed his long teeth. "I suspect my brother, Raul, has one or more of your people." Ryan's one-eyed glare stayed fixed but his guts went cold. The baron saw past Ryan's poker face. "The black woman and the albino can be the only two. Which one waited outside to cover your escape? And which did you send to secure a boat? I think I can guess."

Ryan gave the baron a very cold smile of his own. "I'll chill you all."

"You will try, but let us negotiate as men of quality, and let us negotiate realistically. You will chill myself and perhaps my son, but you will not leave this room alive. Should you be so lucky, you would still not leave my manse, much less this island alive. Upon my or my son's death, Dr. Tanner's demise is assured. He will be bled and slaughtered in the bed he is bound upon. As for the black woman? It is possible that I may be able to negotiate for her return in, how shall I put it, an unsullied state? But upon my death her fate will be brood mare or beefsteak to the sort of nightmare I believe you may have seen before in your Deathlands. As for the albino? He cannot fight an entire island or sail the great ocean alone." The baron knew he held all the cards. "I suggest you think very carefully upon your next move."

Ryan shot Sylvano twice in the chest.

He snapped his muzzle over and gave the baron two more of the same. The closest sec men ignored his slung longblaster and slapped leather for the double-blaster thrust through his belt. He was fast and Ryan staggered as two loads of rock salt ripped into him. Ryan repaid the favor in lead with a double tap of his own. The second sec man gave Ryan both barrels in the gut. Ryan grimaced in agony but kept his feet. The sec man dropped his double-blaster and spun his longblaster around on its sling. Ryan put his front sight on the sec man's chest and double-tapped him. The room shook as the supersonic crack-crack-crack of rifle bullets whipped past Ryan's head. Ryan's third shot chilled the sec man cold and dropped him to the carpet.

Ryan's blaster racked open on a smoking, empty chamber.

Barat and his son, Sylvano, both stood tall and apparently untouched with local blasters in their hands. "Alive, my son," the baron said.

The fireblasted bastards were wearing armor. Ryan flung his panga at the baron.

Ryan's aim went askew as Sylvano shot him in the face. Rock salt tore into Ryan's brow, cheek and ripped along his ear and scalp. If he hadn't been blind in that eye already he would have lost it. Ryan snarled at the inferno of pain in his face and reached for the spare mag thrust through his belt. Sylvano lowered his aim and fired his second barrel. The .75-caliber cloud of salt ripped into Ryan's injured gun hand and the empty blaster fell to the floor. Sylvano dropped the double-blaster and drew his sword. Baron Barat took aim with his weapon and dropped hammer. Ryan staggered as he took a load of rock salt in the front of his right thigh and wobbled as Barat gave him the second in the meat of his left. Ryan could hear the pounding of boots and shouting throughout the house. He drew the slaughtering knife from his boot.

Sylvano knelt by a fallen sec man and took up the double-blaster.

Ryan tottered a step forward. Sylvano's double discharge toppled Ryan out the door. The one-eyed man held on to his knife as he did a backroll and came up onto his feet. He wasn't going to win a knife fight with a pair of swordsmen, and Doc was downstairs. Ryan charged down the hall on burning legs.

A half-naked woman staggered out of a door in front of Ryan as if shoved. She screamed at the one-eyed, blood-covered chiller that came for her. Her hair was blond and her skin golden-brown from a life lived under the sun. She dropped to her knees in terror and covered her head with her hands. Ryan vaulted her terror-genuflected form. The man behind her was older, chill-pale and dressed in a nightshirt. His dagger wavered in fear as he gaped in long-toothed horror at the bloody avenger hurtling down upon him. Ryan twisted midleap away from the clumsy thrust, and his forearm clotheslined the man across the clavicles and slammed him to the floor in passing. Men were boiling up the stairs. Clearly the trap had been set for the bottom floors. Half a dozen men shouted as Ryan appeared at the top of the landing and raised blasters.

Ryan leaped over the banister.

He dropped two floors. Rock salt tore at him. Two screaming islanders were kind enough to be standing beneath his boots and break his fall. Ryan pushed himself up from the tangle of broken, moaning men. The floor next to him erupted in splinters as someone above took a shot at him with lead. Ryan scrambled to his feet as boots slammed down the stairs. Servants screamed and fled in his wake. Ryan pounded for the door. He flung it open and took the steps down four at a time. Whistles began blowing upstairs and were answered by the men outside guarding the perimeter. The wag driver stood by his vehicle and raised a blaster. Ryan charged across the gravel drive. If it was loaded with lead, he was a dead man.

The driver fired a barrel and stinging fire ripped into Ryan's shoulder. His lips skinned back from his teeth like a wolf's. He almost stumbled as he took the second load center-body. The driver screamed and reached for something beneath his long coat. Ryan's panga flashed across the driver's throat and ended his caterwauling. Ryan slid behind the wheel of the wag. Any ville with a still could make alcohol for the purposes of either entertainment or fuel. The problem with getting a wag moving since skydark was that almost no one could produce batteries of any power. Most wags had been converted to hand-crank or cartridge ignition.

Ryan grabbed for the keys. Three, small single-shot blasters and a powder horn lay in the well where the armrest had been. They were all the same caliber and had a locking lug for a front sight. He shoved the barrel of one down the hole where the cigarette lighter had been. The one-eyed man turned the blaster to lock it in place and pulled the trigger. The gunpowder charge sent its blast down the pipe and kicked the engine over. The cold engine coughed, sputtered and died. Ryan waited for the bursts from the auto-blasters to tear him apart as he ripped out the starter blaster, but maybe the sec men were reluctant to destroy what was perhaps the ville's only working wag, much less the baron's pride and joy. Ryan shoved in the second starter blaster, turned it and pulled the trigger. The smell of brimstone filled the wag interior and the engine turned over, sputtered and roared as Ryan gave it some juice.

He caught motion in the corner of his eye.

The driver's window shattered beneath the pommel of a sword. Ryan snatched up the third starter blaster as the sec man drew his blade back for the killing thrust. Ryan pointed the weapon and fired. There was neither lead nor salt in the weapon but at two feet the starter charge sent superheated smoke and gas searing into the sec man's face. He fell back screaming as Ryan shoved the wag into gear. He flung open the door and picked up the fallen sword. The act saved his life as glass erupted in geysers across the windshield. The sec men with auto-blasters had lost their shyness about shooting into the baron's ride. Ryan flung the sword on the passenger seat. Gravel spit beneath the tires as he floored it straight for the gate. He kept his head down as bullets ripped through the rear windshield.

The wag skewed as it hit the gate, but where the iron bars held the ancient mortar, the firmament holding them in place failed. Ryan rose and fought the wheel as the wag fishtailed on the wet road. The iron bars slewed off in a shower of sparks from the roof of the wag and Ryan brought his ride under control. He swung off the road and onto the grass of the grounds beyond the fence. The wheels tore up turf as he brought it to a halt beneath the tree. Ryan leaped out. "Mildred!" He stared up the rope and saw nothing but darkness in the bole of the tree. Ryan almost went up the rope but his foot stepped on something hard. He picked Mildred's target revolver out of the wet grass.

Mildred was gone.

Ryan flung himself back in the wag and stepped on it. He lost a rear window as longblasters cracked from the manse. A dozen armed men ran for the broken gates. Ryan roared past and the wag took a broadside, but it mostly resisted the rock salt and lead buckshot. In an instant Ryan was beyond the range of the lights of the manse and in the inky darkness beneath the trees. He made the curve in the road mostly by memory and hit the lights. Light bulbs were in short supply in the Deathlands and most wags' headlights had been modified to a type. The push of a lever allowed some hot gas from the engine into the fuel of the lamp reservoirs. The lever next to it closed the damper and extinguished them. Ryan pushed the lever. The engine made a hiss and clicking noise. The oil lanterns burned into life and the reflectors behind them intensified and threw their yellow beams.

Horror stood in the headlights.

It was female with the gigantic breasts and belly of a fertility goddess. Its ghost-white features were Neanderthalic, and it had the grotesquely muscled shoulders and arms of a gorilla. It charged the wag screaming and wielding a club the size of a sapling. The wag's engine roared as Ryan downshifted and stomped on the accelerator. Ryan rammed the she-thing dead-on. The hood crumpled and the besieged windshield buckled as the huge mutie made its tumbling run over the wag. Ryan didn't look back. He was too busy fighting the wheel and trying to see out of the collapsing and spiderwebbed windshield. One headlight had been smashed and burning oil sputtered and smeared along the right fender with the wind of the wag's passage.

Ryan did some dead reckoning. Islands were all the same. They usually had one or two roads that criss-crossed out of the main ville, and most had a predark belt of road that circled the coastline. Ryan weighed his options. Mildred was missing and the hag-thing told him the night was uncertain at best. What was certain was that nothing but hundreds of islanders with blasters and swords waited for him back at the ville. Ryan chose the uncertainty of the night. He took the next turnoff on the road, which led into the hills.

He could only hope it would lead him to the coast.

Chapter Thirteen

Doc opened his eyes to gunshots and screaming. It was a far too frequent occurrence in this third, and he suspected, final life that fate had dealt him. Despite the Blood of the Lotus addling his mind, he knew the violence was relevant to him. In fact the narcotic in his bloodstream calmed him and allowed him to focus, even if that focus was tinged with a warm and somewhat welcome fuzziness around the edges. People were shooting and screaming on the floor above. Men were moving and shouting on his floor and the one below. Blasterfire cracked out on the grounds outside and Doc heard a crashing noise by the gate. Resignation passed through Doc's soul as the key turned in the door. He managed a small smile. He had fenced the match of his life. He had done his best. He wished his companions could have seen it. Doc closed his eyes as the door opened.

He prayed his friends were alive and inflicting confusion upon the enemy. For himself he prayed for strength to withstand what was to come. He knew Baron Barat would not be gentle. He was surprised when he felt someone sit on the bed. He smelled the scent of crocus flowers for the first time in centuries. A hand as soft as silk touched his cheek.

Doc opened his eyes and beheld an angel.

A single candle lit the room, and in its light the woman's skin was even whiter than the cotton nightslip she wore. The thin garment did more to accentuate than hide the lush, pale curves beneath. In startling contrast her eyes were of deepest black and her hair was so black it seemed almost blue in the soft glow. She might well have been the ghost of some beauty in a Gothic romance, except that her lips were as red as blood. She smiled at Doc, and when she did her scarlet lips and long canine teeth conspired to turn her from ethereal beauty to succubus.

Her voice was dulcet as she spoke his name. "Dr. Tanner?"

Despite the narcotic Doc was well aware of the family resemblance.

"I am the daughter of Baron Barat. My name is Zorime."

"A pleasure, I am sure. I had feared you were the baron come to coerce my cooperation. I see instead he has sent a more gentle form of persuasion."

"The men my father would use to break you are occupied elsewhere at the moment."

"I see." Doc sighed.

"As you may surmise the attempt to rescue you met with failure."

"May I ask of my companions?"

"No, you may not."

Doc took that to mean they were still alive and at large. If any of them had been captured or killed he suspected Zorime would have told him. Doc tried to laugh carelessly. "I fear you have me at a disadvantage. I am drugged, bound and bespelled by you."

The huge dark eyes narrowed slightly. "Do not treat

me like a foolish girl, Doctor. I am aware you made every attempt to kill my father and brother."

"I protest, my lady. I engaged both your kinsmen in honorable single combat, and offered quarter and succor in exchange for parley and the safety of my companions."

Zorime's black eyes stared luminously into his own. "This is known to me. It took Herculean efforts to staunch my brother's wounds, yet still he speaks highly of you."

Doc went to the point. "What is it you wish of me, Lady Zorime?"

"Nothing less than your utter cooperation, Dr. Tanner."

Doc swiftly retreated from the point. "You speak in a most courtly fashion."

Zorime blushed once again. "My father the baron insisted that I learn English that I might read Shakespeare in its original language."

"Then I pray you, my lady, tell me the tale of your islands, in both tragedy and triumph I am sure they rival the Bard."

Zorime regarded Doc for long moments. "As you have seen, Doctor, we often rely upon steel on this island. My brother speaks for you in this regard. Peradventure my father has a number of books in Latin that require translation, and we always seek to improve our education on the isle in every area we can. There is a comfortable life here for you as a master should you wish it."

"So your noble father has intimated. Yet I beg my lady's favor for the tale again."

Zorime's pale cheek quirked delightfully. "I am not sure my father would completely approve, but I will tell you a story, Dr. Tanner."

"I am your rapt and undivided audience."

Zorime gave him a dark-eyed look of wariness, but Doc knew he had hit a vein of gold. Baron Barat's daughter wanted to talk. "Our isle survived skydark. No fire fell upon us, and while the earthshaker weapons dropped some islands and raised new ones in the Atlantic, our island chain remained relatively untouched." Zorime examined her ghostly hand. "However, we did not remain untouched by the black rains nor the chemical storms."

Doc knew the story all too well. "Many of your people became sterile."

Zorime dropped her gaze. "Yes, and inbreeding became both endemic and unavoidable unless we were to become a zero point population."

"And porphyria, a recessive gene in your already somewhat isolated population, became dominant."

"Yes."

"Many in my time claimed the legend of vampirism came from the victims of porphyria." Doc scowled. "However, even in my time it was medically accepted that the ingestion of blood gave no relief to its symptoms."

"The recessive porphyria gene became dominant on our small island, as you suggested Dr. Tanner." Zorime's huge dark eyes stared at him steadily. "And it mutated."

"I see."

"Frequent transfusions of untainted blood, along with infusions made from the local narcotic do ease the symptoms, which other than the need to protect our flesh from direct sunlight allow us to lead relatively normal lives."

Doc tried to rein in his scorn. "Except that it has also

left you not only with blood upon your hands but upon your lips, as well."

"There is a taste for it. A...craving." Doc was horrified as Zorime unconsciously licked her lips. "I admit I am not immune to it."

"And what of the people on the other island? How have they remained immune?"

"This island is dependent upon the lakes up in the hills for water. Come skydark fallout settled in it. We catch rainwater in cisterns, but in dry years we must draw upon the lake. We filter the water through charcoal, but though diminished the taint is still there."

"And the other island gets its water from natural springs, where the bedrock of the isle forms its own natural filter," Doc guessed.

"Yes, we import their water in some years of great need. However its levels are variable, and its ability to sustain Sister Isle is always near the brink."

"Thus you seeded the isle with millet, which requires little or no irrigation, and goats, which can subsist on forage rather than fodder."

"Yes."

"And how did you seed Sister Isle with such willing blood donors?" Doc gave Zorime a shrewd look. "Surely they are outlanders."

"According to our history, a refugee fleet came out of the west."

"From Brazil? Or Amazonia, as it is now known?"

"No, they came from your United States, the Deathlands. They had been badly mauled fleeing whatever it was they sought to escape, and had been forced to battle pirates on their voyage, as well. Many of the adult men and women had been killed or wounded in the fleet's defense. Nonetheless they still had close to a thousand souls under sail."

"They made landfall on your island."

"Yes."

"And so?"

"At first they were grateful. Relieved to find a sanctuary."

"I assume friction soon developed?"

"Our ways, our language and our…condition were alien to them. They knew little about fishing and less about farming. Their men expressed interest in our women, but their women considered our men repulsive. They considered us a damaged and diseased population. More of us spoke more English than they knew. We knew that some of them spoke of taking whatever they wanted and sailing on. We outnumbered them, but they were much more heavily armed and others among them spoke of simply taking over. My forefathers decided they had to act."

Doc shifted uncomfortably in his bonds. "Act?"

"A feast was held. The Blood of the Lotus was introduced into the food."

"There was…" Doc felt sick as the word passed his lips. "A culling?"

Zorime could not meet Doc's gaze. "Every male over the age of nine was killed."

Doc closed his eyes.

"Every woman of child-bearing age was…distributed. The women who were too old were hobbled, put to work as slaves, and bled."

"And you set the orphaned children upon Sister Isle. Whereupon you gave them a new language, a new occupation and a new religion."

"It takes but one generation to cut the cord of culture,

Dr. Tanner, and children are easily molded, particularly when they are utterly dependent. English was forbidden. Though we took it on as a second language here. A simple mythos of the island across the strait was devised that our priests promulgated with weekly sermons. The gifts of wine and the narcotic gave the religious rites power."

"The narcotic, you call it the Blood of the Lotus?"

"There is a plant on this island that has been used for medicinal purposes since time out of mind. It is believed to be related to the mainland nettle. Its leaves, fruit and 'milk' were long used by our local midwives and herbalists. Scientists from the mainland were actually studying its properties just before skydark. Afterward the efficacy and potency of it grew and we learned methods to distill it to even greater power. Every man, woman and child of my people is addicted to it."

"I see. Might I ask whom these nightwalkers your father spoke of may be?"

What little color Zorime's face had, drained away. "You may have noticed that after skydark many women give birth to horrors."

Doc had seen mutations that spanned the gamut from the pathetic to the horrific. "Yes. The Deathlands have their share, I assure you."

"You have seen some of the mutations our population faces. Sometimes among us, even if the child seems utterly normal and healthy by our standards, at the onset of puberty, a…change comes upon them. Among some it is subtle, among some it stabilizes and stops, and for some…"

"Horror," Doc whispered.

"Yes, Doctor." Some of her father's coldness entered

Zorime's black eyes. "Gigantism, sociopathy and a greater intensity in the craving for blood…and flesh."

"Your people let this happen?"

"Given the times we live in, it is easy for most to kill an infant who is clearly deformed, but when the change starts during the flowering of adulthood, in a child you have raised and loved all its life, it is far more difficult."

"I understand."

"You understand nothing!" Tears spilled down Zorime's flawless cheekbones.

Doc's heart broke at the sight, and at what he intuited. "You fear for yourself."

Zorime gazed upon her reflection in the mirror over the dresser for long moments. "You find me beautiful?"

"It is no exaggeration to say that you are without doubt one of the most beautiful women I have ever been privileged to look upon."

"You sink to flattery, Dr. Tanner."

Tears stung Doc's eyes as memories rose unbidden. "Only my wife was more beautiful." Doc's throat tightened. "And my daughter, who had the good sense to take after her mother."

Doc's emotions were plain to see. Zorime gazed upon him intently. "I will tell you, Dr. Tanner. But a few years ago I was a fat, happy little girl. The runt of the Barat litter. Now I grow taller. The chubby little hands my father so loved?" Zorime held up a hand as graceful as any concert pianist's. "Grow longer."

"Mayhap my lady is simply flowering into womanhood."

"So my father and Dr. Goncalves say, and so I pray." Zorime closed her hand. "For if not, my fate is to be driven from the ville, to live in the caves with the other nightwalkers, brooding more abominations like myself." The beauty shuddered. "I am sure as the night baron, my uncle Raul will take me first."

"Your uncle Raul, he...changed?"

"Yes. It had never happened before among the baronial line, but the change came upon my uncle Raul, and my father became first in line for the barony, and first for my mother's hand. My uncle did not take it well. He found a way through the caverns into the catacombs, and then into the manse. He took my mother and killed her."

"And after such an action why did your father not rid the isle of the nightwalkers once and for all?"

"My father was about to purge the caverns with fire and sword, but then the island was invaded by raiders from the continent. It went ill for my father and his forces, but come nightfall my uncle Raul and his brethren rose from their lairs and fell upon the pirates. Between my father and my uncle the pirates were annihilated, and despite the terrible blood between them, an accommodation was reached. The nightwalkers are a form of insurance. Three times since, the island has been attacked and twice it was the terror that my uncle and his people wreaked in the night that told the tale."

"Yet your uncle and his brethren, the nightwalkers, they seek blood and flesh in the night?"

"Sooner or later they must. We put food, wine and the Blood of the Lotus by the cave mouths, but the craving for blood and flesh is too strong to resist indefinitely."

Doc felt the sting of his wounds. "Thus at any given time most of your weapons are loaded with rock salt."

"Sufferers of porphyria fear wounds, Doctor. We bleed. Yet the rock salt does not wound deeply. It is usually enough to drive them away if they are driven to attack the ville or the outlying farmhouses."

"So—" Doc shuddered "—they slake their lust among the slaves."

"They are allowed a certain amount of…depredation," Zorime admitted.

Doc could no longer look upon the beauty in front of him.

Zorime lifted her chin in challenge. "You are appalled."

"I have seen far worse things in the Deathlands, but you cannot ask me to approve."

"Your approval is neither here nor there, Doctor. What is required is your cooperation."

Doc sought to steer the conversation away from that dreaded topic. "Your brother, Sylvano, he suffers the change?"

"He takes after his grandfather, who was a very large man. Sylvano is also an active physical culturalist and engages in lifting grotesque amounts of weight when he is not practicing his sword mastery and marksmanship. In some ways it is almost like he has made himself in the image of the nightwalkers. I was too young, but Sylvano remembers our mother. I fear when he becomes baron he intends a reckoning."

"And so—"

"And so you will give my father your cooperation?"

"I fear I must resist the baron with all my might."

"Then I fear tomorrow you will be broken." Zorime rose from the bed. "I have a blaster of my own, Dr. Tanner. Your cooperation is necessary for the safety of my people, I will not impede your interrogation, but once my father has what he wants of you, I fear you will be the subject of low sport, blood and finally food come the night. I tell you now, when you have given up your last secret, look for me in the crowd, and I will end your suffering."

Doc took a long breath. "I thank you, my lady."

Fresh tears spilled from Zorime's eyes as she turned away. "I will pray that you see reason come the dawn."

"May the condemned make a last request?"

Zorime stopped at the door. "He may ask."

"You can read Shakespeare in the original language?"

A hint of a smile crossed the young woman's face. "I can."

"Then the condemned asks to spend his last night beholding beauty, with his ears caressed by the verbiage of the Bard."

"I am currently reading *Much Ado About Nothing.*"

Doc glanced helplessly at his bonds. "As ever I am your undivided audience."

"Then let the request be granted." Zorime smiled. "I shall fetch the book and a carafe."

Chapter Fourteen

Ryan stood bare-chested in the rain. He would have given almost anything for Vava and Eva's poultices and salves, a hot fire and a bowl of gruel. He would have sold his soul to feel Krysty's healing hands upon him. Instead he let the downpour dissolve the chunks and crystals of rock salt crusting the wounds all over his body. Ryan lifted his head into the deluge and let the cold water sluice across his burning, ravaged face. Thoughts of Krysty focused him despite his pain and exhaustion. Ryan examined his liabilities. He was lost, the road had dead-ended and he could see the lanterns and torches of searchers behind him. He was busted up pretty bad. Doc was drugged and tied to a bed in the baron's manse. He had to assume Mildred was a prisoner. Krysty and J.B. were going to mat-trans into an ambush. The cave chiller and the baron's brother were out and about; and Ryan had a bad feeling they were one and the same. From the baron's talk, the cave-chiller had friends. Ryan was pretty sure he had run one of them over.

Ryan examined his assets.

He hefted his sword. It was on the short side with a brutal, diamond-shaped point for thrusting and two good edges that could lop off a limb if the wielder was strong and went for the joints. It was the weapon of a warrior rather than a duelist, and that was just Ryan's game. He had Mildred's target blaster with six rounds in the chamber. It bothered Ryan that she hadn't gotten off a shot. The starting blasters were single-shot muzzle-loaders but like just about everything in the Deathlands they were multitaskers. He had found a small leather sack of .410 gauge lead balls in the glove box. They weren't ideal, but at spitting distance they would put a .40-caliber hole in both man and mutie where their life had resided. He had three of them. He had his panga, and he had a wag.

Ryan slid back into the vehicle. He turned on the heater and was pleased as warmth from the alcohol-burning engine washed out of the vents. He loaded the starting blasters with lead as the heat washed across his cold, bleeding flesh, while keeping an eye on the lanterns in the distance. Ryan put the wag into Reverse and took it off the road into a stand of trees. The idea of leaving the warmth of the car was ugly but there was no other choice.

Ryan drew his sword and went for a walk.

Evading the search parties in the rolling, wooded, rain-washed hills wasn't hard, but a half mile into his hike wounds, exhaustion and cold reasserted themselves. Ryan knew he was going to have to take a risk. He descended into a valley, which was dominated by a fortified farmhouse. Ryan ignored it and made his way through the fields of grain toward the slave quarters. The people of the other island had been hospitable and willing to help. Ryan had to hope that subsequent enslavement hadn't ruined that attitude. Ryan approached the long building and listened at the door. People inside were talking. Ryan knocked on the door. *"Olá!"*

All talk within stopped.

"Olá!" Ryan pounded the pommel of his sword against the wood. *"Olá!"*

People within whispered fearfully. "Fireblast..." Ryan muttered. "Ago!" He shouted. "Vava! Eva! Marco! Nando!" Ryan shook his head. "Boo!" he tried.

The whispering stopped.

"Ago! Vava! Eva! Marco! Nando!" Ryan repeated. He sagged in exhaustion against the door. Boards and beams thumped and rattled on the other side. Ryan nearly fell forward as the door opened. Warmth and light washed across him. Men and women dressed in plain tunics regarded Ryan in fear and wonder. All of them had a club or a stone in hand. A gray-haired woman stepped forward tentatively. "Vava?"

Ryan nodded. "Vava."

She led him to an empty stool by the fire while others secured the door. Ryan counted fourteen people all between the ages of thirty-five and sixty-five. There was nothing in the room other than some crude wooden stools, a communal table and bunks along the walls. Ryan sheathed his sword and stuck a thumb into his chest. "Ryan."

The woman nodded. "Moni."

"Vava was your..." Ryan made a baby rocking motion at Moni. Moni burst into fresh tears and nodded eagerly. Ryan grunted to himself. It was the first piece of luck he had caught since stepping onto this pesthole rising up out of the Lantic. "Vava is..." Ryan made a fist and thumped his chest. "Good, *bueno.*"

Moni nodded hopefully. *"Bom?"*

"Bom," Ryan agreed.

Moni seized Ryan's hand in gratitude. Her voice lowered to a whisper. "Feydor? Galina?"

His luck was holding. The Russian revolution had been here, as well. "Feydor?" Ryan shrugged. "Galina?" He shook his head. The slaves lowered their heads in mourning. Ryan's eye widened as he looked over his hosts. The slaves wore crude sandals, and each had been hobbled by having the toes of their left foot cut off. All bore wounds and scars old and new on their inner elbows. A woman took Ryan's coat and shirt and hung them by the fire. The slaves shook their heads at the number and severity of salt blasts Ryan had taken. Another woman went to a shelf and took up a crude earthenware jar. The one-eyed man sighed as she began applying some kind of salve to his wounds. The pitted scars on the slaves' arms and legs showed they were no strangers to the less than lethal kindness of the islanders' blasters.

Another woman filled a wooden bowl from a pot over the fire and gave it to Ryan. He ate. It was a thin stew of vegetables, stale bread and tiny shreds of meat Ryan made to be rat or squirrel. It wasn't the hearty food of the other island. These people were slaves and they lived like it. They were given what the ville didn't want and had to scratch out anything else in the small plots around their quarters. Ryan cleaned his bowl, made contented noises and nodded his thanks. Everyone smiled and nodded as the woman refilled his bowl.

A younger man stepped forward questioningly. "Ago? Nando?"

"Ago, Nando." Ryan made a fist. *"Bom."*

The man nodded and gestured as he spoke. All Ryan could make out was that he knew them but perhaps wasn't directly related. Everyone was nodding and smiling nervously. Ryan finished his stew and got to business. He held up his bandaged right fist. "Ryan." He held up his left. "Barat." Ryan punched his fists together. The slaves stared as if hypnotized. Ryan opened his left fist and waved his hand dismissively. "Barat." The slaves looked at one another in shock. Ryan pointed at them. "You." Ryan pointed at himself. "Me." He held up his right again and made a fist in unity. The slaves broke into excited talk.

A demonic howl cut the conversation like a knife. It rose above and then fell below human vocal range. The sound froze the blood in Ryan's veins. A second, horrifically feminine ululating shriek answered from farther away in the hills. The slaves sagged. Some moaned and covered their heads with their hands in despair as a third roar tore the night from the direction of the ville. The sound was half summons and half victory.

They were hunting screams.

Something had picked up Ryan's trail, and it was triangulating on the slave dwelling with two of its friends. Ryan spoke a single word. "Raul."

The slaves flinched as a unit.

A second round of hunting screams tore out over the wind and rain, and all of them were closer. If whatever approached was anything like the abomination he had run down in the wag then he knew he was in no condition to fight three of them. Whatever revolt the Russians had tried to foment among the slaves and the sister islanders had died with them. Ryan reached into his coat and took out one of the starter blasters and slammed it on the table. The slaves stared at it as if it were a snake. Ryan suspected handling a weapon was a death sentence for any slave. Looking around, he didn't see a single ax or shovel or tool. The only knives were short and rounded for utility.

Ryan closed his fist and jerked it upward in an obscene and unmistakable gesture of violation. "Fuck Barat."

The slaves stared, dumbstruck.

Ryan pulled out a second blaster. "Fuck Raul." He set down the third. A third round of screams shook the night outside. They were getting close. Ryan filled one hand with Mildred's target blaster and the other with his sword and rose. He took a step toward the door and jerked his head. "Who is with me?"

No one moved.

Ryan shook his head. "Fireblast." They were too conditioned to fear and servitude.

"Ryan." The biggest man among the slaves stepped forward. He was white-haired, weathered and bent by untold years of labor, but still strong. When he rose he could look Ryan in the eye. "Cafu."

"Cafu." Ryan held out his hand. Cafu shook it. The man turned and gingerly picked up one of the little starter blasters. He stared at it in wonder. His knuckles suddenly went white around the grips. Tears spilled down his seamed face. Ryan could only imagine how many of Cafu's friends and loved ones he had seen worked and bled to death, much less how many times hunting screams had filled his nights with terror and how many of his people he had seen taken. Cafu's voice shook as he spoke his new word. "Fook…Barat."

Moni seized up a blaster in both hands. "Fook Barat!"

The man who had asked about Ago and Nando took up the third. He thumped his chest. "Renan!"

"Renan." Ryan nodded.

Renan gave Ryan a savage grin. "Fook Raul."

"Bom," Ryan said. He looked around at the rest of the slaves. *"Bom?"*

They all nodded and said *"bom"* or "fook" in the affirmative. Ryan watched as they filled their hands with clubs and stones. He considered the she-thing he had seen. Sticks and stones might drive off a nightwalker, but probably not before it had snatched a victim, and Ryan knew in his bones this night was a far more serious affair. He considered their arsenal. The starter blasters were woefully underpowered and inaccurate, purely a point-blank proposition. Mildred's target blaster wasn't much better. It had six shots, but it was Mildred's deadeye accuracy that made it such a premium chiller rather than any stopping power. Nine shots against three abominations, and three of the shooters had never held a blaster before. Ryan kept the grimace off his face.

It was going to end up a brawl, and one they were very likely going to lose.

Cafu picked up a stool. Ryan stabbed his panga into the tabletop and one of the slaves took it. The one-eyed man overturned the table and arrayed Cafu, Renan and Moni behind it. He went and drew an *X* in the dirt six feet in front of the door. He spit on it and then pointed his blaster at the door. He nodded at those holding stones and pointed at the *X*. They all got it. Whatever came through the door was going to take everything they had in a volley. Mebbe killing one would be enough to dissuade the others. If not, Ryan knew he would have to take point and hope the slaves would pile on. He ran his eye over the bunkhouse. The walls were heavy timber. The ceiling was thick boards. Mebbe it would hold. Mebbe—

Ryan whirled and the women screamed as timbers rent and tore. Rain and wind lashed into the bunkhouse as the back corner of the roof was ripped open to the sky. The nightwalker was female. Her filthy, milk-white face was a giant witch face of brutal knobs of chin, cheeks and brow. Fertility fetish breasts slopped down nearly as long as a man's arm. The hag's hunting scream froze every slave in their tracks. A woman howled as the she-creature reached down a huge, dripping white hand and seized her by the hair.

"Moni!" Ryan roared. "The head!" He tapped his own skull with his blaster. "The head! The head! The head!"

The spell broke. Moni scurried to the back of the bunkhouse as the nightwalker pulled up her struggling prize. The thing boomed something at Moni in Portuguese. Moni held up her blaster in both hands and screamed in answer. "Fook Raul!" She closed her eyes and pulled the trigger. Moni's blind blast tore away most of the hag's lower jaw. Moni screamed and fell backward as violet blood rained upon her. The she-creature made a horrible noise and dropped her prey. Moni and the woman clutched each other as the thing toppled backward and fell off the roof with an audible thud. Ryan kept his eye on the door.

It exploded into kindling.

A six-foot-tall and five-foot-wide thing burst into the room. It was bloated, bald and bullet-headed, and moved far too fast for its bulk. The nightwalker's grotesque rolls of fat leaped and jiggled in all directions as it charged. It held a yard-long club crudely shaped into the form of a blaster stock. The business end was studded with Orca teeth. The massive mutant was past the *X* before any of the slaves could act.

Ryan shot it twice in the chest as it hurtled forward. Renan fired wildly and missed. Cafu took a concerted extra second to aim. His blaster boomed and the nightwalker dropped its war club as blood exploded out of its neck. It screamed and came on. Ryan braced himself and rammed it through as it came across the table. The thing bowled Ryan over anyway. Every ounce of air blasted out of Ryan's lungs as four hundred pounds of filthy, screaming, bleeding, milk-white flesh fell on top of him.

The slaves piled on.

A forest of legs surrounded the pile. The slaves screamed and shouted out their long-suppressed rage. Clubs and stones rained blows on the nightwalker's head and back. It flailed and screamed, but it was wedded to Ryan by the blade through its ribs. Renan lifted a hearthstone the size of a loaf of bread in both hands and brought it down against the nightwalker's skull with crunching finality. He wheezed as its deadweight collapsed against him. The slaves roared in triumph. They shouted their defiance to the storming heavens above.

They were no longer slaves.

Ryan took a gasping breath as they rolled the vast bulk off him. They continued beating the corpse. Ryan shook off the cobwebs and got a knee underneath him. The shouts of triumph were instantly eclipsed by screams. Ryan blinked as one of the slaves flew overhead as if she had wings. The woman smashed into the far wall with the snap of breaking bones.

Horror surpassed itself.

The third abomination was eight feet tall if it was an inch. Like a giant scarecrow, its arms stretched out in an all-encompassing wingspan nearly as wide. Its knees came up to its chest as it folded like a spider to fill the bunkhouse from floor to ceiling. Renan charged it with his stone in both hands. The nightwalker slapped the stone away with ease. Renan's head disappeared as a giant hand closed around it. Women screamed as the nightwalker ripped Renan's head from his body. Blood geysered across the bunkhouse. The nightwalker upended the youth's corpse like a goblet and gulped blood and fluids from the neck.

Ryan shot it in the chest.

The mutant's head snapped around and it gave Ryan its undivided attention. He shot it twice more center-mass. Pinholes of purple blood appeared but without effect. Ryan raised his aim for the head shot, and the nightwalker flung Renan's body at Ryan in response. The one-eyed man dodged most of it but Renan's leg still clubbed him brutally across the chest. Stones pelted the creature and two more slaves attacked with clubs. The nightwalker closed a hand the size of a bunch of bananas into a fist. It hit the leading man like a battering ram and crushed the cage of his chest. The second man swung his club. The nightwalker caught the club and the hand holding it. The mutie ripped off the man's hand at the wrist. The attacker staggered back, screaming. The nightwalker took the commandeered club and crushed the mutilated man's skull.

Ryan raised his blaster and fired his final round.

Blood blossomed on the nightwalker's forehead. It dropped the club and clapped a hand to its skull as it reeled back a step. Ryan lowered the empty weapon. The nightwalker lowered its hand. Bulging eyes regarded Ryan out of a purple mask of blood. The soft lead .38 bullet had caromed off a brow ridge of bone thicker than a thumb and filleted away flesh along the side of the nightwalker's skull.

The Deathland's warrior dropped the smoking, empty blaster and ripped his sword from the flesh of the fallen fat one at his feet. His eardrums tried to meet in the middle of his head as the nightwalker loosed its hunting scream in the closed confines of the bunkhouse. The caterwauling was cut short as Cafu flung a stool into the screaming mutie's teeth. Cafu picked up the dead nightwalker's war club in both hands and looked to Ryan desperately. "Ryan!" The women had retreated to the back of the bunkhouse. The two remaining men hung back, to guard them and out of sheer terror.

Ryan shambled forward.

Cafu cried out, "Ryan!" and followed. The two men behind joined the attack. "Ryan! Ryan!" The giant nightwalker's hands shot forth to rend Ryan limb from limb. The one-eyed man dived beneath them and rolled up in a crouch. He slashed his blade beneath the knob of one giant, misshapen knee. The mutie screamed as tendons parted and it tilted back off balance. Cafu took the cue and swung his club like an ax. The tooth-studded weapon shattered the mutie's patella. The nightwalker collapsed backward, kneecapped, and its screams registered fear. It raised a warding hand and Ryan slashed off the offered fingers. The mutie screamed again as Ryan's backslash opened its elbow to the bone. Cafu pounded its other hand to pulp with his club. Fingers and bones broke under his assault. The other two men dodged the mutie's flailing legs and landed blows wherever they could.

Ryan lunged hard and low.

The diamond point of his blade rammed underneath the nightwalker's jaw, piercing the soft flesh beneath and crunching through the hard palate into the brain. The giant went limp. The bunkhouse was suddenly silent except for the ragged breathing of the victors. Cartilage cracked as Ryan ripped his sword free. He tottered toward the door. Cafu leaned on his club, gasping. Ryan stepped out into the rain. The she-creature had not gotten far. It crawled on three limbs through the mud of a garden plot, mewling and cradling its jellied lower jaw. The hag wasn't even aware of Ryan until he yanked her head back by the hair and cut her throat. The female fell unmoving into the mud. Ryan returned to the bunkhouse. He felt like he'd been pounded like a nail, but there were no injured to attend to. There were only the living and the dead.

Ryan gestured at the clutch of sobbing women. "Moni?"

Moni got the four women moving and they gathered their few possessions. They pulled their rough cloaks around themselves. Moni got it across in pantomime that they would go to another farm. They said their goodbyes to the men and scurried into the night. Cafu and the surviving two men gathered around Ryan. Cafu made introductions. "Leto, Luis." Leto wasn't much younger than Cafu. Luis was about Ryan's age and a head shorter. Ryan retrieved his panga, then reloaded the starter blasters. He kept one for himself and gave one to Cafu and one to Leto. Luis would have to make do with lumber until they could find him something better. Ryan examined the three men. They all looked angry. They all looked ready. Ryan now had local guides. He had the start of an army. The revolution had begun.

Ryan also had a wag that seated four. "Hey, you guys wanna go for a ride?"

The three men nodded grimly with no idea what was being proposed.

Ryan took a ragged breath. "Good."

Chapter Fifteen

Jak made landfall just as the storm really started to kick in. He figured no one would be stupe enough to take a boat out in a gale like this besides himself, so the Sister Isle, as Father Joao termed it, was the safest place to be. It took some persuasion to convince Father Joao to make himself useful, but they made it across the strait and got the boat up on the sand and tied off to a boulder. Father Joao peered up into the lashing rain. "Do you wish to take shelter or shall we just stand here until dawn?"

Jak was tempted to slash him again, but they needed to get out of the storm. "Where?"

Joao shrugged. "My church?"

Jak's eyes slitted. He smelled a trap, but he was pretty sure he had Father Joao under control, and Ryan had said there was food, wine and supplies there. Jak shoved him. "Go."

They slogged up a muddy path through the fields. Occasional lightning flashes lit the pounding darkness. Several times they wandered off the path and had to correct as they trod down millet grain. Father Joao mostly knew the way by heart. A pair of lamps hung high above the highest hill. Lightning showed Jak the church in stark relief. "Why lit?"

"It is always lit at night. It can be seen from most of the villages. It is a symbol. The light in the darkness."

They trudged through the muck and Joao opened the door. “Sacrilege!” Father Joao shook with rage as he took in the chopped-up pews. Portuguese profanity spewed from his lips in a torrent. “Nini!” He stamped his foot. “Nini!”

A frightened girl came out of one of the cells in the back. She was hardly any older than Jak and had a bruised look about her. Joao grabbed the girl, shaking her while screaming questions. Jak ended the interrogation by slashing the barrel of his blaster across Father Joao’s kidney. He gasped and buckled to one knee. The girl stared wide-eyed at Jak and ran across the church. Jak let her run. “Who she?”

“Nini, a servant,” Joao gasped. “She lights the lamps at night. When I am here she…” Joao trailed off uncomfortably.

“Bed warmer,” Jak finished. “You—”

The clang of the steeple bell rang off the walls deafeningly. Jak gave Father Joao another clip across the kidneys to keep him honest. He turned and pointed the weapon down the church at Nini, who paled and dropped the bell rope. Jak twitched the muzzle of his blaster and Nini very reluctantly approached. Jak gave the priest his attention. “You order that?”

Father Joao pressed a hand to his back. “You attacked her priest, did you not?”

The priest had a point, but Jak still wasn’t buying. “Who coming?”

“Probably most of the population.”

Jak stuck his head out the door. He squinted into the wind and rain and saw torches by the dozens moving in the little valleys. They were all winding up toward the church like fiery snakes in the darkness. Jak knew he didn't have much time. He also knew he couldn't fight the entire island. He would have to talk his way out.

"Nini." Jak pointed at the lamps and candles within the church. She looked at Father Joao. He nodded and the girl began lighting up the church.

The islanders began arriving and several stuck their heads in warily. They looked like hedgehogs in the bushy grass capes and crude straw hats they wore against the rain. They had arrived at the sound of the late-night alarm bearing clubs and stones. Jak motioned them inside. The islanders saw Father Joao and another pale main islander they didn't recognize. They began filing inside out of the rains in ones and twos. Jak spoke quietly to Joao. "Tell I not like you."

Joao sighed resignedly. "Take off your hat."

Jak took off his hat. Several islanders gasped. Joao pointed at Jak and spoke a few words. A ripple of fear went through the throng and out the door. Clubs and stones were raised. Jak wasn't getting the reaction he wanted. They had been friendly with Ryan and Doc. Jak suspected the color of his skin had something to do with it, and Father Joao wasn't helping matters. The priest gasped as Jak snaked his arm under his chin into a choke and screwed the muzzle of his blaster into his temple. "You said?"

Father Joao's voice came out in a hiss. "I told them to look at your white hair and demonic eyes, and know that the change was upon you."

Jak pressed the blaster harder against Joao's head. "Change?"

"You haven't yet made the acquaintance of our night-dwelling brethren. There has been an unpleasant strain of mutation on the main island. It manifests itself in young adulthood, and encourages some very aggressive behaviors and habits. You are a bit old, but they do not know that. All they know is that several times one of the nightwalkers managed to make it onto their island and reeked great devastation before they were brought down."

Jak kept the muzzle of his blaster screwed to Father Joao's temple. "Big island's supposed to be heaven."

"It was easy enough to incorporate some devils into the mythology. Heaven must have its hell. It helps them to see us as protectors, and dissuades them from attempting to visit the main isle without sanction. They see you, a young man with red eyes and white hair, threatening their savior."

"Tell I not."

Father Joao winced at the pressure of the blaster against his head. "They might suspect my change of story was…coerced."

The islanders eyed Jak's blaster fearfully but they slowly kept filing in. Jak wished he had his back against a wall, but he wasn't about to back up, and if it came to a brawl he wanted room to move. Father Joao got some sneer back in his voice. "Go ahead, start shooting, see how well it serves you."

"Shoot you first," Jak promised.

"And you will be torn apart. They are a docile people, but they think you are a nightwalker, and must be stopped at any cost. Come now, let me go and we will negotiate your surrender."

The congregation was thirty and growing, and Jak could see a forest of torches outside. Jak raised his voice. "Ryan! Doc!" The islanders inside froze. Jak took a chance. "Ago!"

A big man with a big piece of wood jumped at the sound of his name.

Joao started to hiss something, but Jak choked it off. Jak kept his eyes on Ago. "Vava, Galina, Feydor." Ago nodded with each name. "Boo," Jak said.

Ago's jaw dropped.

Jak shoved Father Joao to the ground and flung off his cloak with a flourish. The assembled islanders gasped at his field jacket, canvas pants and combat boots. He was wearing the clothes of a stranger. Jak thumped his chest with his fist. "Ryan, Doc." He flexed his limited Mex. *"Amigos."*

The effect was galvanizing.

"Amigos?" Ago asked.

Jak nodded. He took a huge chance and uncocked his blaster, spun it like a gunfighter and thrust it through his belt. He stuck out his hand. *"Amigos?"*

Jak had to restrain every fighting instinct he had as the big man stepped forward grinning like an idiot and heaved Jak up in the air in a rib-crushing bear hug. *"Amigo!"*

Jak allowed himself a small smile as Father Joao muttered imprecations from the floor. The priest was a bargaining chip, but he bore watching.

MILDRED WANDERED blindly through the womb of the earth. It was cold, hard, wet, inhospitable and as black as ink. Rage fought with terror in her breast as she slammed her head into the ceiling for the tenth time and a sob almost escaped her. Raul had abandoned her. She had awoken alone with a splitting headache and her throat a bruised pipe that had difficulty drawing air. She hated the cream-colored son of a bitch for leaving her alone in the cold, but she feared his return even more. He was probably hoping she would cringe whimpering in the darkness and stay put like a good girl while he went off and hunted Ryan. Part of Mildred hoped Raul found Ryan. If anyone was going to chill Captain Blubberknife, Ryan was the man.

Mildred clutched her throbbing head. She still had her clothes on and, other than her morale, she was unviolated. That was about the only good news. Her pack was gone, everything had been taken from her and she couldn't see jack shit. Mildred abandoned dignity and began crawling and crab-walking like a blind, four-legged and very fearful spider over the wet expanses of rock. Her fingers fluttered ahead of her like antennae. The going was interminable. She was pretty sure she had been moving for about half an hour, but— Mildred snarled as her foot slid down through a crack in the rocks and punched through, snapping driftwood that tore at her leg. She shuddered as she reached down and her hand brushed over the smooth dome of a human skull and a sprung rib cage. Claustrophobia began pulling at her. She could feel the cave walls closing in like the cold earth of the grave. She realized she was hyperventilating. Mildred fought the urge to curl up and start sobbing hysterically. The past twenty-four hours had been pretty rough even by Deathlands standards.

She took a shuddering breath and centered herself.

The rock she was sitting on was wet and cold. She ran her hand across it and licked her fingers. Cave water usually had a bitter mineral or acrid alkali tang. Mildred allowed her herself a small congratulatory smile in the dark. She wasn't a veteran rock-licker but this one definitely tasted like sea salt. Mildred gave the rock a little more love. In her experience caves were some of the sharpest, lumpiest, jagged places on Earth. The rock here was worn smooth. The only thing that was likely to have done that was tidal action. Mildred spider-walked on and nodded to herself as she clicked past panic and into survival mode. She was definitely going downhill.

Mildred stopped again and took a breather. She was sweating with exertion, but the moment she stopped and wasn't panicked she could feel the cold draft blowing in her face. She crawled on, grinning savagely as the hoped-for sound of the surf stopped being an ambient hallucination and became clearly audible over the sound of her breathing. Mildred moved forward into the breeze that got stronger and stronger and the pounding surf and the moaning of the wind blocked out all other noise. She knew she'd hit pay dirt when her hand suddenly clawed into wet sand. She was close. Mildred stood cautiously. She rose on tiptoe and stretched up her hand but still couldn't touch the cave ceiling. Mildred moved sideways until she found the cave wall. It was smooth and rounded and carved by millennia of tides coming in and out. She marched out toward freedom.

The physician yipped as she stepped into a hole and plunged waist-deep into seawater. "Bastard!" she snarled. She slogged forward through the sizable puddle and a dozen yards farther was on relatively dry sand again. The rainstorm was still in full force outside. Mildred gasped as a lightning stroke flash-framed the entrance to the cave in front of her. It disappeared in the split-second strobe but salvation lay one hundred feet ahead.

Mildred whirled, her fists blindly cocked at the sound behind her.

She tried not to breathe. She couldn't be quite sure

what it had been. A splash? A crunch of sand? It didn't matter. Mildred knew with absolute certainty that there was someone or something behind her. Her heart hammered in her chest as she stood frozen, listening. The wind howled on and the waves crashed in a world just a short distance away from this brutal burial chamber.

Mildred whirled and ran for it.

Sand flew beneath Mildred's feet in the darkness. A lucky second lightning flash showed her the cave mouth again, and she corrected her headlong flight for it. Mildred plunged out into the rain and wind. It was raining and overcast, but it was a definite improvement over the stygian darkness of the caves. Mildred didn't stop running until the surf splashed around her boots. She turned to face her pursuer. The wind blew her plaits and she was soaked again in moments, but no pale hands reached for her. There was no flensing knife in the dark. The next bolt of lightning revealed a narrow strip of beach and the stark cliffs and the mouth of the cavern she had left. Mildred noted a pile of driftwood in the flash and fumbled up the beach toward it. She selected a slimy hunk of wood by feel and heft.

Mildred stood shivering and waiting with her bludgeon.

Nothing happened.

She looked left and made out the glow of the ville and its harbor lights to the south. Mildred did some math and she shivered as she realized she had just been a guest in the cave of the chiller that Ryan had talked about. Mildred gazed north into the dark. If she followed the beach about four miles, she would hit the rendezvous point, and if Jak had gotten his milk-white ass in gear and stolen a boat, he should already be there patrolling off shore. Failing that, she might try the raft and take a chance on paddling to the island of dumb healthy people who by reputation lived in a land of barbecued goat and warm huts. Mildred leaned into the wind and splashed north along the tidal line. When she was well past the cave she moved inland until her fingers found the cliff face and she hugged rock wall for what little protection from the elements it offered.

Mildred lost track of time as she trudged miserably. The rain slowly ebbed and died. The moaning wind kept up but at least it tattered the emptied clouds to reveal patches of cold starlight. She marched on, hugging herself and her length of wood. She looked upward and sighed. Since waking up in the Deathlands, she had learned to read the sun but navigating and telling time by the stars were still out of her skill set. She thought maybe the sky was a little more purple than black.

Mildred stopped and adopted a batter's stance as she perceived a strange lump in front of her. It was strangely square and— Mildred ran forward. She plunged her hand through the curtain of seaweed and felt spars and wooden barrels. Mildred pumped her fist skyward. "Yes!"

She had found the raft. She was at the rendezvous point. Score one for Mrs. Wyeth's child prodigy. Through caverns and storms she had tracked…

Mildred spun around with her club on high again.

Her tracks. Mildred's stomach clenched in dread. She had left a mile of tracks from the cave mouth in the wet sand. Mildred fell to her knees in exhaustion and shame. The party had split up. The enemy knew they were split up and the paper-faced bastards had known in their chilly little hearts there had to be a rendezvous point. Raul had let her escape. Mildred's cheekbones burned in shame despite the cold. Raul had listened in amusement to her whimpering, crying, worm-blind trek through the caverns he knew by heart and laughed at her triumph at finding the raft. Jak would be bringing the boat at dawn, and they would be waiting. Ryan would be coming island-side and they would be waiting. She had nowhere to go where there would not be a welcoming committee.

Mrs. Wyeth's child prodigy had been played like an amateur.

Mildred screamed in rage into the wind and night. "Fuck you!"

"In good time, Dr. Wyeth!" Basso profundo amusement boomed off the cliffs from out of sight in the dark. "In good time!"

Chapter Sixteen

Cafu, Leto and Luis could hardly contain themselves. If Ryan hadn't commanded their awe before, the fact that they were driving around in Baron Barat's wag, beat-up as it was, had cemented his godlike status. Ryan hadn't quite gotten around to telling them yet that they were headed back to Baron Barat's manse, and he was frankly worried what that might do to morale, much less the entire revolution. He really didn't see much other choice. He had a few hours to chill before making his dawn rendezvous with Jak on the beach. Mildred had gone missing on the manse grounds, and Doc was still a prisoner inside. Doubling back was just about the only plan that made any sense. Ryan was betting the baron and his son were out in the night hunting him, and only a skeleton crew would be guarding the grounds.

Cafu suddenly got wise. His hands slammed on the dash and he stared at Ryan in shock. He started babbling in rapid-fire Portuguese, and Leto and Luis went all excitable, as well. Ryan rolled his eye. Cafu started gesticulating wildly. Ryan grabbed him by the hair and yanked the wheel savagely. "Down!"

Twin blasts of lead ripped across the roof. Another tore at the fender as someone got smart and went for the tires. Ryan floored it and dark figures flung themselves out of the feeble headlight's glare and out of the way.

They swung around a curve and left the hunters shouting and blowing whistles behind them. Cafu rose and looked at Ryan sheepishly. They drove for a few more miles in silence. Twice they heard nightwalker hunting screams in the distance and the island men clutched their weapons tightly. Ryan cut his headlight as he caught the glow of the manse up on the hill. He stopped a few hundred yards from the gate where the woods and curve of the hill concealed them. Ryan chinked open his lighter. It was a risk but he had no common language with these men and he had to get the strategy into their heads. The three island men sighed at the wonder of the light in Ryan's hand. He handed it to Cafu and started talking and making pantomime with his hands. "You're going up the hill. Luis? You tell them you've seen me, *comprende?* You, tell them, you've seen me. Ryan."

Luis watched Ryan point at the hill, point at his eyes and then himself. He nodded slowly. He pointed at Ryan, Leto and Cafu as he replied and made a circling gesture with his hand.

"That's right." Ryan nodded. "You tell them you've seen me. Then me, Cafu and Leto—" Ryan punched his fist into his palm "—we sneak up on them from the side. *Bom?*"

The men nodded. *"Bom."*

Ryan took back his lighter and stepped out into the rain. They slogged up the hill, staying by the side of the road. Another scream tore out of the darkness, but it was far away. They stopped as they neared the edge of the grounds. Two men with auto-blasters stood sentinel in front of the shattered gate. Ryan put a hand on Luis's shoulder. *"Bom."*

Luis handed his club to Leto and ran out into the

road. His sandals slapped on the wet cobbles, and he began waving his arms and calling out. The sec men snapped up the muzzles of their blasters. Luis raised his hands and did a good job of cringing fearfully. He bowed and scraped and would not meet the sec men's eyes. One rammed the muzzle of his blaster into Luis's gut and dropped him gasping to his knees for his trouble. Ryan had Cafu and Leto shuck off their sandals, then they broke from the trees. They were out in the open but circling wide in the darkness. The wind and rain covered their approach. The wet grass beneath their feet made no noise as they charged forward in a hobble. Luis had the sec men's full attention. He yelped and flinched as the sec men gave him a few kicks to help the questioning along.

The sec men never saw what hit them.

Ryan rammed his sword through the kidney of one. The man went as stiff as a board and dropped his blaster. Ryan tore his blade free and chopped it into the side of the sec man's neck. Cafu's war club nearly took the other sec man's head off his shoulders. They dragged the dead sec men back into the darkness beneath the trees and Ryan went over their find. The two autoblasters were rebuilt from a make he wasn't familiar with but they were heavy, .30-caliber, and each sec man had a spare mag. Both carried a short double-blaster in their belt and had another of the short stabbing swords on a baldric. Beneath their coats the sec men bore leather purses holding powder, lead shot and rock salt. One man had a set of heavy iron keys. Ryan held out a sword to Cafu. The old man hefted his tooth-studded club and shook his head. The old man had been swinging axes, mattocks and mauls all his life. He was old but as strong and gnarled as an oak. The gunstock club with its pointed ivory pegs was right up his alley. Leto and Luis both took a sword eagerly and Ryan handed out the doubles to Cafu and Luis.

Ryan hid the extra auto-blaster under a dead man's cloak for later retrieval and hefted the remaining one. He took a moment in the gloom to familiarize himself with the selector and mag eject. He tucked the two spare mags away. They were as ready to mount a rescue as they were going to get. "Let's go."

Ryan and his team moved past the gate and into the inner perimeter. All the lights were on. He stalked up the steps. His tiny squad of revolutionaries looked at one another fearfully at their own temerity. The door was locked. Ryan quietly tried keys and the second one fit. If it was bolted they were going to have to start climbing. He turned the key, swung open the spiked, oaken door and swept into the foyer.

The baron's expansive living room had been turned into a field surgery. Three dead men lay in the corner shrouded in purple-soaked sheets. The sec men Ryan had attacked lay on pallets moaning with broken bones. The old man he had clotheslined in the hall sat on a couch nursing a broken collarbone in a sling. Two sec men with slung, bolt-action blasters stood nearby grimacing. Two old and bent servants were mixing and passing out jiggers of the wine, Blood of the Lotus and blood mixture. The sec men Ryan had given the powder charge to the face lay on the table snarling while a balding man applied dressings. One of the most hauntingly beautiful women Ryan had ever seen held the injured man's hand. Her arms were purple up to her elbows from surgery. She murmured soothingly to Ryan's victim.

Ryan spoke softly. "Nobody move."

Cafu, Leto and Luis filed in behind Ryan. The woman and the healer stared in shock. The two sec men shouted in open outrage and Ryan's cohorts cringed. The click of Ryan flicking his blaster's selector switch to full-auto was unnaturally loud and the shouting stopped. Ryan pointed his blaster at the woman. "Lady Barat."

The woman stared down Ryan's blaster imperiously and shouted in Portuguese. Her voice rang with the unmistakable tone of command. Luis and Leto began to lower their weapons in long-conditioned subservience. Ryan brought his blaster to his shoulder. "Lady, I'm gonna—"

Cafu stepped forward. A plaster bust of Baron Barat stood in prominence by the entrance of the room. Cafu swung his club with a roar and the baron's effigy shattered like shrapnel. Cafu shook with rage as he pointed the club at the woman. "Fook Barat!"

Cafu had had enough.

Lady Zorime shook her head in cold anger. "You are no gentleman."

"No," Ryan agreed. "I'm not a gentle man. I want Doc. I want Mildred, and I want our blasters. Now."

"Maybe—"

"No, mebbe. Now."

The pale beauty lifted her chin in defiance. "And should I refuse?"

Everyone in the Barat barony seemed to have a fondness for rhetorical questions of defiance. Ryan's blue eye burned into Zorime's dark gaze. He knew she was willing to die for her family. "I won't hurt you. You're valuable." Ryan cast his gaze over the injured men triaged on pallets on the floor. "I'll kill your people. One at a time. Until you give me what I want."

"I believe you would."

"Tell your men to drop their blasters."

Zorime nodded at her men. Their longblasters clunked to the floor.

Ryan jerked the muzzle of his blaster. "Swords." The swords clattered to the wood. "Luis, Leto." The two men gathered up the weapons beneath the scathing glares of their former masters. "Your men," Ryan prompted. "On the floor."

Zorime's fists clenched. Her men understood. They were equally enraged but they grabbed floor under Ryan's baleful blue eye and the black muzzle of his blaster.

"Now our blasters," Ryan ordered.

Zorime went to a locked cabinet. She opened it with a key from a ring on her waist. Inside the gun cabinet were a number of blasters of old and new manufacture, including his and Doc's. Ryan slung his Steyr over his shoulder and hung the familiar weight of his SIG-Sauer on his belt. He stuffed his coat with spare mags and ammo.

Zorime and her people stared on frostily.

Ryan shoved Doc's LeMat under his belt and handed his sword cane to Luis. Ryan glanced at the man tending the sec man's face. "He's your healer?"

"Dr. Goncalves." Zorime nodded. "What of it?"

Ryan examined the lady's bloody hands and nightshirt. "He trained you?"

"Yes."

"Here's the deal. You go up. You get Doc. You bring him down. You come alone. If you don't, no matter what, I blow your healer's head off. Understand?"

Zorime's fists clenched. "I understand."

"Hope you do. Get Doc."

Zorime marched stiff-legged up the stairs.

Other than the occasional moan of the drugged and injured men the silence in the room grew uncomfortable. Dr. Goncalves gestured at Ryan. "Your injuries. Are—"

"Just fine," Ryan finished. He looked toward the ceiling as he heard Doc's voice. He shook his head. Doc was apologizing to Lady Zorime for the inconvenience. Doc looked a little wobbly and he was favoring his side as he came down the stairs. He smiled happily at Ryan. "You came for me."

"Twice," Ryan admitted.

"I knew you would."

Ryan shrugged.

Doc looked Ryan up and down. "Your injuries?"

"I tussled with some of their nightwalkers." Ryan glanced at Zorime. "Killed four of them."

Zorime gasped.

Ryan didn't even want to think about the swathes of his flesh that had been blasted into bruised and bloody ground meat. "Got rock-salted a few times."

"Yes." Doc winced and put an empathetic hand to his side where the baron had given him both barrels. "They saw fit to season me, as well."

"You all right?"

"I have been well dosed with their Blood of the Lotus."

"And?"

"To be honest, I believe it is doing me some good."

It hurt his face, but Ryan gave Doc one of his rare smiles. "Saw you put your mark on the baron and his boy."

"I wish you had been there, my friend." Doc grinned exultantly in memory. "It was something to see."

Ryan handed Doc his LeMat, cane and backpack. "We gotta go."

Doc checked the loads. "How shall we proceed?"

"I got the baron's wag."

"Capital!"

Zorime scoffed. "You have nowhere to go."

"Mebbe. Could stay here," Ryan countered. "Wait for your kin to come back."

Zorime's eyes flared in sudden fear. Ryan looked at her long and hard. She was easy on the eyes. Ryan had a very serious distaste for hostage taking, but it was almost dawn. The people of the ville and their rad-blasted monster brethren were both hunting him. He had a rendezvous to make with Jak, and if they were right about the timer on the mat-trans, then Krysty and J.B. would be coming through come morning. Lady Zorime was an edge he needed. "Best put on your traveling clothes."

Zorime flushed with anger. "I will not!"

Ryan's voice dropped. "You can come along or you can be carried."

Zorime took a frightened step back. The two sec men on the floor started to push themselves up, but Cafu and Luis stepped on them. Zorime looked about herself helplessly. "I will come."

Chapter Seventeen

Mildred huddled miserably on the beach. The storm clouds had been replaced by dreary overcast devoid of warmth as the sun rose. At some point exhaustion had overtaken fear and she had fallen asleep for a few hours. Raul was gone when she awoke. Mildred reread his message. The gargantuan son of a bitch had walked right up to her as she slept and written in the sand with his whale-butchering blade: You sleep like an angel.

She shuddered as she read his postscript.

Soon…

His sasquatch-size footprints went down to the water's edge and disappeared so she couldn't tell which way he had gone. If he had gone at all. Mildred clutched her driftwood club tighter. Like it was going to do her a lick of good. She jumped as a rope flopped down the side of the cliff beside her. "Dr. Wyeth, I presume!"

Mildred glanced up to see another gigantic son of a bitch staring down at her. This one was dressed all in black rather than a loincloth. The man leaned jauntily on his sword and doffed his hat. He was huge, but he wasn't a deformed monstrosity like Raul. He replaced his hat and smiled down past his smoked lenses. "Will you join us?"

Mildred hung her head. She had nowhere to go unless she wanted to start swimming. One look at the heaving gray mush of the sea and the dim shadows of the other island in the distance told her she would never make it. She once again considered swimming out to one of the buoys and waiting for Jak there, but she was already chilled to the bone. She didn't think she could make it, much less hold on long enough. "Fuck you," she managed.

It sounded lame even to her.

"Come now, Dr. Wyeth. You truly have nowhere else to go. Unless you would prefer to sit there and wait for night to fall once more…?"

Mildred shook her head and felt like crying again.

"There is no reason for you to be miserable while we await your friends. Come, we have blankets, freshly baked bread and mulled wine. As long as you behave, I give you the word of Sylvano Barbosa Barat that you shall have my hospitality and protection. None shall molest you."

Mildred stifled a sob as she took the rope.

"Please be so kind as to leave the lumber below," Sylvano cautioned.

Mildred dropped her club to the sand. She shook with the sense of betraying her friends and herself. She stood on the knot and twisted against the cliff as the big man and two of his friends hauled her up. She couldn't meet their shaded gaze as they lifted her to the cliff edge. Someone draped a shaggy wool blanket over her shoulders. Sylvano himself pressed a cup of hot, spiced wine into her hands. Mildred nearly sagged as the hot wine bloomed its warmth in her stomach. Another man pulled a biscuit the size of her fist from a covered basket. It was still warm from the bakery. Mildred tore into the bread knowing that she looked like a starving, homeless wretch who had surrendered. "Listen, I…"

Mildred gasped as she looked around her. She counted about two dozen men. Except that everyone was dressed in black, it looked like a civil war reenactment from her time. Long-barreled, single-shot blasters with bayonets fixed stood in tripods ready for instant use. The men all wore swords on white leather cross-belts and had put jaunty feathers in the bands of their wide-brimmed hats. A pair of men with optics scanned the sea. The cannons were the most disturbing development. Four of them sat on spoked wheels facing the channel. Plungers, powder kegs and pallets of ugly iron spheres the size of croquet balls were all at the ready. Mildred eyed a pair of ancient, highly modified Unimog flatbed wags.

Sylvano gazed upon the cannon proudly. "My father's innovation. I was but a boy, but we nearly lost our last battle with invaders. They came with predark weaponry. We were routed. Indeed it was Raul and the nightwalkers who turned the tide. We simply do not have the wherewithal to manufacture machine guns or other heavy armament. So my father looked backward rather than forward. Even predark our island had a blacksmith and a forge. My father has several books in his library about the Napoleanic Wars, some included specifications of rifled muskets and cannon." Sylvano smiled bemusedly. "There was some initial trial and error, I admit, but in the end we perfected the ancient craft of artillerymen. Do you see the buoys? They ring the island, and serve another purpose besides guiding boats through the rocks of the channel."

Mildred shoulders sagged wearily. "They're range markers."

"Yes!" Sylvano was delighted. "Did you know my father has made me master of the cannon?"

Mildred was too depressed to come up with a snappy comeback. "Good for you."

Sylvano was too happy with his artillery pieces to be bothered with Mildred's sarcasm. "I tell you, when the self-styled Vikings came some years ago, they sailed into the harbor, firing their blasters in the air, waving their axes and howling like the berserkers of old to Odin." Mildred flinched as Sylvano made a huge triumphant, black-gloved fist. "We blasted them into matchsticks with our shore batteries!"

Mildred sighed despairingly. "Like you're going to do to my friends here."

"Yes." Sylvano lowered his hand. "I can see how these are no glad tidings for you. Let me offer you what silver lining I may."

"And what would that be?"

"You are a medical doctor?"

Mildred didn't bother denying it.

"Then I suspect you well know you are far too valuable a commodity to be wasted. My father has authorized me to offer you terms. Both you, Dr. Wyeth, and Dr. Tanner would be considered assets to the community."

"You know something, Sylvano? I've heard this speech before."

"I'm sure you have. So consider wisely. Here you would be treasured and respected, working at your chosen profession with Dr. Goncalves, my sister, our interns, nurses and midwives. Think of Dr. Tanner. Would he not be more comfortable here? He could live out his remaining years, surrounded by books, a respected teacher of science and the sword. Like you, he might initially reject my proposal, but I suspect he would settle in quickly enough."

"And you'd trust me to just settle in?"

"You would initially be on parole." Sylvano shrugged. "However, once you had children I suspect you would become invested in our community."

Mildred recoiled. "Yeah, right."

Sylvano gestured out at the sea. "We have occasional visitors to our isles as you know. We know of your Deathlands, Dr. Wyeth. Is there any place there you truly wish to return to? Do you truly wish to continue randomly hurling your body through the void, from mat-trans to mat-trans until your luck runs out?"

"No offense, but this island wouldn't exactly be my first choice."

"None taken, I am sure you have seen many. However, in our defense, here everyone is well fed. The air is clean. We have survived, and thrived in our own way. Sometimes in this world compromise equals survival." Sylvano gazed down at Mildred from his great height. "And in the end? You really have no choice."

"What about the rest of my friends?"

"Tell me about them," Sylvano suggested.

She remained silent.

"Then, I can only speak for the fate of Ryan and the albino. They have proved themselves very dangerous men. Even hobbled, I do not believe they could be trusted among us."

"So you're going to slaughter them. Just like you always planned." Mildred shook her head bitterly. "Not much of a bargain there, Sylvie."

"There is more. I give you my word on this, and I have the authority to speak for my father, the baron, as well."

Mildred couldn't think of any other plan than to keep him talking. "Do tell."

"The fact is, no one in living memory who has gone through the mat-trans on the escarpment has ever returned. Whether this means that it hurls them to some terrible fate or the machinery has been programmed to prevent it, we do not know. If you help negotiate the surrender of your companions, the male warriors among your party? They will be sent through."

"Just like that?"

"We will keep their blasters, and any valuable tech they have, of course."

"Great, a blind jump with jack shit for the other side."

"They will have each other, Dr. Wyeth, and they will be sent through alive. Along with food, water, kit to make fire, and I will give each a sword in hand to face whatever awaits them." Sylvano's face grew hard. "This is the limit of my generosity. Should you refuse, you will next deal with my father, the baron, and you will find him a far harder bargainer."

Mildred already knew everyone's answer. Ryan and Krysty would both rather die than be parted. When the islanders found out J.B. was an armorer, they would hobble him and put him to work. Jak had come up the very hardest way in the Deathlands. There was nothing more important to him than loyalty. Mildred knew he would never willingly leave her or Krysty behind. Doc might agree to the bargain if he thought it would save his friends, but he abhorred human iniquity in all its forms. In the face of the slavery and the blood harvesting, it wouldn't be long before he tried something stupid. As for herself? Mildred had to admit she loved J.B., but she wasn't quite ready to settle down. Particularly here on goddamn vampire island.

Sylvano waited for an answer.

A lookout's cry gave Mildred a moment's reprieve. "Sylvano!"

Sylvano ushered Mildred firmly toward the cliff edge. He took the offered binoculars and scanned the gray sea. He handed the optics to Mildred and pointed obligingly. "Dr. Wyeth?"

Mildred's spirits sank as she looked out to where Sylvano pointed. An open boat was cutting across the strait. Three men and a woman in the local peasant garb clutched the sides as well as staves. A man in black sat among them. It was hard to tell at this distance, but it looked like his hands were bound. A smaller man sat in the back with his hand on the outboard. He was dressed in the local ville black, but white hair fluttered beneath his hat and Mildred would recognize Jak's silhouette anywhere. A dog stood at the prow with his paws on a tiny cannon and his snout lifted to the breeze.

"It seems your friend has done some recruiting, and, as suspected, he has Father Joao."

Mildred felt a glimmer of hope. "You want to talk a trade, Sylvie?"

"You?" Sylvano snorted. "For Father Joao?"

"Why not?"

Mildred's stomach sank as Sylvano and the lookout both laughed. "I fear you are far more valuable than the good Father. I also fear that Sister Isle's society and spirituality have been corrupted, first by the Russians and now irretrievably by your friends. I fear a far stricter social order will have to be put in place. I fear..." A cold smile crossed Sylvano's face. It was pretty clear he had very little use for the good Father. "Father Joao may need to be martyred in the name of the island."

The lookout laughed.

Sylvano took back the binoculars. "You can save both if you wish, Doctor."

"Oh, how's that?"

"You will go back down onto the beach. You will entice them to land. Your friend is brave, but I think if he suddenly finds himself looking down the barrels of a dozen rifles and four cannons, particularly if you are down on the beach with him, he will surrender. If we have you, Dr. Tanner and the albino, and this Ryan sees the escarpment blockaded, then perhaps he can finally be brought to heel."

It was Mildred's turn to snort. "No one brings Ryan Cawdor to heel."

Sylvano's voice dropped again. He was tiring of the conversation. "Then he will see reason, or he will see his friends exterminated, if he has not been slaughtered already by Raul and his clan. Now, enough of this. I wish an answer from you." Mildred struggled for something to say. She stepped back as Sylvano drew his sword. "And I warn you, Doctor, whatever you choose, I do not wish to hear the words *fuck you* cross your lips again."

Mildred gulped.

Sylvano took a step forward and Mildred found nothing but the edge of the cliff beneath her heels. Sylvano's voice thundered. "The moment they cross the buoys, I fire! If you wish your friends to live any longer, you must choose! No matter what transpires, you will serve the ville! You must choose whether you do it willingly, or you whether you must be hobbled and broken to it! But you must choose!"

Hot tears stung Mildred's eyes. "I..."

"Choose!" Sylvano roared.

"I..."

Sylvano lowered his sword and shook his head sadly. "I am not a cruel man, Dr. Wyeth. I will not make you watch." He nodded to the lookout. "Rafa, bind her and put her in the cab of one of the trucks where it is warm. Put a man to watch her."

Sylvano raised his voice. "Filho! Alexandre! Ready your crews! Prepare to run out the guns! All else, to arms!"

"No!" Mildred sank to her knees.

Sylvano cocked his head. "No?"

Mildred wept. "No."

"If your friend surrenders, he will live. Those with him will not face reprisal. You have my word. Regardless, you will not be harmed, and your life among us will be made as pleasant as possible." Sylvano put a hand on her shoulder. Mildred no longer had the wherewithal to shake it off. "I do admire you, Dr. Wyeth."

Mildred felt like nothing but a coward and a traitor, but she saw only a single option. Keep Jak out of the cannons. Keep him alive a little while longer. Mildred wiped her eyes and took the rope Sylvano handed her. They lowered her down to the sand. Mildred picked up her driftwood club for no other reason than it made her feel a little better. No warning came down from the cliff. She turned and the rope was gone and there was no sign of the ambush above. She scuffed her feet through Raul's love note as she walked slowly to the surf line and waited.

It wasn't long before Jak's boat appeared out of the gray. Mildred raised her club and waved it. The Sister Islanders all waved happily. Mildred's stomach clenched as Jak piloted the boat past the buoy marker but no salvo of cannon fire tore the dawn. Mildred half wished a dozen rifles would blast into her back and end her misery.

Mildred just about jumped out of her boots as the cannons cut loose up above. Three detonations rippled one after the other. Mildred whirled and screamed up the cliff. "Bastards!" Mildred screamed over the cannonade. "You bastards!" Jak rose from the tiller with his blaster aimed at the cliff. Mildred was surprised to see the young man not blasted into matchsticks. She was shocked that no geysers erupted out of the waves where the cannon rounds hit. Up on the cliff men shouted and screamed. Mildred gaped as one of the cannons rolled smoking and burning over the cliff's edge and plunged sizzling to the sand.

The fourth cannon didn't fire at all.

A sudden silence fell upon the beach. Mildred and Jak looked at each other in confusion across the surf. Ryan's voice echoed dimly along the cliffs. "Mildred! Run!"

Mildred flung away her wood and broke into a dead sprint. Jak slewed the whaler around hard to parallel her course. His stainless-steel blaster gleamed as he kept it pointed at the cliff line. Mildred ran like she had wings. She wanted to shout out, but she saved her breath. She needed to gain distance.

No one brought Ryan Cawdor to heel.

Chapter Eighteen

Ryan glared through his Steyr's optic. It wasn't good. Two dozen men, four cannons, and all squatting over the rendezvous point. Sylvano and two other sec men had auto-blasters. The rest were carrying single-shooters, but they all had bayonets fixed of all rad-blasted things and every mutie in this pesthole was suicidally in love with sharp points. They all had sawed-off doubles and swords, as well. Cafu, Leto and Luis were three hundred yards back up the road with the wag and the baron's daughter.

Doc whispered as he lay next to Ryan in the gorse. "We are outnumbered."

Ryan nodded. "When aren't we?"

"Indeed, but they also have artillery. If they have grapeshot then they can rake us at this range once we begin firing."

Ryan continued to scan the enemy position. He reckoned it about two hundred and fifty meters. "What's grapeshot?"

"You see the cannons?"

"Yeah."

"Imagine them laden with several hundred buckshot rather than a single iron ball."

Ryan gazed at the black iron cannon. "That could be a problem."

"What do you believe would remedy it?"

Jak and J.B. geared up and in a bad mood would be a good start, but Ryan wasn't going to hold his breath. Last time he'd shot Sylvano the man had been wearing armor. Ryan figured he was wearing it now. He let out a long breath. Two hundred and fifty yards with a stiff ocean breeze. A head shot would be problematic. Ryan had exactly three black-tipped, armor-piercing rounds. Sylvano was a big man. There was a good chance Ryan could put three rounds into his chest or back and drop him. "I could drop Sylvano. These guys don't have a clue yet that you're free and we're out and about with Cafu and the boys, much less have the lady. I drop Sylvano and hightail it. Mebbe they chase me in force. You and the boys work your way down. Take out whoever they leave behind. Warn off Jak and have him meet us farther down the coast. I'll double back when I can."

"I am not the best of wag drivers, Ryan."

"All you got to do is keep it on the road and head north. You link up with Jak. I'll catch up."

Doc's breath hissed inward. "Ryan!"

Ryan snapped up his rifle and watched Sylvano and two men haul Mildred up over the cliff with a rope. "Fireblast."

They watched as she was given food and drink. Sylvano was questioning her closely. Mildred looked like she'd had a rough night. Ryan could hear the big man's roar. "Choose!"

Ryan's blood ran cold as Mildred fell to her knees. They yanked her up and lowered her back down the cliff.

Doc choked with emotion. "They are using our dear Mildred as bait!"

Ryan raised his blaster for the long shot on Sylvano.

"The dawn rises!" Doc cried. "Jak will be here in heartbeats!"

"Doc..." Ryan took aim.

"The people of this ville are using black powder!" Doc's brow beetled in furious thought. "If only we could sneak down and set one or two kegs alight! That might be diversion enough to allow us to affect a rescue and—"

Ryan's chewed-up face arranged a smile. "Doc?"

"Oh, I am sorry." Doc flushed in sheepish embarrassment. "I will endeavor to keep my prattle to a minimum."

"You're a genius."

Doc blinked. "You know? A few people, and they were in the minority mind you, used to be of that opinion a few hundred years ago."

Ryan took out his remaining five red-tipped U.S. Military tracer rounds. He ejected his mag and racked the bolt to take out the bullet in the chamber. He put a tracer in the breech and let the bolt fly home. He shucked out seven rounds from the mag and back-loaded the three armor-piercing and topped off with the four remaining tracers. Five rounds to make something to go boom. Three rounds for Sylvano's rad-blasted ass if the deal went sour.

"Doc, you work you way back up around the hill. Have Cafu and the boys push the wag up to just around the bend. Then you bring me Zorime."

"And then?"

Despite the fact they had commandeered a trunk-load of blasters Ryan knew he was the only one who could hit something from this distance. "You wait. Move, Doc. We don't have much time."

"I understand, my friend." Doc kneed and elbowed backward until his bony frame disappeared in the shrubbery. Ryan waited. If Sylvano got impatient, he'd punch him burning and screaming over the cliff edge. Minutes crawled like hours. Doc returned. The old man had a problem with laying his hands on women, which was probably why Cafu had come along and was prompting Zorime along by a handful of hair. The lady took a single look at the situation and scoffed. "You will be annihilated. Let me go to my brother and—"

"You behave, and I let your brother live."

"Are you mad?"

"Watch and see." Ryan put the post of his optic on a powder keg.

The Steyr cracked. By night the tracer would have been a laval red line through the air. In the gray dawn it was a dull orange streak. Splinters flew as it impacted the powder keg. Sec men snapped around and reached for their blasters. Then the keg, the pallet of shot and the man standing next to it disappeared in orange fire and pulsing clouds of gray smoke.

Zorime screamed and clawed at Ryan. Cafu heaved her back by the hair. Ryan stayed on station and swung on to the next cannon position. He took several heartbeats to steady his aim and squeezed. The tracer lasered across the three hundred yards and impacted the next keg. A man and his arm flew into the air separated by blood and smoke. Ryan tracked his aim to the third position and fired. The powder keg was right next to the cannon. As it exploded, the cannon jumped its chalks on a column of smoke and rolled off the cliff.

Sylvano and his men had flung themselves flat. Ryan put his post on the fourth keg but held his fire. Choking gray smoke rolled across the cliff and bits of wood and human continued to rain earthward. Ryan filled his lungs and shouted across battleground. “Mildred! Run!”

Ville sec men snatched up their stacked longblasters. Ryan still held his fire. “Lady, your brother is right next to the fourth cannon. If you don’t stand up, I shoot.”

Tears spilled out of Zorime’s eyes. She shot Ryan a look of pure hatred over her glasses, but rose.

“Doc, take her hat.”

“Ryan, surely—”

“Doc, do it!”

Doc rose and plucked away the lady’s hat. Her dark hair flew in the ocean breeze. She whimpered even in the feeble ultraviolet radiation of the overcast dawn and covered her face. Doc swiftly put her hat back on. The quick reveal was enough. Sylvano’s voice was ragged with emotion as he shouted in both Portuguese and again in English for Ryan’s benefit. “Hold fire! I Command you! Hold fire!”

Ryan never took his sights off the powder keg. “Doc? I need you to draw steel, walk down there, and tell me Mildred’s and Jak’s disposition. Can you do that?”

Doc pulled himself up and drew his rapier from his cane. “I can.”

“Tell Cafu to put his blaster to the lady’s head.”

Doc made a blaster out of his hand, pressed it to his head and spoke a few words in Latin. Cafu put his short double against the base of Zorime’s skull. Doc walked down the hill with sword and blaster drawn. Well over half the sec men had rifles and bayonets to hand but none fired and none rose. Doc threaded his way through the sec men as the ocean breeze dissipated the black powder smoke. He leaned over the cliff and his sword glittered as he pinwheeled it around his wrist. He waved. "They make their way north! They saw me!"

"C'mon back!"

Doc made his way up the hill. When he was safely back, Ryan stood. "Sylvano Barat! You hear me?"

Sylvano stood with his sword and short blaster filling his huge hands. He made no effort to move away from the powder keg. "I do!"

"Me and my friends! All my friends! We enter the mat-trans and we go! That's the only way your sister lives! You got me!"

"You touch her! You touch a hair on her head! I will crucify you, Ryan! I will crucify your friends! I will light a bonfire on the beach and leave you nailed in spread-eagled invitation to my uncle!"

Ryan didn't doubt it. "Fair enough!" he shouted. "So let's make this work!" Ryan kept his sight on the keg.

"Doc," he whispered, "back to wag." Doc and the islanders retreated with Zorime.

"Listen to me, Ryan!" Sylvano shouted. "You had—"

"You and your men had best get away from that keg, Sylvano! I'm counting to three!"

Sylvano and his men scattered from the fourth gun emplacement as if it were pumping rads. Ryan squeezed his trigger and blew it sky high. He trained his sight on their wags and blew out the tires facing him. Ryan rose and broke into a lope. The islanders and Zorime were packed in the wag. Doc folded himself in beside Zorime as Ryan slid behind the wheel and gunned the engine. "Put the lady's head out the window!"

Doc reluctantly shoved Zorime's head out the passenger window. Cafu put his blaster to it without being told. Ryan shoved the wag into gear and roared down onto the coast road. He whipped the wag around the bend and drove straight at the milling sec men. Some leveled their blasters. Sylvano shouted and waved his sword for them to lower their weapons. Ryan blasted past through the smoke and confusion and shot down the road paralleling the sea. Luis and Leto wahoo'ed triumphantly. Ryan eyed his gas gauge. He was down to little more than an eighth. He continued a mile down the road and pulled off on an ancient scenic spot. Steep, heavily eroded steps long missing their railing led down the beach. They piled out of the wag and, looking south, they could see Jak moving up the coast. Ryan looked through his scope and saw Jak had picked up Mildred.

"Doc?"

"Yes, Ryan?"

Ryan held out Mildred's blaster. "Take the boys, take Zorime and get on the boat with Jak. You pick up Krysty and J.B. and head to Sister Isle."

Doc's brow furrowed with concern. "Ryan, once J.B. and Krysty are through, should not we all leave together? Whilst we can?"

"Ago and Vava helped us out across the channel. Cafu, Leto and Luis and others helped us here, and Baron Barat is going to rain on them like a chem storm for it. If we leave, we don't leave things square."

"As always, my friend, you are right."

"Way I figure it, mebbe the mat-trans sends us all off, or mebbe it does us two by two again. If so, then four of us on the escarpment are easy pickings."

Doc nodded. "We must win the Ryan Cawdor revolution for Sister Isle."

"Only way we leave it square, and the only way to be sure."

"Then by all means! Let us thrash them!"

Ryan made an amused noise. "You're awfully full of piss and rads this morning, Doc."

Doc opened his coat to reveal a pewter flask. "I am awfully full of the Blood of the Lotus this morning. I purloined the supply from my room."

Ryan gave the flask a hard look. "Word is that local jolt is habit forming, Doc."

"If it gets me through the revolution, then I will consider its duties fulfilled, and once we jump I suspect my opportunities to exposure myself to it will be severely curtailed."

"Good enough. I want you to take all the swords and blasters from the wag and get them down onto the beach. Hook up with Jak and Mildred, pick up J.B. and Krysty. Get to Sister Isle. Get our boys here talking to them about what's really happening, then get them ready for a fight."

Doc gave Ryan a searching look. "You are staying, then?"

"Someone's got to keep the fight going here."

Doc gave him a wary look. "Krysty will not be pleased."

"It's gotta be done."

Doc's hands fluttered like birds as he tried to impart this information to the three Sister Islanders. Zorime made an impatient noise and began speaking in Portuguese. Ryan almost slapped her mouth shut but Cafu suddenly stepped forward and began speaking impassionedly to him. Zorime rolled her eyes behind her dark glasses. "Cafu says he is old and he does not know anyone on the Sister Isle anymore. He says this is his island. His people are here, and you will need him. He wants to stay with you."

Doc chewed his lip. "I believe that was the gist of it."

Ryan loomed over Zorime. "You're translating for me because?"

"My brother loves me. However, neither my father nor my uncle will endanger the island to save me. The quicker you go about your business, the quicker one or both will kill you."

"Fair enough. Doc, get the lady on the boat. Cafu and I'll do what we can here then steal a boat and link up."

"Very well. Godspeed, Ryan." Doc, Luis and Leto armed themselves down with blasters and cutlery and escorted Zorime down the steps to the beach. Ryan raised his blaster to Jak as they loaded onto the boat. Ryan could tell by Jak's posture the young man didn't like it, but the albino teen had been a guerrilla fighter almost from the cradle and he knew it had to be done. He raised his Magnum blaster in salute and headed the boat back into the channel.

Ryan turned to Cafu. "You want to have some fun?"

The grizzled old man nodded uncomprehendingly. Ryan went back to the wag and put it in Neutral. He got out and put his back to the bumper and began pushing. Cafu dropped his club happily and leaned his brawn into the act of vandalism. The black wag crunched across the gravel of the vista point and they both jumped away as it nosed over the cliff. It fell thirty feet and hit a boulder with a tremendous crash. Cafu stopped short of jumping up and down and clapping his hands.

Ryan had to admit pushing a wag off a cliff had its own unique appeal. "You like that?"

Cafu nodded vigorously.

"That was good fun?"

Cafu kept nodding. "Fun?"

"Oh, yeah." Ryan clapped him on the shoulder and pointed inland. "Let's go have real some fun."

Cafu scooped up his club and followed Ryan into the trees.

Chapter Nineteen

Metal screamed as the overhead ducts failed. The six-foot section fell through the overhead lighting in a shower of sparks and wiring with dead stickies and smoke trailing out of either end. J.B. whipped his scattergun around. He and Krysty had needed only a few more minutes and they would have been gone. They weren't going to get it. A fresh stickie fell through the roof and flopped onto the piled bodies of its brothers and sisters. The stickie's rubbery musculature hunched and popped as it relocated its limbs. J.B.'s blast smeared its skull across the corpse-littered floor. Another stickie was flailing its legs up in the wiring, the front half of its body still jammed in the torn duct. J.B. unrepentantly filled its rear contact point full of lead. The legs went limp and the Armorer leaped aside as the section fell. Arms flailed out of the other end, and J.B. pumped buckshot into the eight-foot section.

"J.B.! Look out!" Krysty snapped up her blaster. A stickie crawled like a four-legged white spider in the wiring. Krysty put three rounds through its head and it hung, crucified from the conduit risers by its suckered hands and feet that continued to clamp on even in death. Metal continued to rend and scream. Stickies hooted and shrieked, and the ceiling and walls thudded with bumps and crashes. The ducts were falling section by section. The stickies were in the walls. J.B. pushed fresh shells into the action of his M-4000. He was starting to run uncomfortably low. J.B. checked the loads in his Uzi and unzipped his bag of tricks. "Krysty, get by the door."

The statuesque redhead moved into a covering position. J.B. stayed in the control room. His eyes flicked in constant scan from the ceiling to the two ducts they'd covered. The glued-on seats twisted as the ducts they covered were torn from their moorings. One popped away beneath a stickie's pale fist. The hooting stickie shoved its head through the enlarged hole and J.B. blasted it. He pulled the rip fuse on an improvised pyrotechnic. The nylon mag-pouch began to hiss in his hand. The dead mutie was yanked aside, and J.B. blasted the one behind it and stuffed in his smoking package. One helpful, suckered stickie hand snatched up the charge greedily. J.B. jumped back as the wall thumped and the stickie hoots and coos turned into shrill, trilling screams. It was another white-phosphorus package, but rather than a slow smolder J.B. had rigged it for a nice out-of-control burn and seasoned it with a little high explosive to spread it around.

White smoke poured out of the hole, but it was white-hot and it billowed upward on its own updraft into the ceiling, carrying winking and burning fireflies of white phosphorus with it. A blackened spindly arm covered with yellow fire whipped and flailed in the ragged opening. Stickies might be as resilient as rubber tubing, but the rad-blasted pests still had to breathe, and you took a lungful of white-phosphorus smoke just once. The problem was J.B. and Krysty had to breathe, as well. The Armorer watched the dense smoke crawl across the gutted ceiling of the control room like a creeping white carpet. A stickie fell out of the wiring choking and clawing at its throat. It fell on a pile of bodies and thrashed. J.B. didn't waste a cap.

Krysty cried out as the other duct seal failed. A stickie shoved its head through, and Krysty's slug caromed off its skull. J.B. pulled another home-rolled Willie Pete as the stickie went limp. "Cover me!" The stickies in the walls snatched back their dead horde-mate. J.B. ripped his pull-fuse. The package hissed in his hand, and the Armorer shoved it into the ruptured vent.

A suckered hand wrapped around his wrist with a squidlike grip.

J.B. yanked his arm back but the stickie wouldn't let go. It would anchor him even in death in a petard hoisting that would leave J.B. a blackened mummy. He put his boots against the wall and heaved, at three seconds on a five-second fuse.

Krysty ran forward. "J.B.!"

"Stay back!" He shoved the muzzle of his scattergun against the stickie's inner elbow and fired. He topped backward with everything below the elbow still attached to his arm like some gruesome fetish. The suckered hand constricted against his wrist. J.B. rolled across blood and corpses as white smoke and yellow fire pulsed out of the wall in a jet. Searing heat washed across him, and dead stickies ignited in his wake. Krysty grabbed J.B. and hauled him up. She handed him his hat and he instinctively slapped the fedora across his thigh and perched it back on his head.

J.B. surveyed the battleground. Most of the control-room lighting was out. Dead stickies blackened and burned and threw off flickering orange and yellow light. The smoke above was beginning to creep down in curtains. The walls glowed with heat. The brimstone smell of burning phosphorus competed with the charnel house smell of death and horrific new stench of burning flesh. J.B. was not a religious man, but he knew about the concept of hell. He knew he'd painted a fairly close approximation.

Krysty snarled in exasperation as three stickies dropped down from the ceiling. "Gaia!"

"Dark night!" J.B. agreed. The stickies were coughing and hacking but seemed little worse for wear. There was someplace in the ceiling they were coming through that wasn't being inundated with smoke. They turned their weeping, unblinking black eyes on J.B. and Krysty and bounded forward. J.B. blasted two of them off their feet. Krysty let the last get uncomfortably close and took it with a head shot. J.B. dropped his empty scattergun on its sling. He was out of shells. He unslung his Uzi and pushed the selector from safe to automatic fire. "Time?"

Krysty checked her chron. "Three minutes." She broke open her blaster and grimaced. "I'm out." She ejected her spent shells and put the brass in a pocket of her coat and holstered her blaster. Krysty drew a long, curved skinning knife. A stickie dropped through the smoke, followed by another and another. They didn't bound forward. These swayed and eyed their prey. More kept falling into the room. J.B. pulled a heavy, bulging gas-mask bag out of his satchel and kicked the nearly empty carry-all into the mat-trans chamber. Nearly a dozen stickies slowly began to come forward, stepping over their dead brethren.

"Now!" J.B. shouted. Krysty dived into the mat-trans chamber. J.B. yanked the pull-fuse and tossed his charge. A stickie snatched it out of the air and peered at the hissing olive drab bag. J.B. hurled himself into the mat-trans chamber and rolled to one side of the door and hugged the wall. The stickies hooted as they surged in pursuit. J.B. stuck his thumbs in his ears and covered his eyes.

The chamber shook as J.B.'s charge went off.

It was the last of the white phosphorus, the last of the high explosive and every screw, nut, bolt and small metal part J.B. had managed to scrounge from the control room all in one overstuffed and glue-sealed gas-mask bag. Heat and overpressure rolled into the mat-trans chamber like a wave. Bits of metal ricocheted off the armaglass walls. J.B. opened his eyes. He yawned to clear the ringing in his ears and instantly began to choke. He dropped to the floor and crawled over to Krysty. She had one hand over her mouth, but she reached out the other and gave J.B. a squeeze. Over the ringing in his ears J.B. could hear screaming and shrieking. He took up his Uzi and risked a peek through the door. Just about everything in the control room was on fire. The smoke was thick, but J.B. could see that his improvised charge had done its work. Most of the stickies were burning and blown apart. One thrashed about in the corner like a flaming, spastic scarecrow. Two more remained alive but they were badly torn up. They were bleeding out of their eyes and ears from the blast effect and could do little more than twitch and moan.

"Time?" J.B. choked. He couldn't hear whether the mat-trans control was peeping or not and he couldn't see the control panel through the smoke.

Krysty checked her chron and gave J.B. a very weary smile. "Time." She pointed her knife at the filthy, suckered paw still wrapped around J.B.'s wrist. "Let's cut that thing off."

"Let's get out of here," J.B. countered.

Krysty didn't need convincing. She covered her mouth, hurried forward and closed the door. The mists descended and darkness enveloped them.

MILDRED LOOKED AT HER chron out of habit and realized for the tenth time that Raul the Gargantua had taken it along with every other thing of use she owned. She hunched against the ocean cold and looked back at Jak. He stood with his hand on the tiller looking like a diminutive and very pale Captain Ahab. Doc was chatting with the natives and appeared to picking up the local lingo pretty quickly. When they weren't chattering away in what mostly sounded like vowels, the natives stared at her in wide-eyed wonder. Doc had filled her in on the story of the islands. Any African-Americans who had come with the original refugee fleet from the Deathlands had been bred into the population generations ago.

As usual, Mildred Wyeth and her pleasing light brown complexion was quite the novelty. They probably thought she was a mutie. Father Joao sat bound, bruised and pouting amidships. Zorime stared enigmatically out across the waves and kept her own counsel. "Jak, how long on J.B. and Krysty?" Mildred asked.

Jak lifted his ruby gaze to the watery light coming through the overcast. "Soon."

Mildred reached out and scratched Boo behind the ears. The dog thumped his tail against the side of the boat happily. Vava beamed. Like most world-class marksmen Mildred had far better than average vision. She jerked up in alarm as she saw the smudge in the distance. "Jak!"

Jak threw back his cloak and loosened his Colt in its holster. "Boat?"

Mildred squinted into the distance. "Definitely, coming from the ville and headed for the escarpment."

Jak put the whaler on an intercept course. Doc snapped out his brass telescope. "It is a whaler, like our own." Doc lowered his spyglass and shook his head. "I count a dozen men under arms aboard, and their engine seems larger than ours."

Jak went to full throttle. "Mildred!" The albino teen made a blaster out of his fingers. "Motor!"

Mildred raised her hands helplessly. "I'm empty, Jak."

Jak instantly drew his stainless-steel Colt and tossed it to her. Mildred caught the heavy blaster awkwardly. She looked at the straining little outboard powering their craft and considered the Magnum revolver in her hand. "You'll have to get me close, Jak. Fifty yards, closer if you can, and keep me there."

Jak nodded as he gauged distance. Their courses would intersect, but the ville men had a bigger engine and more blasters. He wouldn't be able to stay close long and if he didn't they probably wouldn't survive it. "Doc! Cannon!"

"Indeed." Doc nodded. "They have a swivel gun much like ours."

Jak rolled his ruby-red eyes in exasperation and pointed at the little cannon mounted on the prow. "'Poon them!"

"What? Oh, yes, I see." Doc frowned. "Why should I…poon them?"

Mildred rolled her eyes, as well. "Doc, just do it! Below the waterline if you can!"

Doc was startled by this new, weird and wonderful turn of events, but he handed his spyglass to Mildred and went to work. He threaded a line through the eyelet of one of the short, iron harpoons in a fairly efficient fashion and coiled the line so it wouldn't tangle when it flew. He stared at the weapon for a moment and then began measuring powder from the little cask. Mildred prayed he knew what he was doing. She used Doc's glass to get a good recce on the enemy. They were ville sec men all right, a dozen with blasters. They were aware of the pursuit and had throttled up. Their craft threw spume as it took the tide on the chin. Mildred folded the spyglass and took point next to Doc. "Doc, this is our asses, and J.B.'s and Krysty's. Don't screw this up."

Doc took a nip from the flask in his jacket and gave Mildred a startlingly confident smile. "Dear Mildred, my naval gunnery shall rival Nelson at Trafalgar."

Mildred took a look at the enemy. They were aware an engagement was imminent. Black-cloaked blastermen lined the gunwhales, waiting for Jak to bring his whaler within range. "Doc, you better tell those islanders to get low and stay low."

"As you say." Doc spoke to the natives and they hugged the deck. Jak brought them in closer. Mildred started getting very nervous. A lot of guys in black hats and shades were pointing blasters but the only sound was the noise of the motors. "What are they waiting for, Doc? Why don't they shoot?"

"Those are muzzle-loading arms they bear, Mildred. They load from the front and it takes time. They want to hit us with volley fire."

The sec man at the helm yanked his tiller hard to bring the prow and his swivel gun into play. The men along the port gunwale all suddenly knelt and the men on the starboard side of boat stood and presented arms.

"Now!" Jak shouted.

Doc sighted down the crude rib atop the swivel gun.

"Now!" Jak shouted again. "Mildred! Down!"

Blasterfire popped and crackled like a string of fire-crackers across the water. Mildred flung herself to the deck. "Doc!" Splinters flew like shrapnel as lead balls raked across the whaler and the swivel gun clanged as a ball hit it. Mildred reached up to yank Doc down. "Doc!"

Doc was still sighting. He suddenly smiled and yanked the firing cord. Flint scraped and powder flashed in the pan. The prow of the whaler shook as the swivel gun recoiled against its mooring. Mildred peeked over the rail. Line whipped from the coil as the cruelly barbed iron rod streaked across the sea. The second line of sec men leveled their blasters as a unit. The boat was just coming around enough to bring the gun on the prow into play and no harpoon was mounted. It would be throwing lead and a lot of it.

The harpoon threw up a geyser of spume as it hit the water a yard from the hull and skipped. A sec man screamed and toppled over as the lugged iron punched through the hull and did him a terrible disservice. "Ha!" Doc shook his fist in triumph. "A hit!"

"Goddamn it, Doc!" Mildred yanked the madman to the deck as a second volley hit their boat. Vava screamed. More splinters flew and a hole appeared next to Mildred's head. Jak's hat had been blown off his head and was sailing out to sea. Jak reached up and through the throttle into Reverse. "Doc!"

Doc tied off the harpoon line to a cleat. "Lay on, Mildred!"

Mildred took a seated shooting position next to the smoking swivel gun. The line between the two whalers went taut and held them in a tug of war. In that moment they couldn't bring their own little cannon to bear. Nearly all of the sec men were desperately slamming rammers down the muzzles of their weapons. Mildred had asked for fifty yards and a still target and gotten it. One of the sec men drew his sword to hack the harpoon line holding them together. Mildred cocked Jak's revolver. It was a service model rather than target, but a Colt Python, even a hundred-year-old one, was one of the more accurate revolvers ever made. Mildred took in a breath and let half of it out. She slowly began taking up the trigger…

The barrel went vertical with recoil and tiny geyser shot up as she hit water. Mildred cocked the hammer as the barrel dropped back into the firing plane. She took half a second to raise her aim a hair and fired again. Sparks whined off the motor casing across the water. Doc drew his LeMat and began cocking and firing. Someone across the water figured out what Mildred was trying to do. Half the sec men abandoned their longblasters and started drawing and firing their short doubles. Lead began whizzing and snapping through the air in earnest, and all of it had Mildred's name on it. The big Magnum blaster recoiled brutally in Mildred's hand and across the water the enemy outboard began screaming and clanking.

"Doc!" Jak shouted. Doc took up the hatchet in the prow and chopped through the line. The whaler surged backward in Reverse. The enemy whaler was almost obscured by the clouds of powder smoke. The smoke lit up orange as they discharged everything that was still loaded. Jak got the boat turned and moved swiftly out of range. Mildred moved back along the boat and got to work. A rifle ball had shattered Vava's arm, Boo was barking hysterically and Jak had lost his hat. They had gotten off light. Jak was giving the enemy whaler a wide berth as he headed for the escarpment. Smoke boomed from the prow of the enemy boat. Mildred made a concerned noise as she looked up from her patient and saw the tennis ball–size piece of iron skip past across the water a few yards to stern.

"Doc?" Jak called.

Doc had his spyglass to his eye once more. "The enemy is putting to oars, four to a side."

"Way?"

"They continue their pursuit of us, or more to the point, the escarpment appears to remain their goal. However, the current is against them. We should make landfall with a comfortable lead upon them."

Jak throttled back just slightly. He could feel the heat coming off the little outboard despite the cold ocean wind and they had a lot more sailing to do. He was already considering how they would whip the Sister Islanders into any kind of fighting force and he wasn't seeing a lot of options. He was really hoping J.B. would come up with something.

Chapter Twenty

Cafu was having the time of his life. His killer whale-toothed club was caked with dried blood and hung from his shoulder on an improvised sling. He had a pair of double-blasters thrust through his belt as well as a sickle and a hatchet he had purloined from a toolshed. He lay next to Ryan on a hillock and peered in wonder through Ryan's collapsible telescope. The one-eyed man scanned the compound through his blaster's optic. It consisted of two large, interconnected barnlike buildings, a couple of sheds, a well and stone bunker. They were just a couple of miles outside the ville. Cafu had made it clear that he had never seen these buildings before and neither had any of the other slaves on the main island. Ryan could understand why. One, you didn't want your powder mill accidentally blowing up inside town, and, two, you didn't want to have your oppressed population knowing where your gunpowder was being manufactured. In fact it was best that they had no idea what gunpowder was. All they needed to know was that you had blasters and they didn't. Cafu lowered the telescope and squinted at Ryan hopefully. "Fun?"

"Cafu," Ryan said, "if you like pushing wags off cliffs, you're going to love lighting this place up."

Cafu blinked in happy incomprehension.

"Big fun, Cafu." Ryan smiled and held his hands wide apart in measurement. "Big fun."

Cafu savored his newfound grasp of English. "Big…fun."

Ryan had seen black-powder-producing plants before. There would be mills inside with some kind of nonsparking grinding apparatus, either stone, bronze or lead to grind and mix the nitrate, charcoal and sulfur. The well and the sluice leading to the barn told Ryan they were wetting their powder, forming it into mill cakes and then corning it into granules that made it more powerful than loose powder and easier to load. Ryan had a very reasonable suspicion that the stone bunker was a munitions dump that neither the nightwalkers nor the slaves could get into. Cafu started to rise, but he pressed him down as the wide, double doors to one of the barns opened and a buckboard wag rolled out. Ryan had been wrong. Some slaves had seen the powder mill.

It was the last thing they had ever seen.

Eight men, mostly in their prime and probably recently taken from Sister Isle, were yoked like oxen to the wag traces. Unlike the other slaves, they had not been hobbled and none of them were tied in place. There was no need for it. Each man's eyes had been put out. They lived for but one purpose, and that was to labor in the hidden mill and haul powder into town. The driver gave most of his directions with a whip, but there was little need. The wheel ruts were deep from an untold number of runs, and the slaves had trod the path untold times. A sec man with a long double-blaster rode shotgun and two additional sec men walked alongside the wag with their blasters over their shoulders and bayonets fixed.

Cafu surged up with a snarl of hatred, and Ryan had to forcibly shove him down. "No, Cafu! Wait!"

Cafu stayed down, but he stabbed out his finger at the human draft animals in outrage. "Nuno! Real! Pedro!" He knew some of them. Given their age, probably when they were children.

Ryan pointed to where the dirt road disappeared into the trees. "There."

Cafu still shook with rage but nodded. They waited as the wag faded from sight. "Now," Ryan said, "let's go get some fun."

"Big fun," Cafu said. He wasn't smiling anymore. The words from his lips were a death sentence. Ryan backtracked down the hill and Cafu limped after him. They circled through the trees and cut back toward the road. Ryan found a wide alder tree next to the road and planted Cafu behind it. Ryan pantomimed. "You wait here. I hit them from behind. No blasters."

Cafu answered by unlimbering his club.

Ryan moved back, skirting the road. He ducked behind an alder as the creak of the wag and the groans of the slaves became audible. It was punctuated by the crack of the whip and the ugly laugh of the driver. Ryan thought he liked his job just a little too much. The one-eyed man drew his panga as the wag passed and waited for it to approach Cafu's position. Ryan broke cover and loped out onto the road, his boots making little noise in the soft earth of the road. He vaulted up into the back of the wag, hurdled the pallet of powder kegs and chopped his panga into the side of the shotgunner's skull. The blade bit into flesh and bone. Ryan put his boot between the driver's shoulder blades and sent him sprawling out of his seat and down among the slaves. Ryan dived at the footman to starboard. The panga twisted down past the sec man's collarbone and found his heart. Ryan hit the ground with a corpse for cushioning and rolled up with his blaster in his bandaged hand.

He needn't have bothered.

The remaining sec man had barely unshouldered his blaster when Cafu's club snapped his spine. The sec man keened like an animal and went rigid as he fell. Cafu had to put his foot in the man's back and heave to rip the four-inch whale teeth free. The driver was thrashing and swearing among the slaves and trying to untangle himself from the traces. The slaves were crying out in blind fear and incomprehension. The driver managed to stand, then shut up when Ryan pointed his blaster in his face. "Cafu."

Cafu came forward and put a hand on one of the draft slave's shoulders. The man jerked but calmed as Cafu said his name. "Real..." Cafu named others. "Nuno, Pedro, Miguel." Cafu started talking quietly in his native language. The slaves had neither eyes nor tear ducts to weep with, but they sobbed and choked as Cafu told them the situation. Ryan tore away the driver's short blaster and sword, and flung him to the dirt. He kicked off his hat and slapped away his smoked glasses. Even in the overcast light beneath the trees he clutched his face.

"Speak English?"

"No!"

Ryan pinned him down with a foot to his chest. "Want to live?"

The driver contradicted himself. "Yes!"

"How many sec men at the mill?"

"Eight! Eight men!"

"How many workers?"

"Twelve!"

"How many slaves?"

"Two more teams! Sixteen!"

"Tell Cafu what you told me." Ryan calculated as they spoke in Portuguese. Twenty hostiles, and all he had was surprise. Ryan watched as Cafu asked a few pointed questions of his own. He also had Cafu, and he had promised the man big fun. Ryan stripped one of the dead sec men of his hat, cloak and glasses. He nodded at Cafu to do the same. "Cafu, we're riding in the wag. You tell Real, Nuno and Pedro they have to pull us." Ryan fired off rapid-fire hand signals and Cafu began speaking to the blind men. It was heartbreaking to watch, but the men put themselves back under the yoke without complaint for what would be a short haul, and the last.

Cafu looked at the driver and hefted his club. Ryan shook his head. A deal was a deal. He put foot to ass on the driver to get him moving. "You, head for the ville. If I see you again, I'll kill you."

The driver covered his head with cloak and stumbled down the road whimpering and covering his eyes. Cafu tossed his club into the back of the wag and helped Ryan drag the corpses into the trees. Ryan put his long-blaster in the back of the wag and took up the whip. The slaves turned the wag around with the ease of long practice and headed back to the powder mill. "Blasters?" Cafu inquired.

"Oh, yeah."

Cafu put the double-blaster across his knees. They pulled their hats low over their faces as they approached the mill. The double door was still open as they pulled into the mill yard. A man walked out with a whip in his hand and shouted a question at Ryan. Cafu gave the overseer both barrels in the chest. Ryan took up his Steyr and hopped off the wag as shouts broke out in the mill. Cafu dropped the spent scattergun and pulled the handblaster from the dead overseer's belt. They walked into the barn. Ville men looked up in horror as Ryan and Cafu walked in. The barn appeared to be for storage and lading. Half a dozen men were mill workers wearing aprons and work gloves. Two sec men sat at a table drinking wine. They rose, spilling their goblets and going for their blasters. Ryan sat each one back down with a burst through the chest.

Two sec men burst out of a side room pulling up their trousers and trying to bring auto-blasters into play. Their flushed, sweaty faces and the tumescence they were trying to conceal told Ryan they hadn't been in the commode. Cafu pulled both triggers and the mill workers gasped as a unit as Cafu missed and put two loads of lead inches above a line of powder kegs stacked along the wall. Ryan didn't miss. One man fell in the tangle of his pants with his heart blown out. The second fell twisting and screaming, trying to hold in his torn guts. A single blaster crack ended his suffering.

"Ryan!" Cafu shouted.

Ryan spun and a heavyset, bald ville man wearing an apron froze in place with a barrel stave in his hand. Ryan raised an eyebrow at the stave. The big man dropped it. "You the foreman?" Ryan asked.

He eyed Ryan with pure hatred. His accent was very thick. "Yes, I am…foreman."

"Tell the other three guards to come out, and your men, or I shoot all of you." The foreman shouted through the doorway to the other barn. Two sec men came out with their hands up, followed by half a dozen more mill workers. Ryan pointed his blaster between the foreman's eyes. "You're missing a sec man, and in a minute you're going to be missing your head."

"Lucio!" the foreman shouted. "Lucio!"

Lucio was as tall as Ryan and his long black hair was pulled back in a ponytail. He came out of the side room with both his pants and his hands up.

"On your knees," Ryan ordered. The men dropped and Ryan backed toward the side room. His lips curled in disgust. A blindfolded woman from Sister Isle was tied naked to the bed. She was beautiful despite the bruises all over her, like an older version of Vava. Blood spattered the bed all around her from a dozen minor wounds on her limbs and body. There was a taste for blood in the ville. Cutting had been part of the mill workers' fun. "Cafu."

Cafu came forward. His breath hissed in at what he saw. Ryan held the mill men under his gun as Cafu cut the woman's bonds. She flinched as Cafu removed her blindfold. Ryan was just relieved she still had eyes underneath it. The woman broke down sobbing into Cafu's arms and clutched him. "Thais," Cafu murmured. "Thais." They knew each other.

Ryan had the terrible feeling they were related. "Cafu."

Cafu took his stolen ville cloak and draped it around Thais's shoulders. Lucio gave Cafu the evil eye as he led Thais out of the rape room. He said something and the woman flinched and began crying anew. Lucio and his friends laughed. Lucio started telling Cafu something Ryan figured was about how Cafu and all the slaves were going to suffer. Lucio held up his hands and clearly ordered Cafu to free him. Ryan took a step forward to beat him down.

Cafu drew his spare double and shot Lucio in the head.

Lucio tipped backward, missing most of what he had above his eyebrows. Cafu shot the sec man next to him without mercy. The last sec man screamed and turned to flee. He howled as he heaved on the bar of the back door with his bound hands. Cafu unlimbered his club and swung it into the sec man's kidneys. He shrieked like the damned as the great teeth tore into him and fell. Cafu's club rose and fell twice more and the man's screaming ended.

Ryan looked at the mill men. "Anyone else got anything to say?"

No one piped up.

Ryan backed up enough to see into the mill proper. The two mills were human powered with wheels like ships' capstans driven by the blind men who now knelt and huddled in fear beneath the pushing poles. The sluice from the well came through the wall and had taps that fell into vats for wetting the powder. The walls were lined with racks for drying the powder cakes. "Cafu." Cafu kept his glare on the millers as he approached.

Ryan nodded at the blind, huddled slaves by the mills. Cafu walked among them, many of whom he knew by name. Cafu got the mill slaves lined up, each holding the shoulder of the one in front of him, and led them into the yard. He began handing out the swords and blasters to the blind men. Ryan indicated the kegs along the wall and Cafu gave six to the last men in line and then put Thais at the front of the train.

Ryan glanced up at the hills and shrugged at Cafu. "Where?"

Cafu came back and whispered in Ryan's ear. "Moni."

Cafu knew where Moni had gone. Ryan didn't give the blind freedom train much chance, but no place was safe, and if they could get to the farm Moni had taken her refugees from the nightwalker attack to, there was a chance the arms could get into some angry hands and another front could be opened.

Thais waved back to Cafu and got her train moving up into the hills.

"You." Ryan turned to the foreman. "And your people. Your boots. Get them off."

"What?"

Ryan pointed his blaster at the foreman's feet. "Your boots."

The mill workers began to unhappily comply. They shifted from bare foot to bare foot dreading what they suspected. Ryan pointed his blaster out the door. "Now go."

"Go?"

"Get out of here, and without your hats, gloves or shades."

The foreman's face contorted with rage and his men cried out in consternation. Ryan stared them down implacably. The foreman spoke through his long, clenched teeth. "Cloaks?"

Ryan shrugged. "Sure."

The mill men pulled their black cloaks over their heads and clutched them about themselves like monks. They hunched as they gingerly stepped out into the light of day on their fish-white feet. They huddled and bumped into one another, gasping and cringing in ones and twos. Thais and her blind column were making one whole hell of a lot faster and more orderly progress. The foreman was the last to leave. He regarded Ryan bitterly. "You wish to send the baron a message?"

"I'll send it myself." Ryan was going to send his message to Baron Barat skyhigh for the world to see. He watched the foreman go. The millers managed to get into a better assembled mob once they got under the trees. "Hey, Cafu."

"Ah?"

Ryan went over and picked up the fallen shotgun and started reloading it for Cafu. "Didn't I promise you some fun?"

"Big fun?"

Ryan handed Cafu the scattergun and reloaded his handblasters for him. Cafu watched carefully. Ryan considered his options. He went along the wall where the filled kegs were stacked and began pulling out random bungs. Black grains of powder began spilling out like sands through an hourglass. Cafu watched with interest as Ryan took a cask and began drawing a long black line of powder on the floor and walked it into the mill yard. Cafu followed as Ryan kept pouring past the wag and out onto the road. He didn't stop until the cask was empty. Ryan rose and surveyed the long black line snaking back into the mill. He took another cask and the foreman's keys and drew a second line into the stone bunker. It was full of powder kegs. The two lines came to a point in front of Cafu.

It was too bad J.B. wasn't here to see this.

"Cafu." Ryan pointed at the little starter blaster on Cafu's belt. Cafu drew it and stared at Ryan. The one-eyed man pointed to the end of the powder trails in front of them. "Have some fun."

Cafu pointed the blaster and fired.

The charge blasted into the black powder and ignited it. The powder lines rapidly began flashing, snapping and pulsing smoke as each powder granule blew up and ignited those around it. The powder lines popped and hissed and left a trail of gray ash and smoke in their wake. Cafu watched the powder fuses in wonder as they snaked toward the mill and the bunker. His jaw suddenly dropped as he figured out what was happening.

"Big fun!"

Ryan took him by the shoulder and pulled him farther back into the trees. The powder line burned past the wag and into the mill. Ryan crouched behind a tree and plugged his ears. Cafu did the same. They watched as wisps of powder smoke drifted out the door. Several seconds passed. Cafu blinked in disappointment. "Big…fun?"

The powder mill disappeared in smoke and fire. The roof emerged from the fireball and rose up on a column of smoke and fire. The walls blew outward and sections of timber and chunks of stone scythed through the trees in all directions. The wagload of powder went up an eye blink later. The air pulsed with the heat of the double detonations and a solid wall of smoke swept through the trees in a wave driven by hundreds of pounds of black powder fulfilling its destiny.

The bunker went up like skydark.

Ryan hugged the tree against the gale. It was gone as quick as it had come. He opened his eye to find Cafu sitting stunned on the ground, blinking and yawning. His face was a mask of black powder smoke out of which shone glazed eyes and grinning teeth. Ryan was pretty sure that even down in the ville the baron had gotten his message.

Most of the trees had been stripped of their leaves by the blasts and they fluttered down in a shower. Bits of stone and metal began raining to earth and pattered through the treetops. One of the brass millstones returned to earth like a molten meteor and thudded into the road. Ryan and Cafu watched for long moments. Smoke continued to rise, but there was little in the way of fire. Most things that were combustible had been blown to smithereens. The wind shifted and showed them a pair of blackened, smoking holes in the ground where the powder mill and the powder bunker had once stood.

Ryan helped Cafu to his feet. "Big fun?"

Cafu shook his head in wonder at the pillars of smoke rising into the sky. "Fireblast," he agreed.

"Cafu."

Cafu slung his club and hoisted his new blaster. "Ah?"

"The blood." Ryan held up a finger and shoved it against his inner elbow. "Where do they draw the blood?"

KRYSTY'S FIRST THOUGHT as she spewed her guts was that despite the terrible wrongness of being broken down in one place and reassembled in another, this time the jump had gone right. She and J.B. had definitely gone somewhere this time.

"J.B.! Wherever we're going next, we're taking wags."

J.B. managed a groan in agreement as he sat up.

"You okay?"

The Armorer nodded.

"Let's recce," she suggested.

J.B. pushed himself to his feet. "Right."

Krysty shoved the lever on the door to the mat-trans. It swung and two men in dun-colored tunics and sandals nearly got shot. They had clubs in their hands, but they shrank from J.B.'s blaster. Krysty and J.B. were coated from head to foot with smoke particulate crusted with just about every form of filth and fluid a stickie could excrete. It showed on the strangers' faces. The bigger one nodded hopefully and poked himself with his thumb. "Nando." He nodded at his compatriot. "Enzo." He looked at J.B. and Krysty hopefully. "Jebbee? Kreestee?"

J.B. and Krysty looked at each other. Krysty nodded. "Yes."

Nando clapped his hands. *"Reean? Doke? Meeldraid e Jak? Sao mues amigos!"*

Krysty perked an eyebrow at this. "Amigos?"

Nando nodded vigorously. "Amigos!" He presented Krysty a piece of paper like a bold talisman and nodded knowingly. "Jak!"

Krysty and J.B. gave each other a suspicious look. Jak wasn't exactly known for his written correspondence. Krysty unfolded the note and read the terse, unfamiliar handwriting out loud.

"'Krysty, J.B.
Get Ryan, Mildred, Doc. Ville enemy. Islanders OK. Trust no black hats. Back soon.
Jak.'"

Krysty raised an eyebrow at the postscript: "'Written under duress, Father Joao.'"

Krysty doubted Jak could have proofread Father Joao's letter but it sure sounded like Jak at his most chatty. Nando and Enzo continued to nod and smile. "I say we go with them," J.B. said.

Krysty and the Armorer gathered up their packs and followed the two men out of the tiny redoubt. Krysty's knees almost went weak as the breeze played across her. After the blood, smoke and filth of the stickie siege the clean, cold ocean air was a gift from Gaia.

J.B.'s head snapped up. "Hear that?"

Krysty cocked her head. She did, in the distance she heard the sound of men trying to give each other the gift of lead. "Blasterfire."

Nando squinted out into the channel and nodded. "Jak."

J.B. heard the crack and boom of firearms he didn't recognize, but the clouds of white smoke told him they were burning black powder, and J.B. would recognize the crack of Jak's .357 Magnum blaster anywhere. The battle seemed short and inconclusive from shore, and one of the boats came about and began making for the escarpment. J.B. deployed the folding stock on his Uzi. He lowered it as Doc's lean figure stood in the prow and waved. The boat puttered up to the concrete quay. Doc threw Nando a line and everyone boarded the boat.

Everyone in the boat looked at Krysty and J.B. in horror.

"We really need a bath," Krysty whispered.

J.B. was all too aware of that. "What do we have, Jak?"

"War," Jak replied.

"A revolution," Doc said.

"The short end of the stick," Mildred stated. "As usual."

Krysty shook her head in disappointment. "Where's Ryan?"

"He is upon the main isle," Doc answered. "He rescued myself and Mildred, and then stayed on to organize resistance."

Krysty rolled her gorgeous green eyes. "Typical."

"J.B.," Doc continued, "Ryan asks that you and Jak organize the natives of the Sister Isle for war. We can expect the ville to launch an invasion quite soon."

J.B. sat exhaustedly as Jak took the whaler back out. "Give me the whole story."

"Well," Doc began, "as you know, Ryan and I were first of our party through the mat-trans, whereupon we found ourselves alone save for a puffin. He was quite a handsome specimen so I sketched him. Then my—"

"Mildred?" J.B. interrupted. "Give me the short version."

Chapter Twenty-One

Ryan and Cafu crept through the field. He hadn't quite been sure what he expected, perhaps a blood "plantation" with people in pens. What Cafu brought him to was a fortified predark clinic. The road here was cracked and raddled pavement rather than the cobblestone of the old ville. Most of the parking lot had been ripped up and turned into a field. The walls of the clinic had been buttressed with brick and stone. The electric glass doors had been replaced with iron-bound oak. The ambulance roundabout still existed, and Ryan was surprised to see a red-and-white ambulance that looked to be in good shape parked beneath the portico. Ryan looked over at Cafu. Despite his bull-like strength, Cafu was an old man, and a man with half a left foot wasn't made for marching. Ryan figured the ambulance would make a fine war wag.

It might also solve the problem of egress.

This raid would have to be fast. They were dangerously close to the ville. Ryan was hoping one whole hell of a lot that their sec men were at the powder mill right now with their hands on their hips staring at a smoking hole in the ground. Ryan glanced backward at the column of smoke still rising to the east.

Blowing up the powder mill had been big fun.

Ryan turned his attention back to the clinic. "Cafu." Ryan pointed. "You been in there?"

Cafu exposed his arms to show the scars dotting his inner elbows. The old man had been "harvested" many times. He pointed at his mutilated foot to show that drawing blood wasn't the only operation going on inside.

"What do you say, Cafu?" Ryan gestured at the clinic with his blaster. "You want to have some more fun?"

"Big fun." Cafu tapped his club into his palm several times as he gazed bitterly at the medical building. "Fireblast."

Ryan doubted they could go nukecaust on the place as they had the powder mill, but if they could bastard up both the ville's munitions and meds situation, the revolution was going to have a leg up on things. "Want to go for a ride?"

"Ride?" Cafu asked.

Ryan did some finger pantomime of steering wheels and crashing. "Cafu, we're going to take that wag and drive it right through the doors."

Cafu started chattering rapid-fire and shaking his war club. He stopped short of jumping up and down and clapping his hands, but it was clear he was excited about the plan and thankful to be a part of it.

"Let's do it."

Cafu nodded and the two men continued their creep forward through the field.

Seven and a half feet of nightwalker erupted out of the earth behind them.

Ryan whirled. Two more exploded up out of their hides and their hunting screams shook the air. They were using spider holes. Wicker frames supported stiffened blankets covered with thatches of field stalks and brush that concealed their lurking pits. The nightwalkers had swathed themselves from head to foot in strips of ville fabric like black-clad mummies. Their heads were heavily turbaned, and thinner black gauze covered the slits they had left for their eyes. The closest nightwalker reached for Ryan with one hand as it raised a splitting maul in the other.

Ryan's blaster burned on full-auto as he held down the trigger. Bullets walked up the mutie's body in a line of bloody purple geysers. The mutie's spider hole became his grave. Ryan put five rounds into the second nightwalker, and his blaster racked open on a smoking empty chamber. Cafu gave the creature both barrels. The third nightwalker was female by the shape beneath its wrapping, and swung a stolen oar from one of the whaler's like an ax. Cafu's ribs cracked like kindling beneath the blow and his spent scattergun went spinning away. The oar blade flashed and Ryan narrowly avoided a skull crushing. The she-thing screamed and swung the oar down like an ax. Ryan barely got his empty blaster in the way. Splinters flew as the blade hit the barrel. Ryan grimaced and buckled to one knee as the force of the blow shocked down both arms. There was no time or opportunity to go for his SIG-Sauer. The next blow would finish him.

Cafu rose behind the nightwalker. He groaned horribly as he swung his club into the nightwalker's back.

It was a weak blow, but the weight of the weapon did most of the work and the orca teeth sank in a line across the nightwalker's liver. The creature's shriek was deafening. For a second she went rigid with shock, and Ryan slapped leather for his SIG-Sauer. The blaster barked once in Ryan's hand and the nightwalker toppled with a smoking, purple-stained hole in the gauze covering its eyes.

Cafu's knees buckled. Ryan slammed a fresh mag into his blaster. Sec men were spilling out of the clinic. "Cafu! We have to go!" Cafu tried to pull his club free of the dead mutie's flesh, but he didn't have the strength. Ryan hauled him up. "C'mon!" Cafu took two agonized wooden steps forward. Ryan shook his head. "Fireblast." He groaned as he slung Cafu's heavy frame into a fireman's carry across his shoulders.

People burst out of the clinic. A blaster cracked and a bullet whipped past. Ryan trotted toward the trees. A gully spilled out to irrigate the field, and beneath the trees was sheltering darkness. Another shot rang out and Ryan gritted his teeth beneath his load and shambled into the creek. Mud splashed beneath his boots as he staggered into the gloom under the trees. The eroded walls of the gully topped his head and provided cover. Ryan slid Cafu off his shoulders. The gully was a narrow defile, and he had a modern blaster with an optic. He could hold off a lot of sec men from here. "Cafu!" Ryan pointed upstream. "Go! I'll catch up!"

Cafu shook his head and drew his two handblasters.

"Cafu, you have to..." Ryan's eye flew wide. He had been too busy carrying Cafu to notice. It was too dark beneath the trees. Ryan looked up. The overhanging trees had grown into each other; and someone had taken the further step of weaving them with netting and brush to form a canopy to block the sun. It was a perfect observation point for someone to watch the clinic during the day.

And it was a trap.

An inhumanly deep voice spoke from around the bend in the gulch. "Now."

Ryan spun. Above him the canopy shook and

snapped. Four anvil-size rocks plunged through the branches above as the trigger line holding them was cut. Heavy netting was strung between them. Ryan sprayed a burst up the gully as the net fell across him. The trawling net was woven of heavy strands of hemp, made to hold catches of Lantic cod fish. Ryan struggled to stand beneath the net's weight. He fired another burst and clawed his slaughtering knife from his boot. Ryan sawed the razor-sharp blade against the strands weighing down his rifle.

Feet splashed at the entrance to the gully behind him.

Ryan tried to turn but the netting snagged on his rifle. He turned his head to see a nightwalker filling the entrance to the gully. It spun a casting net around its head like a gladiator. The net was smaller, weighted with round stones around its circumference and opened like a flower in the air as the nightwalker cast it. The netting fell over Ryan's head and shoulders. The mutie heaved back on the cords tied to its wrist and the net contracted against Ryan and Cafu. Cafu fired his blaster up the gully at something. A third net fell across them. Ryan heaved at the piles of rope clogging his every movement. It was nearly impossible to raise the muzzle of his blaster. He could hear the nightwalker behind him splashing through the creek. He managed to punch his blade out through gaps in the mesh, but the giant easily avoided the thrust. The nightwalker grabbed Ryan and Cafu and bodily lifted them both off their feet, nets and all, then slammed them facedown into the creek. The giant hand against Ryan's back pinned him in place like an insect.

Ryan tried to push up but he stood no chance. His lungs began to burn as his face was pushed deeper into the mud and gravel of the creek bottom. Huge hands lifted the edges of the net and ripped away his weapons. Ryan's vision was blackening when he was yanked up out of the mud and hurled against the wall of the gully like a sack of refuse. He bounced off the slick clay and fell back to the mud.

Ryan rose with a rock in his hand.

Three nightwalkers were arrayed against him. Two were as tall and straight as saplings, and they looked almost identical in conformation beneath their wrappings. Except one clearly had breasts. The third was far larger, like a misshapen titan out of mythology, and carried something with a huge blade much like a medieval polearm. It turned gauze-shrouded eyes on the rock in Ryan's hand.

This was the cave-chiller.

A laugh like distant thunder rumbled out of its giant chest as it reached down and pulled up a rock the size of a watermelon from the creek bed with one spatulate hand. "Shall we have another exchange of stones, Ryan? I believe you are currently a point up. In the interest of fairness I shall let you have the first throw, so—"

Ryan threw.

He was beaten and exhausted, but hatred had always been a good motivator for him. Ryan flung his rock like it was his last act on earth, aiming at Raul's skull. The rock hit low but with a meaty thud into his adversary's collarbone. Raul's chunk of stone fell from his nerveless fingers.

The only thing missing was the snap of bone.

Raul sank his blade into the mud and brought a huge hand to his shoulder. He slowly circled his arm in its socket several times and sighed, then unwound his turban and pulled away the gauze covering his eyes. Raul wore wooden snow goggles like those who still hunted what remained of the icepack in the Arctic Circle. He pulled them down to reveal the charcoal he had smeared below his eyes. Raul's eyes were the same color as Ryan's single orb. The difference was that Ryan's glacial gaze was that of a man who had seen and survived the worst the Deathlands had to offer. Raul Barat's burning cobalt stare was that of a creature that slaked its thirsts by inflicting them. The charcoal smeared around those eyes made them pop with even more insane clarity. "I now owe you for two rocks, Ryan."

The one-eyed man was too weary to respond. He made a mental note to go for Raul's eyes or his balls, whichever presented themselves first, assuming he survived the first heartbeat of the engagement.

Raul's smile was horrible to behold. "To tell you the truth, once I put my wrath upon you, I do not think I will be able to control myself, and sad to say, my dear brother wishes to speak with you, and I have promised to deliver you onto him alive."

Raul turned his horrid glare on Cafu. The old man wheezed and bubbled blood between his lips. "I shall slake my thirst for blood and pain on this poor slave you dragged to his doom." Raul pointed a huge, black-wrapped condemning finger at Ryan. "As for your chastisement, allow me to introduce the twins, Niolao and Xadreque Andrade. Xadreque, my love, please educate Ryan in his inadequacies."

The woman unwrapped her turban and pulled down her goggles. Waves of black hair spilled around her shoulders. Gray eyes gazed insanely at Ryan out of the charcoal masking her eyes. It was obvious that once she had been beautiful. Her cheekbones were pronounced, and she had the chin and widow's peak of a witch, but she had not yet achieved the Neanderthal-like physique of the other nightwalker women Ryan had seen. She was young, most likely in mid-transformation, and was still exotically attractive, except that she was running six foot nine in height. "Crippled, my Baron of the Night?" Xadreque suggested. "Emasculated?"

"Beaten, humiliated and compliant," Raul suggested. "We mustn't disappoint my dear brother. At least not quite yet."

Xadreque was on Ryan in two strides. He tried to go for the eyes, but the insane she-thing was too fast and too strong. He had to cover up as the first blow came at him, and it nearly broke his arm and drove him into the wall of the gully. The sky seemed to open and rain sledgehammered. Ryan saw stars as Xadreque's open palm cracked across his face like an iron skillet. He buckled as her huge fist hit him in the belly like a battering ram. Ryan fell back and rammed his boot into her belly in return, but it was like kicking a steel wall. She picked Ryan up in both hands, pressed him overhead and hurled him across the gully. She crossed the creek in three strides and repeated the process three more times. Ryan was a rag doll in the mutie's hands. After the fourth toss, Xadreque stepped back to examine her handiwork.

Ryan rose, swaying like a drunk.

"He is a strong one," Raul observed.

"Is he?" Xadreque's hand shot around Ryan's throat, and she lifted him a foot off the ground. Another giant, feminine hand slammed up invasively between Ryan's legs. Xadreque smiled to show her growing teeth and purple gums. Her squeezing hand stopped just short of crushing his testicles. "Yes, he is a strong one." She slowly pulled her hand back until Ryan's organs strained against their moorings in his body. Ryan's vision went white. "And a big one, my baron." Xadreque giggled and dropped Ryan gagging back to the mud. She suddenly squatted on her heels beside him. Her voice was a hiss. "When the false baron is through with you, Ryan, you will watch, screaming, as my teeth tear your manhood from you."

Ryan had nothing left. He tried to rise and another crushing slap sprawled him back down in the chill water.

The hunting whistles of the Baron Barat's sec men were suddenly close. Raul tapped Cafu's crippled, wheezing form with his flensing blade. "Let us hasten, my love."

Ryan rolled over and once more tried to push himself up, but his muscles hung like brutalized meat off his bones. Xadreque tore off Cafu's tunic. She buried her face between his legs and Cafu's body spasmed in shock. Xadreque leaned back, her lips smeared with blood, and threw back her head, swallowing like a crocodile gulping a fish whole. Raul flipped Cafu over and with the tip of his weapon ripped open the right side of Cafu's lower back. Raul tore out Cafu's liver with his bare hand, shoved it into his mouth and cut off the excess with a flourish of his weapon. Raul gave a third to Xadreque and tossed the rest to her brother.

Xadreque swallowed and knelt over Ryan with Cafu's blood staining her lips and chin. "I want him now."

"Wait, my love." Raul piled Ryan's weapons out of reach. "My dear brother comes, and we shall render unto Caesar that which is his, for now, and when my brother renders Ryan back unto us, broken upon the wheel, you may take your every pleasure of him. We go."

The giants took up their nets and Cafu's body and were gone up the gully in an eyeblink. Ryan made an effort to crawl to his blasters, but the clinic sec men reached the gully and were on him before he could make more than five feet through the mud of the creek. The stomping they gave him was completely superfluous, but after what had happened to the powder mill, they were in a bad mood. Ryan really didn't feel much of it.

His last coherent thought was of Krysty. For her sake he hoped J.B. and Jak had a plan.

J.B. AND JAK SURVEYED their collection of weapons. It was laid out in its entirety on a single blanket. They had two auto-blasters with four mags between them. They were Heckler & Koch G-3s, heavy, .30-caliber weapons that would shoot till Doomsday. They were in decent condition, and still firing a hundred years after skydark. That was the best of it. Beyond that they had two bolt-actions with ten rounds apiece, two of the long, single-barrel, single-shot blasters, four of the short doubles, two automotive starter blasters and five swords. None of the regulars in J.B.'s army had the slightest idea how to use any of it, and there wasn't enough ammo or powder to teach anybody even the basics. Krysty was out of .38 ammo.

According to rumor, the enemy had cannons.

J.B.'s artillery consisted of a single swivel gun with two harpoons.

The Armorer shook his head. The situation wasn't good. In the Deathlands guerrilla war would've been the obvious answer, picking up much-needed weapons and experience in a series of running fights and ambushes. Jak was a past master at that kind of war. But they were on a small island. There just wasn't room to run. The windswept rolling hills of Sister Isle didn't provide much cover, and there were no subterranean cave complexes to hide in. J.B.'s biggest problem was that the Sister Islanders had been raised pacified. Luis and Leto had spent the past twenty-four hours running from hamlet to hamlet and telling their tale of what happened to those who were taken to the main island. The Sister Islanders were outraged and angry, and they knew they would be defending their families, but there was very little time to teach them how. The only two advantages J.B. could claim was that he would have the invading force outnumbered, and by all accounts most of them would be using single-shot blasters. There was no way around it. It was going to be a stand-up fight.

It was a fight J.B. was pretty sure he couldn't win.

J.B. wished Ryan were here, but by the same token the only real hope was that Ryan could make something happen on the main isle.

Jak squatted on his heels, staring at the small assortment of weapons. "Spears?"

J.B. nodded. "Yep." It was going to come down to that, and they didn't even have anything from which to make a decent spearhead. They would have to make do with sharpened sticks with the points hardened in fire. Driven with a will, you could certainly kill a man with one, but Jak had told him most of the ville men carried swords. Worse still, Doc had reported the sec men at the cannon emplacement had bayonets. J.B. was already having nightmares of a few, select sec men shock troops rolling up the entire revolution with a single volley and a bayonet charge.

They would also have the support of the cannons, and while by all reports the number of predark blasters the enemy had were few, it would only take a few to turn the entire battle.

Zorime sat in the shadow of the nearest hut and echoed J.B.'s worst fears. "You are going to make my father very angry, Senhor Dix. You are going to get these people slaughtered, and yourselves nailed to wagon wheels and given to the mercies of the nightwalkers."

J.B. ignored her. He stared at the dismounted swivel gun and the small keg of powder that had come with it off the boat. "We load that with nails, preposition to break a hole in their lines, mebbe sweep a gun position. I'll make a bomb with the remaining powder. I'll figure out how to deploy it later."

Jak nodded, searching his own swamp-fighting experience for some kind of edge. The situation was pretty cut and dried. It was bad, and he couldn't see any angles to play.

Doc leaned over the strategy session. "I fear we must be mauled in any exchange of musketry."

J.B. refrained from rolling his eyes. When Doc had a firm grasp on anything at all, it was all too often the obvious. "Yep."

"Slings?" Doc suggested.

J.B.'s first instincts always ran toward blasters and explosions, but he was aware of slings. "Takes time to get good with one, doesn't it?"

Doc pursed his lips in thought. "Must our brave island confederates be good? If the enemy confronts us in formation to give us volley fire, and we release hundreds of stones at their center, then surely with even the vaguest of aim it will have a deleterious effect, and would it not also give us a much-needed element of surprise?"

J.B. looked at Jak, who shrugged. J.B. frowned up at Doc. "You know how to make one?"

"Use one?" Jak asked even more pointedly.

"Oh, as a lad my playmates and I whiled away many a happy hour with our homemade slings and slingshots. Church bells were our most cherished target. I received many a thrashing by our good parson for—"

"Doc?" J.B. asked.

"Yes, J.B."

"How come you never mentioned this before?"

Doc searched about in his damaged mind for an answer. "It…never occurred to me."

J.B. just let that one go. "What do you need?"

"Oh, lengths of leather, plaited hair or wool." Doc scratched his chin. "Even simple cloth will do except that it will tear after a prolonged session of slinging."

"Whatever happens won't be prolonged. What else?"

"Well, we have neither the time nor the wherewithal to cast proper, elliptically shaped bullets of lead or clay, so we must rely upon stones. Best if they are smooth and approximately the size of hen's egg. I suspect the beaches will provide them."

Jak shrugged. Military strategy wasn't usually Mildred's purview but she spoke up as she saw an angle. "This could work. The ville can't afford to slaughter these people. They need them as labor and as a blood source. They don't want a war. They'll want to end this quick. Like you said before, they're expecting all it will take is a volley and bayonet charge. Our guys scatter.

They round up the women and children and our guys surrender unconditionally. They crucify a few people, us included, as examples, and they're back to business as usual."

"Our dear Mildred is right," Doc agreed. "Despite the Lady Zorime's imprecations to the contrary, if we can surprise them, bloody their noses, give them a real fight, then they will have to rethink their entire strategy. It will buy us time, and Ryan."

J.B. looked at Jak. The albino teen was grinning. J.B. nodded. "Doc? Get the women making slings. Get the children into rock-gathering gangs. Krysty, get me a head count. I'll need every man over the age of fourteen. Jak, get the men to cutting straight boughs and making spears. No time to teach them to fight in formation so make them short. Each as tall as the man wielding it."

Doc translated to Ago and Nando.

Jak rose without a word and drew his heaviest knife. He nodded at Ago to follow him. Mildred looked at J.B. ruefully. "J.B., give me any kind of blaster and I'll do my best."

"Rather you set up a surgery. Get the island midwives together. Lot of people are gonna get hurt whichever way this goes. Stay at the church. Stay in the light. You know you're a valuable commodity. If it comes to it, you surrender."

"J.B.—"

"Millie, you have to promise," J.B. insisted.

"Promise me you'll be careful."

"Deal."

Chapter Twenty-Two

Ryan strained against his bonds, but he was strapped to a gurney by predark medical restraints designed to hold violent patients. He hadn't the strength to tear free from the heavy-duty webbing, and his fingers couldn't reach the multiple buckles. Ryan sagged back in his restraints. The interior looked like the med lab of a lot of redoubts he'd seen except that the electrical lighting had failed long ago and lamps and candles lit the room instead. Dr. Goncalves sat at his desk, and his witchy-looking nurse leaned against the edge of the desk looking Ryan up and down as though he was some new breed she didn't recognize.

Baron Barat stood over Ryan, gazing down upon him with cold-blooded interest. Four sec men lurked behind him. "I gather my brother took your accomplice," Barat said. "Cafu, was it?"

Ryan glared silently up at the ceiling.

"How many others among the slave population have you suborned?" A sneer curled Baron Barat's lips. "Besides women and blind men?"

Ryan inwardly had to admit not nearly enough.

Barat read Ryan's mind. "Word of your capture and the death of the slave Cafu have been sent to all the farms. Your revolution is over. All that remains is to crush Sister Isle. I will have you know that you are going to get a large number of the people you sought to save killed."

"Their choice." Ryan rolled his eye onto the baron. "And better dead than in here."

"Speaking of in here, I am going to have Dr. Goncalves bleed the rebellion out of you. Then he will take his amputation knife and hobble you. Thence you will be taken across the strait to Sister Isle where you, any of your surviving male companions and a suitable number of rebellious Sister Islanders shall be broken upon the wheel to make an example that will be remembered for generations. Finally, you will all be brought back and crucified on the beach outside the cave where you first encountered my brother. Bonfires will be lit, and Raul and the brethren will commit acts upon you that no one will want to remember."

Ryan stared upward stoically, but he couldn't help think of Xadreque's promise and her long teeth.

Barat whirled. "I leave him in your charge, Doctor. The fleet leaves tomorrow with the outgoing tide. Have the clinic prepared. We may well take casualties subduing Sister Isle. Mr. Cawdor saw fit to put something of a dent in our powder supply." Barat gave Ryan a scathing look. "However, my son and his cadre have been putting great effort in their bayonet drills. I will have you know that Sylvano has taken an even dimmer view of you abducting Zorime than I have. I believe he is prepared to be quite ruthless."

Ryan deigned to look at Barat. "My friends won't hurt her. They won't let anyone else hurt her, either."

"You know? I rather believe you, Mr. Cawdor. I shall likewise spare the women in your party."

Ryan knew that short of being killed outright, there was very little chance that Krysty and Mildred would be spared. Barat stalked out of the clinic and left two of his sec men behind. Moments later Ryan heard a wag drive off.

Dr. Goncalves ran a hand over his bald head, wiped his lips and regarded his subject with unhealthy interest. "You are quite a remarkable specimen for having come out of the Deathlands, Mr. Cawdor," he remarked. "The last few Deathlanders that came through the mat-trans were in terrible condition. According to the annals of my predecessors, even the refugee fleet that came long ago showed signs of great privation. You nonetheless seem quite robust. By report, so are your companions."

Ryan reserved comment. He had grown up healthy in Front Royal, and since then the Deathlands had hardened him. He had taken more wounds than any man should, and later in life, if there were any later, it would cost him. However, at the moment he was one of the hardiest and most dangerous specimens the Deathlands could produce short of radical mutation.

"Let us see." Goncalves took Ryan's bound wrist in one cold, soft, sweaty hand. Ryan's forearm was striated with veins, scars and muscle. "A well-pronounced median cubital vein. Always a good sign." He poured brandy onto a clean bit of cloth and disinfected the extraction site on the inner elbow.

Ryan didn't bother to struggle as Goncalves prepped a syringe. His blue eye fixed on the ville healer in cold-hearted hatred. "I will chill you."

Goncalves laughed. "You are a refreshing change, Mr. Ryan. The Russians and Deathlanders begged, and the Sister Islanders?" Goncalves scoffed. "They just weep."

Ryan watched unflinchingly as the needle slid in and Goncalves drew back on the plunger. Ryan's blood filled the tube. "You wouldn't happen to be aware of your blood type, would you?"

Ryan spit in Goncalves's face.

The two sec men swore in Portuguese and raised the butts of their blasters. Goncalves waved them off and withdrew the needle. He put no pressure on the wound and blood drooled down Ryan's arm. Goncalves smiled as he wiped his face and took a fistful of cordial glasses out of a medical cabinet. He expressed ten cc's of Ryan's blood into each glass and mixed it with a shot of brandy. The red blood congealed in the alcohol and sec men each happily took a glass. Goncalves swirled the glass and held it up to the lamplight. The mixture looked like bloody clouds in a sunset sky. He held the glass out in mocking toast. Ryan watched coldly as the ville men tossed back his blood. Goncalves set his glass down. "Nurse Pauleta, let us begin with a thousand cc's." A sick gleam entered his dark eyes. "Let us see if that cools the fire in his blood."

Ryan had seen Mildred draw blood before. Five hundred and fifty cc's was the usual medical maximum.

Nurse Pauleta was every inch the antithesis of the healer. Goncalves was short, round, and his bald head and chalk skin made him look like an egg. Nurse Pauleta was tall and willowy in a black nurse's uniform. Her face was emaciated and her black hair was pulled back in a severe bun. She trailed her finger up Ryan's slowly bleeding arm and licked his blood from her finger. "Yes, Dr. Goncalves." She prepared a gleaming bronze needle that looked entirely too large for the operation. Ryan grimaced as she slid the needle into his vein and tied it in place with a bandage. The nurse dropped the trailing tube into a Mason jar on the medical tray next to the gurney.

Ryan's blood began spurting into the jar in a stream. He controlled his mounting rage. Thrashing around would only earn him ruptured veins, and Goncalves was already going to put a big dent in his blood volume. He was a mess after all the beatings and rock saltings, and soon he was going to be a quart low. The only advantage Ryan could see was that just like the overseers and sec men at the powder mill, Goncalves and Nurse Pauleta seemed to enjoy their jobs just a little too much. Ryan knew he had to keep it together, make the thousand cc donation and hope for an opportunity to present itself.

Ryan's heart sank as two sec men walked in. One had his hand on Moni's shoulder and the other sec man gripped Thais. Each had a blaster against the women's backs. Goncalves clapped his hands delightedly. "Oh now, look, Mr. Cawdor, a reunion. Dear Thais I know all too well, as does Nurse Pauleta. She enjoyed her so very much before she was given to those rough mill workers, didn't you?"

Nurse Pauleta looked long and knowingly at Thais, who shuddered in revulsion. Barat's sec men took this news with keen interest.

"Such a rare flower cannot escape notice. And this other?" Goncalves lifted Moni's chin. "This must be Moni, poor Cafu's lady love." He let go of her face and shook his head in dismissal. "They all look the same to me after the bloom of youth has faded."

Looking up from the gurney, Ryan could see something Goncalves couldn't. He could see beneath the broad hats the sec men had pulled low. The two men's skin was tanned like leather from years of pulling wags beneath the sun, and both men were carrying a refurbished Uzi Ryan recognized from the powder mill. They were not holding Moni and Thais to control them. They held the women's shoulders because beneath the stolen smoked glasses the two men were blind. Barat himself had said that word of Ryan's capture and what his fate was to be had been sent to all the farmsteads. Moni was mounting a rescue with the only assets she had.

Things were about to get interesting.

Goncalves dismissed Moni's existence. "Nurse, strip Thais and put her on the table next to Mr. Cawdor."

Nurse Pauleta yanked Thais away from the sec man holding her. He almost reached out for her blindly but stopped himself. The nurse cranked Thais's arm back in a cruel hammer-lock and yanked her head back with a handful of hair. The woman knew something about controlling slaves. Thais whimpered as Pauleta bent her over the steel table and began cutting away her tunic with a pair of medical shears. The baron's two sec men watched with avid interest.

Thais moaned plaintively as she was stripped. "Moni…?"

Moni looked at Ryan and desperately flicked her eyes at the two powder slaves clutching blasters beside her. She spoke quietly but firmly. "Ryan."

The two blind men lifted their chins expectantly. If any of the ville men had been looking at them they would have seen their tanned faces. Everyone was too busy watching Nurse Pauleta's ministrations. "Yes," Ryan said. The two blind men's shaded gazes snapped around at the sound of his voice and located him. "I am here."

Moni produced a stolen kitchen knife from beneath her tunic.

Goncalves laughed. "Mr. Cawdor cannot help you,

he—" Goncalves jaw dropped as he noticed the blade in Moni's hand. He shouted at the baron's sec men. "Miguel! Waldir!"

Miguel and Waldir looked around in confusion.

Moni dropped to hands and knees shouting at her own sec men. "Ferno! Gil!"

Moni scuttled across the floor as Ferno and Gil cut loose. Miguel and Waldir shouted and went for their weapons. Glass cabinets shattered and medical supplies exploded under the blind salvo of autofire. To their credit their weapons never swung Ryan's way. Moni slashed through the strap holding Ryan's right arm. Nurse Pauleta hurled Thais to the floor and rounded on Moni with her hands curled into claws. She screamed as Moni slashed her palm open to the bone. Nurse Pauleta clutched her hand to her chest, howling imprecations in Portuguese. Thais hit her from behind and took her to the ground. Moni cut through Ryan's leg restraint. The one-eyed man took the knife and cut his other arm free. A lucky bullet sheared away the side of Waldir's skull and the sec man dropped.

Ferno's and Gil's weapons clacked open on empty mags. They dropped the blasters and drew swords. They stumbled forward swinging at any sound. Miguel raised his blaster and Ferno went flying backward as the musket ball hammered him. Ryan ripped the needle out of his arm and leaped from the gurney. Miguel drew his sword. Gil took two wild swings at him, and Miguel ran the blind man through with ease.

Goncalves screamed and shot Ryan twice. The one-eyed man stumbled backward with each blow and turned a baleful eye on the doctor. Ryan was growing very weary of being rock-salted. The healer dropped his blaster and ran screaming from room.

Miguel came for Ryan warily. A knife was no match for a sword, and Ryan flung it. Miguel dodged. The Deathlands warrior picked up the gurney and charged him. The sec man thrust, and his point punched through the frame inches from Ryan's head. The one-eyed man used his superior size and his remaining strength to drive his adversary across the room. Miguel fell backward and both Ryan and the gurney fell on top of him. Ryan reached out for Ferno's fallen Uzi, raised the empty auto-blaster and drove the butt into Miguel's face until he stopped moving.

Ryan freed Miguel's pinned sword and rose to his feet. He put a thumb against his spurting left vein. "Moni, Thais." Moni held Nurse Pauleta's legs while Thais sat astride her and slammed the nurse's head into the floor again and again. A spreading purple puddle haloed the nurse's head. "Moni," Ryan repeated. "Thais."

Thais let go of the woman's hair. The nurse's pupils were two different sizes, and she was reduced to feeble twitches and jerks. Moni gasped as she looked at Ryan and leaped to her feet.

"Moni..." Ryan's vision swam. Blood was still spurting beneath his fingers. Moni ran to Ryan. Only her arm kept him from falling. Thais covered herself with a cloak and began gathering swords and blasters. Ryan exhaustedly turned his head at the sound of a scuffle outside the door. He leaned heavily on Moni and limped to the door. He pushed it open with the point of his sword to see what was going on in the reception area.

Goncalves was shuddering on the floor in a fetal

position while two blind men pounded him mercilessly with their fists. Apparently their job had been to tackle anybody who came out the door unannounced, and they had succeeded. "Moni," Ryan said.

The men stopped pounding as Moni spoke their names. "Braz, Martym."

Purple froth bubbled out of the corners of Goncalves mashed lips. "Listen, Ryan, I tell you—" The one-eyed man drove the sword down through the healer's chest and gave it a twist. Goncalves shuddered and died.

Ryan yanked the blade free. "Told you I'd chill you."

With Moni's help Ryan rummaged through drawers and found dressings. Moni got the bleeding stopped, bandaged his arm and put it in a sling. Ryan took a lantern and they opened doors until they found stairs to the basement. The old generator had been moved out, and now it was a cold room lined with shelves of Mason jars. Many were filled with blood. They hobbled upstairs and Ryan threw his lamp against the wall. The oil ignited and the flame crept upward. He broke the rest of the lanterns and spilled oil barrels. Black smoke began to roil against the ceiling, and Ryan motioned it was time to go. He kept his arm over Moni's shoulder, while Thais led Braz and Martym. Both men were loaded down like pack mules with weapons.

Moni pointed up toward the hills as they walked outside. Ryan pointed at the ambulance. Moni and Thais were dumbstruck at the idea. He tugged on Moni and they limped over to the med wag. Ryan tried the door. It was open and a starter blaster was in the ignition. He and his little band of revolutionaries piled in. Ryan looked at the clinic as smoke began oozing out of the eaves. According to Doc, the blood was a craving for the ville rather than a necessity like the drug, but the clinic was where the blood was drawn and the slaves were mutilated. It wasn't strategically as big as blowing up the powder mill but it ranked pretty high on the symbolic victory chart. So would his escape.

Ryan slid behind the wheel and pulled the trigger on the starter. The med wag's engine turned over and roared like a champ as he gave it gas. Ryan wondered whether they processed the Lotus drug up in the hills or in the ville. He knew without doubt that would have to wait. He had to rest. The next load of rock salt would put him on the ground and the next beating or bleeding would put him under it. He was no good to anyone right now except the four survivors of the clinic battle who had saved his life. There was nothing he could do to stop Sylvano's fleet from sailing.

The next move was Jak's and J.B.'s.

J.B. WALKED DOWN the firing line. The air buzzed with the whirl of scores of slings and downrange the smack of the stones. J.B. narrowly avoided being brained several times by an overeager islander's backswing. Doc had produced better than J.B. had dared hope. The old man had arranged two simple ranges. Fifty yards away he had laid several dozen cloaks in a line on a steep hillside to represent the enemy. The slings hummed and snapped in rapid succession. An embarrassing number of stones impacted the turf all around the cloaks, but by J.B.'s estimation a good half were hitting home, as well. At fifty yards the stones would break bones and crack skulls. Most of the men were getting off an aimed cast every seven to ten seconds. That would undoubtedly be a whole lot slower under combat conditions, but the islanders would still be releasing rocks far faster than the ville's single-shot blasters could be reloaded.

That still left their supporting fire to be dealt with.

The second range was a hillock at one hundred yards. It represented a landing ship or artillery emplacement. All the islanders had to do was to hit any part of it. At a hundred yards the slinging went from direct to arcing fire. J.B. watched the island men let fly. The sling stones were losing a lot of velocity, hardly hitting much harder than a strong man could throw them. Still, even without a head shot two or three thrown rocks would take most people out of a fight, and the islanders would be raining them down by the hundreds. The men of the island had been broken up into three detachments of 250 each. They were taking turns slinging. More than a few were sporting bruises where they had smacked themselves midsling or had improperly loaded and slung their stone into their neighbor.

Nevertheless, the islanders were going at it with a will.

The ones currently firing stuck their spears into the ground beside them. The island had been denuded of every straight tree limb and fallen branch of the right size. Each was cut to the height of the man using it and whittled to a needle point. The points were black from being thrust in fire to harden them so they wouldn't blunt and deform after the first thrust. They were still hundreds of spears short and almost a third of each detachment was armed with clubs instead.

J.B. watched a little while longer. He had none of the island language, but he walked the firing line, careful to not get his head taken off, and clapped men on the shoulder who made good casts and gave them encouragement. A woman came up and offered him a half gourd filled with millet beer. J.B. drank and called together his generals. Jak and Doc left their men to their practice and gathered for the final strategy session.

J.B. plucked a blade of sea grass and chewed it reflectively. "We can expect it any time now."

"Figure dusk or dawn," Jak said.

"That's the way I figure it, too."

"I would suggest dusk," Doc said. "We know the men of the ville will prefer to stay out of direct daylight lest they are forced to it. The days have been clearing. Tomorrow may be sunny. The men of the ville do most of their work at night, and they must surely be counting on our army having been taught to fear the dark all their lives."

"They still can't see in the dark," J.B. countered. "Hard to shoot what you can't see. It's in our favor. We scatter, they hunt us by night. By starlight it'll be nose-to-nose fighting, and we have the numbers."

"That's not the way I see it."

J.B. waited for Doc to go into some diatribe about generals J.B. had never heard of. Instead Doc looked at him very earnestly. "I have spoken with Mildred today, and before I took ship with Jak, Ryan told me of his own experiences on the main island, come the night."

J.B. spit on the ground unhappily. "You're talking nightwalkers."

Jak shook his head as he saw it. "We scatter. Sec men march. Take the villages."

"And the nightwalkers take the night, hunting our people," Doc continued. "Our people will scatter once more, but this time in blind panic, fleeing toward their homes or the last redoubt of the church. The sec men will be there with torches and fires, offering to protect them if they surrender, or drive them back into the dark at bayonet point to be slaughtered should they not."

"They take church—" Jak stabbed a knife into the dirt "—they take women, kids."

J.B. nodded. The enemy had all the cards except surprise. "We gotta win the first engagement. We gotta win big and win quick." J.B. took out his knife and drew in the dirt. "We lie low in the dunes. Three columns. Loose spread. Doc, you take the center. Your boys keep slinging. Jak, you and yours take the left flank. I take the right. We all sling them as they come off the boats. Doc, you and your boys are arcing for the cannons nonstop. We take two of their volleys. Hoping we get off five rocks for every one bullet of theirs, then Jak and I charge both flanks in a pincer movement. Doc, you keep slinging, but you're the reserve. If we get bogged down, you come in. Right down the middle."

Jak took a long breath and slowly let it out. "Rough."

Doc nodded. "We shall have surprise, my friends. We shall have numbers. Yet I fear it shall all come down to our men's morale. They must stand and sling in the teeth of the enemy guns, and then they must charge. Should they falter, all shall be blood and horror."

All three men knew what that meant. They would have to lead from the front. And in the event of collapse? They were outlanders. They could be abandoned and later blamed as scapegoats. In the end the islanders were just going to have to want it.

"Got something on that angle," Mildred piped up.

J.B., Jak and Doc looked up from their scratches in the dirt strategy session. Mildred and Krysty were smiling. "What've you got?" J.B. asked.

Mildred held up a rolled piece of native homespun and snapped it out. It was a three-foot by two-foot square of the usual dun brown, but stitched in the middle was a yellow sun with eight triangular spokes.

Doc smiled. "Dear Mildred! You have woven us a war banner! I did not know you were seamstress!"

Mildred gave Doc a tolerant smile. "I'm a woman, Doc. I know something about sewing."

J.B. looked at Jak. Jak was grinning. In spite of the lack of good spear material, Krysty held a mostly straight twelve-foot length of tree bough that had been shaved down to a flagstaff.

J.B. nodded. "Do it." Krysty threaded the flag onto the pole through the loops Mildred had sewn and tied them off with leather cords. J.B. looked to Doc. Whatever else you could say about him, Doc had a beautiful speaking voice and he had more local speak than the rest of them. "Doc, say something inspirational."

Doc took the flag and raised it high. Many of the islanders who weren't actively practicing their slinging skills had been watching the meeting that was deciding their fate. The wind was always blowing across the island. The flag fluttered and snapped in the breeze. Those watching stared, awestruck. Doc's voice rolled out at parade ground decibels. *"Filhos do Sol!"*

"Meaning?" J.B. asked.

"Sons of the Sun," Doc whispered. He bellowed again. *"Filhos do Sol!"*

Seven hundred fifty faces turned and gazed at the war flag. Doc planted the pole by his heel and drew his sword from his cane and held it high. *"Filhos do Sol!"*

Ago drew his new sword and thrust it high. *"Filhos do Sol!"*

Other islanders took up the chant. Doc dipped the banner toward the assembled islanders and then thrust it up at the yellow sun breaking through the clouds. "Sons of the Sun!"

The islanders got it and seemed to like the alliteration. "Sons of the Sun!" they roared.

Doc cut loose in the native lingo. The 750 warriors of Sister Isle wept, roared and shook their spears. Mildred watched in awe. "God…damn, I wish I spoke Portuguese!"

J.B. held up his arm. "No need." He had goose bumps.

Doc strode out among the masses waving the standard from side to side. The mob surged around him. They lifted Doc up on their shoulders and marched him and the war banner around the slinging range chanting their lungs out. J.B. nodded to himself. They would have numbers. They would have surprise. Now they had morale. The enemy would have discipline and firepower.

The revolution would live or die by the setting of the sun.

Chapter Twenty-Three

"Behold their armada in mighty array," Doc said.

The baron's fleet had come across the strait in the late afternoon, just as predicted. They hovered offshore waiting as the setting sun turned from gold to orange. J.B. watched the invasion force through his binoculars with more than a little trepidation. The fleet was a hodge-podge of whalers and fishing feluccas and a pair of barges. He had been expecting that, but it was the flagship that was making J.B. nervous. It was a small tramp steamer, but you could fit a lot of men inside the hold. The sides of the ship were strung with heavy nets for the invaders to climb down. The port side deck was lined with cannons in heavy wooden running carriages.

Jak sighed unhappily. "Gunship."

"Indeed," Doc agreed. "They have configured the vessel for shore bombardment. Note the devices amidships."

J.B. took a look at a series of oversize wheelbarrows loaded with long wooden racks. His heart sank. "Dark night."

"Any culture that can produce black-powder cannons and small arms has the capacity to manufacture artillery rockets," Doc stated.

J.B. imagined rockets screaming into the men

standing and slinging in the dunes. "Our boys aren't ready for rockets."

"No choice," Jak said.

Doc continued his discourse. "Note also toward the back of the steamer, six more cannons up on field carriages. Our enemy intends to bring artillery upon the shore."

J.B.'s brow furrowed in thought. "Whole lot of powder on that deck."

"Ryan demolished the enemy gun emplacements upon the main isle with incendiary rifle fire," Doc mused. "However, I fear we have no such armament to hand."

Jak looked at the ville men in their long black coats and broad hats swarming the deck. "I can."

"Can what, Jak?" J.B. asked.

"Get close. Wear black. Battle starts, go aboard. Burn it."

"You got black?"

The islanders were using blankets to transport their stockpiles of sling stones and supplies. Jak unfolded the one closest to him and revealed his stolen cloak, a pair of shades and Father Joao's hat.

"You figured on this all along," J.B. concluded.

"Figured mebbe," Jak admitted.

"My friend," Doc said concernedly, "you may well be subject to friendly fire. No one shall be calling friend or foe whence we are engaged, and you may well be misidentified, particularly by the slingers at a distance."

Jak shrugged. "Better'n facing cannons like you."

"Hmm, well, yes, perhaps."

J.B. had to admit Jak might actually have the easier job. Except for one little detail. "Jak, you blow that boat, you're taking that boat west."

Jak tapped his temple. "Do it smart." He shrugged fatalistically. "If I can."

They both knew Jak would blow the boat up any way he could even it if cost him his life. J.B. looked around at his forces. The dunes were full of islanders lying out of sight in the sea grass. The center was one hundred yards from the beach. The right and left flanks were at fifty. Some of the leading elements were even closer. It was a classic crescent formation. He looked long at the left flank. "Who's going to lead your men, Jak?"

Krysty piped up from right behind them. "How about me?"

"Ryan wouldn't like it."

"Ryan isn't here, and we only get one shot at this. They release the nightwalkers, and mebbe our boys see a woman going forward with the flag, mebbe taking one or two out?" Krysty flashed her smile. "Might be enough to keep them going."

J.B. looked at Jak, who shrugged. "Right," J.B. agreed. "But, Krysty, you take the center." He looked at their dwindling supply of blasters. "Take the longblaster with the bayonet. Doc? You take the left flank. Give them the swivel blaster and the nails if they charge our center. Jak, get in black, take one of the auto-blasters and start creeping forward. Do it careful, let our boys see your hair till you get close. Don't want any itchy sling finger accidents." J.B. took a final look around. Once the action started just about every contingency plan they had would probably go out the window. They all had to get it right the first time. "Let's get in position."

Jak was already dressed and began kneeing and elbowing through the dunes toward the beach. Krysty moved to take the center with the flag. J.B. put a hand on Doc's arm. "Doc, you tell Ago he sticks with Krysty, and sticks with the flag, no matter what." It wasn't much of an insurance policy, but it was all J.B. could do for Ryan. "Issue him the last two short doubles."

"Color Sergeant Ago, then." Doc nodded. "So be it." Doc grabbed Ago by the shoulder and had a short exchange with him. Ago nodded confidently, took the weapons off the blanket depots and crawled after Krysty with the war banner.

"What about me?" Mildred asked.

J.B. sighed. Everyone was sneaking up on him today. "Field med."

"We only get one chance at this." Mildred pointed out. "You need every gun you can get."

Everyone seemed to feel that J.B. needed reminding of that.

J.B. looked at the remaining auto-blaster and the two bolt-actions. "Take the auto, deploy the bipod, fire from right here. Rake the decks till you're out of ammo. Then you run. Take one of the bolt blasters with you. If we lose, you manage the surrender, and you surrender."

Mildred gave J.B. a hard look.

J.B. couldn't help but remember their night in Ago's hut. He looked out at Barat's fleet and knew all too well it might have been their last. "Promise."

"I promise, J.B." Mildred crossed her heart. "Cross my heart and hope to die. Now give me the goddamn blaster." J.B. deployed the blaster's bipod and handed over it and the spare mag. Mildred took a prone shooting position on the dune. J.B. took a long last look at her. Mildred smiled back from her shooting position. "J.B.?"

"Yeah?"

"We're going to be all right. Now get to your people and let's chill these ghost-faced sons of bitches."

J.B. scooped up the remaining bolt-action blaster and began weaving through the dunes toward the right flank. He reached his position just as the steamer's foghorn lowed three times. The whalers plied their oars and ground right up onto the beach. Sec men leaped into the surf with bayonets fixed. The right flank's second in command was a strapping blond islander named Davi. Davi was shaking in his sandals. J.B. clapped him on the shoulder as more and more sec men deployed. "Sons of the Sun."

"Sons of the Sun," Davi replied, but without much enthusiasm.

The afternoon breeze seemed to die of its own accord. Except for the sounds of the debarking sec men, the shore was eerily quiet. A sec man stood alone at the front of the beachhead. He carried an auto-blaster and wore white cross-belts over his black tunic, and had a plume in his hat. The scout was one of Sylvano's elite cadre. The scout scanned the dunes, but there was nothing to see. J.B.'s army didn't need much encouragement to lie as quiet as rabbits in sea grass. They were scared out of their minds. The scout turned back to the steamer and made a cutting motion with one black-gloved hand. Davi flinched as a sound like a thousand hissing snakes came from the deck of the steamer.

Hundreds of rockets streamed up into sunset on plumes of smoke.

They flew in a very high trajectory over the dunes. They were unguided and other than high and up, their trajectory was close to random. They looped and spun crisscrossing as high as their rocket motors would take them and as their propellant burned out they nosed over and began falling back to earth. J.B. saw their glittering points as they fell from the sky. The enemy was using rocket arrows. They would be much more effective fired at a flat trajectory in a mass of men but that was not the ville men's tactic. They were firing for effect.

Davi screamed as a falling arrow sank into his shoulder.

More screams tore out among the dunes. Some islanders rose and tried to dodge the arrow shower. A man ran away inland.

"Dark night!" J.B. snarled. They had just lost surprise. J.B. rose and fired his Uzi three times on semiauto. "Now! Now! Now!" J.B. shouted. He didn't wait. He dropped to one knee and began emptying his blaster into the milling sec men in the surf. His men rose around him, putting stone to sling. The air thrummed with their massed casting. The center rose as a unit as Ago raised the sun banner. The left flank rose at the same time, and J.B. could hear the flat booming of Doc's LeMat. A deadly rain of rocks answered the rocket arrows and sec men fell. They answered by unlimbering their blasters. Men standing and slinging at one hundred yards or less weren't difficult targets. J.B.'s men began dying all around him. J.B. kept firing in short bursts as another salvo of rockets sizzled skyward. More sec men kept spilling over the side of the steamer and down the netting. Some fell to the surf as stones struck them, but not enough. Many of those hit didn't go down but kept loading and firing.

Doc had told him you could teach a man to sling in a day but it took a long time to get accurate, much less to develop the cast for maximum power. For true killing power they were going to have to get closer. J.B. wondered when the cannons would open up. Instead one of the barge's ramp clanged down. Sec men spilled out in a black-clad wave. Each one had a plume in his hat and white cross-belts strapped their torsos. Each man carried a longblaster with a fixed bayonet. J.B. guessed there were over a hundred of them. By Mildred's description, J.B. knew that Sylvano Barat led them, carrying the biggest sword he had ever seen. The chosen men spread out behind their prince in a phalanx as they came out of the surf and onto the sand. War whistles shrilled and screamed. Sylvano's men didn't bother to fire their blasters.

They leveled their bayonets and charged straight for the kill.

DOC COCKED AND FIRED his blaster as rapidly as he could. Rocket arrows fell. Sec men to either side of Sylvano's charge loaded and fired their single-shot blasters with precision. The battle was turning very quickly. Doc raised his cocked pistol, holding his last round. There would be no time to reload before the lines met. The chosen sec men charged the dunes in a 150-man wedge and Sylvano Barat was the tip of the spear. He had abandoned his blaster and rapier and hurtled forward with a great, two-handed sword held aloft. From point to pommel it was nearly six feet long. Doc knew it was a weapon Sylvano had forged for slaying nightwalkers. Pointed sticks would stand no chance. Sylvano would reap the Sister Islanders like wheat, and his men knew it. Held aloft in sunset, the shining sword was all the war banner the sec men required. They charged in good order, bayonets bright as they followed Sylvano's gigantic burnished blade into battle.

Doc took careful aim at Sylvano. He put his front sight on Sylvano's center body mass and squeezed the trigger. The LeMat revolver cracked in his hand. Sylvano jerked slightly but didn't even break stride. Sling stones struck him and bounced off. The islanders began to panic. Sylvano came on like an unstoppable juggernaut. The wave of sec men behind him came on like a deadly tide. Doc cursed himself as he remembered Ryan telling him that Sylvano and his father had worn body armor during the battle in the manse.

The scholar could feel the courage of the men around him failing. His sword cane was a toothpick compared to the Goliath-size weapon in Sylvano's hand. No man would follow it into the rolling line of sec steel rumbling down upon them. Doc holstered his LeMat, saving the shotgun barrel for the melee. Doc could see only one course of action. He took a deep breath, sighed, and pulled the sling from his belt. His men shouted in alarm as Doc began walking across the sand toward Sylvano and his thicket of bayonets.

"Doc!" Nando howled for him to come back. "Doc!" Yet none of Doc's men followed or made any attempt to pull him back. The islanders were heartbeats away from breaking. Doc was at his limit, as well, and knew it was only the Blood of the Lotus he had been fortifying himself with all day that was allowing him this bravado. Doc comforted himself with scripture.

"'And it came to pass,'" Doc quoted. "'When the Philistine arose, and came and drew nigh to meet David, that David hasted, and ran toward the army to meet the Philistine.'"

"Mine!" Sylvano saw Doc stalking forward and bellowed. "Dr. Tanner is mine!" Sylvano shoved his sword skyward and the blade seemed to catch fire in the sunset. The sec men roared as their champion ran forward, hastening to meet the scarecrow the despised Sister Islanders had sent against them.

"'And David put his hand in his bag—'" Doc spiked his swordstick in the sand and put a hand into his pocket "'—and took thence a stone…'" Doc loaded his sling. Sylvano suddenly saw what Doc was about. He kept his sword aloft but his right hand clawed for the blaster strapped to his hip. The piercing Doc had given that hand made it a second too slow. Doc's sling hummed as he ripped it through the Z-shaped windup that had impressed his schoolmates as a child and awed the islanders. "'And slang it'!" Doc shouted. The polished white sea stone hurtled through the air straight and true. Sylvano's black hat was torn from his head from the concussion.

"'And smote the Philistine in his forehead,'" Doc continued. "'And he fell upon his face to the earth.'" Sylvano stumbled two more steps forward and collapsed. The reflected red light of the sunset left Sylvano's great sword like a snuffed candle as it fell to the sand. "Samuel, Book 1, Chapter 17, Verses 48 and 49," Doc concluded.

The charge faltered as some sec men stopped to defend their fallen captain and the men behind piled into them. Others ran past but looked backward and slowed. The amazed islanders sent a great roar of triumph rolling through the dunes and renewed their slinging. The range was now much shorter and their target a compact mass of men. Only a few of Sylvano's front-rank men had predark body armor or flak vests beneath their cloaks, and they began to fall as sling stones broke bones and cracked skulls. Doc knew if there were to be any moment, it was now, before the sec men could reform. "Nando!" Doc shouted back to where Nando stood by the swivel blaster. "Now!"

Nando yanked the cord and three hundred nails blew out in a bee swarm into Sylvano's stalled charge. Sec men screamed and flailed. Islanders slang. Those who had run out of stones shook their spears. Doc pulled his swordstick from the sand and drew the rapier, thrusting the steel point skyward. "They are unmanned! Their formation is broken!

"Sons of the Sun!" Doc shouted. He turned and stalked down out of the dunes, pointing his blade ever forward, daring his men to follow.

"Sons of the Sun!" tore from every islander's throat left, right and center. The right flank came rumbling out of the dunes like an avalanche in Doc's wake. The left and the center followed within heartbeats. The islanders charged the invaders' blasters in a human wave. "Sons of the Sun!"

"OH...MY...GOD." Mildred hunkered down behind her rifle. For good or ill, a broken-minded man from the nineteenth century had bet the entire battle on a single roll of the dice. Not that it was ever going to come down to anything but this, but Mildred would have been a lot more confident if it had been J.B., Jak or, better, Ryan who had called the charge. Still, Mildred had to admit that Doc was cutting quite an impressive figure marching down upon the beach, pointing his blade like a judging finger from God on High.

A short series of whistle blasts stopped Sylvano's men in their tracks. As a unit they took to a knee, aimed and fired en masse into the charging left flank. The wave of islanders rippled like sea grass. Untold scores of islanders fell. Mildred couldn't see what became of Doc through the powder smoke. The sec men had no time to reload. Instead sec whistles shrieked the battle order and the ragged wedge of black cloaks formed themselves into a square. Howls, shouts and screams lifted to the sky as the lines met and the battle went hand-to-hand.

Mildred cut loose.

She ignored the beach bash and concentrated on the gun crews along the steamer's rails. For some reason the ville men had been husbanding their cannons. Her first shot sparked as it caromed off the black iron cannon barrel. Her second took one of the loaders. The gun crew noticed the flash of her blaster and suddenly took a very dim view of her activities. They raised their aim slightly and traversed the gun a degree in its wooden track. Mildred shot the man cranking it and the man who took up the task. The other three cannons all began traversing her way. Mildred began to feel panic as the gaping black muzzles looked her way. She fired three more times and one of the gun crew twisted and fell. The gun captains yanked their cannon lanyards and the iron guns belched smoke and fire.

"Bastard!" Mildred yelped. She rolled down the back of dune as the crest exploded like a volcano. The slings had been a surprise, but the mission of the enemy artillery remained the same. Sylvano's men would deal with the pointed sticks. The gunners would pound any snipers in the dunes with explosive shells. Mildred found herself drowning in sand as the dune was violently rearranged and a great deal of it fell on top of her.

She did a push-up and shook her plaits, spitting and blinking at the grit invading every exposed orifice. She hacked and coughed in the burning, brimstone fog of black powder smoke enveloping her. She scrabbled blindly for her rifle.

"Shit!" Mildred clawed about in the sand but it was nowhere to be found. "Shit! Shit! Shit!" She found the bolt-action rifle, but the spare ammo was lost in the sand slide. Mildred had five rounds in the magazine and one in the chamber. She crawled back up the sundered dune. The beach was one big brawl. Mildred lay in a firing position. She took aim at the steamer once more, and despite his disguise she made out Jak climbing up the invasion netting draping the side of the steamer. It looked like he was hurt. Mildred settled in and kept her sights on him.

Jak's one-man boarding party now had a guardian angel.

ROCKS FELL OUT of the sky like rain, and now that the battle was engaged Jak was just one more black-cloaked and hated sec man. Two stones had struck him. One had grazed his face and it was swelling magnificently. He no longer had to fake the limp he had adopted as he retreated toward the ships. Stones clanged off the side of the steamer's steel hull and rattled down on the decks. Sec men swarmed down the nets as the invaders deployed their reserve into the battle. Jak splashed through the surf and began climbing up the side. A sec man stopped in midclimb and pointed at him and his auto-blaster and began to shout. Jak didn't see any way around it. He had to get on deck. Jak nodded and handed the man the weapon and kept climbing up the net. The climb was difficult. No bone was broken, but Jak felt like someone had hit him in the thigh with a hammer.

Jak looked up as he reached the top and found himself staring up the barrels of a double blaster. He doubted this one was loaded with salt. The sec man shouted and shoved out his hand. Jak's long platinum hair was tied back and shoved up under his hat. All the sec man saw was a face as pale as his own, half swollen out of all recognition behind smoked lenses and struggling up the net with an injured leg. The sec man grabbed Jak's arm and hauled him aboard. He shouted something encouraging and rejoined his gun crew.

For a moment Jak had freedom of the deck.

Almost every sec man without an artillery task was deploying down the netting. Two men stood in the steamer's wheelhouse, but their eyes were on the battle. The cannon men kept their weapons trained on the dunes. A team of four men had reloaded two of the rocket batteries and were swiftly stuffing rocket arrows down the smoking racks of the third. Jak considered his options. He limped over to the rocketeers. He picked up a rocket arrow and helpfully began to assist in loading. The rocket captain nodded and said something. Jak responded by shoving the barbed arrowhead into the sec man's throat. The other three gaped in shock at the sudden violence. Jak took the opportunity to put a throwing knife into the throats of two more. The fourth rocketeer shouted, and his sword rasped from its sheath.

The man flew backward as though he'd taken a huge invisible fist to the chest.

Jak smiled. Someone out there liked him.

The albino youth went to one of the loaded rocket racks. Ignition was fairly simple. Each row of rockets rested against a wooden tray with a runnel carved in it. Each runnel was laid with fuse cording. A coil of slow cord smoldered in a bucket on the deck. Jak considered the possibilities. The entire device was basically a wheelbarrow loaded with arrows. Jak lifted the handles and found it surprisingly light. He lifted the handles to maximum declination and kicked the wooden elevation stop so that the rocket rack was level with the deck. Jak aimed the rocket battery at the cannon crews. He took the burning slow cord and touched it to the master fuse hole and prudently stepped out of the way. The lines of fusing hissed down each row of rockets, igniting their motors. The rocket arrows hissed out of the racks in a rippling, random swarm. The weapon was hopelessly inaccurate, but it made for quite a deck sweeper. Gun crewmen fell pin-cushioned across their cannons or flopped to the deck. The arrows slammed against the cannons and even the explosive iron shells, but lacked the velocity to detonate anything. The far gun crew escaped most of the carnage. Jak put the cord in his teeth and took his Colt Python in both hands. The remaining gun crewmen died beneath Jak's blaster as they went for their swords. Jak ran to the partially loaded rocket rack.

The wheelhouse door slammed open and the captain and his mate came out with swords and short blasters in hand. Jak aimed the rack at the wheelhouse stair. The captain and mate screamed and ran back up. Jak took the slow cord from between his teeth and lit up. Only seventy-five arrows had been loaded, but they shrieked satisfactorily against the wheelhouse landing. The captain dived through the door. The mate took a dozen arrows in the back and ate stairs. Jak quickly reloaded his blaster.

The captain stood in the arrow-studded wheelhouse and yanked a handle in the roof. His foghorn boomed three times. He staggered backward and half flopped out the window as Jak's guardian angel smote him. Jak looked around. There had to be more crewmen below, at least in the engine room, but for the moment he owned the deck. Jak ran to the side. The battle was still raging. The sec men square had taken a horrific toll. The sand was a sea of dead islanders, but the numbers game had told the tale. The sec men square was down to one-third its number. The reserve from the middle was completely deployed. The crews of the feluccas and whalers were rushing to reinforce them, but sling stones rained down among them and Jak could tell they wouldn't be enough. The square was crumbling and inexorably being pushed toward the sea.

Jak wondered what the captain's horn signal had meant.

He got his answer as the ramp of the second barge slammed into the surf. The belly of the barge gave birth to abominations. The nightwalkers came screaming out of the hold. They were half naked or naked, and their fish-white flesh gleamed like ivory in the dying light. Most carried clubs or spears of astounding size, often inset with sharpened pieces of iron or nails. Others carried stolen picks and axes, and they wielded them in their huge hands like a norm would hold a hammer or a hatchet. The leader was smaller, and still had a veneer of human proportion in comparison to the screaming grotesques he led. He carried a great whaling harpoon in one hand and a crude wooden shield in the other. A net was wrapped over one shoulder.

Jak estimated there were fifty of them.

He ran to the last loaded rocket battery and rolled it forward to the rail.

Chapter Twenty-Four

"Gaia!" Krysty's men were surging past her to join the battle. Keeping a reserve had gone straight out the window. So had covering fire. Krysty shouted as Ago began to run forward waving the flag. "Ago!"

Ago looked back and then eagerly snapped his head around as more men ran forward shouting the war cry. "Sons of the Sun!" The spirit of the all-out attack was infectious. The islanders sensed victory was within their grasp. "Sons of the Sun!" was the clarion call to battle. Ago started to drift forward with attack.

"Ago!" Krysty shouted. She pointed at the flag and waved her hand back and forth. "Tell them to hold!"

Ago turned to face the rush. He waved the flag back and forth in the face of what remained of the surging center. Krysty stood in front of them whirling a sling around her head. She pointed at the enemy fleet. "Sling! Sling! Sling!"

Krysty had already lost over half the center, but J.B. and Doc were probably just as glad to have the reinforcements. The remaining men skidded to a halt in front of the flag and dropped their spears and clubs. They scrambled back to their depots of stones and got back to slinging at the men running up from the boats. Krysty could see fire and rocket trails on the deck of the steamer and knew that Jak had made it and was at his task. "Sling!" Krysty cried, and the islanders who still had stones left slang with a will.

Krysty's blood froze in her veins as the hunting screams of the nightwalkers rent the sunset.

The islanders literally froze in place. Slings went limp. The men holding them almost did, as well. On the battlefield the attacking islanders recoiled from the sec men square. Every islander's worst fear came boiling up onto the beach. Men of both J.B.'s and Doc's regiments threw down their weapons and flat-out fled the scene of the battle in stark terror. The sec men were playing mutant power as their trump card.

Two could play that game.

"Gaia…Earth Mother, give me aid," Krysty intoned, her breathing deepening as she began her trance of power. With each breath, power began to flow from her deepest core. "Give me all the power…let me strive for life…" The power centers within Krysty's body gave bloom. It started in her loins but the sensuality gave way to something bigger, moving into her belly, rising through her solar plexus, her throat, to between her eyes and the top of her head. Power flowed up her legs from the earth. Power flowed into her from the sky with her every breath. Time seemed to dilate and everyone slowed down as her senses became hyperacute.

"Kreesty!" Ago shouted. Krysty drew her sword and picked up a fallen blade from one of the rocket-arrowed islanders. With a sword in either hand, she felt unbearably light as her feet skimmed across the sand. "Sons of the Sun!" Ago shouted, and charged with the battle flag in Krysty's wake. The last hundred or so islanders followed the warrior woman and the war flag. Krysty arrowed straight for the nightwalkers. It was suicide. She knew she could take one or two, and felt the killing lust to make it happen, but even with her help the islanders couldn't beat half a hundred. Krysty saw it with terrible clarity. Each nightwalker would be an individual siege that would take a half-dozen islanders or more to finish. The islander losses would be horrific, and they would break and run. Sylvano's sec men would regroup, retreat to their boats and wait out the night of rape, cannibalism and horror that the nightwalkers would inflict. Come the dawn the nightwalkers would seek refuge from the sun in the church. The shattered Sister Islanders would seek refuge from the nightwalkers by surrendering to the sec men. Nothing short of a miracle would stop it.

The miracle was a sizzling, rippling salvo of rocket arrows from the rail of the sec men flagship.

The hunting screams of the nightwalkers turned to roars and agonized shrieks as the rocket-driven shafts drilled deep into their gigantic bodies. Half their number fell beneath the point-blank barrage. Krysty beelined for their leader. He raised his harpoon in rage and flung it with horrific force. Krysty twisted with the grace of a dancer and the huge, barbed head skimmed inches from her collarbones. The nightwalker bellowed and took his huge wooden shield in both hands to swat Krysty down like a bug. Krysty's body moved almost of its own accord. She threw herself into a slide beneath the blow and slid between the nightwalker's legs. Krysty rolled up to one knee, and her swords crossed as she whipped their points across the back of the nightwalker's knees. He screamed and fell hamstrung to his knees. Krysty rose and slashed her swords like scissors across the nightwalker's neck.

The nightwalker's head fell from his shoulders.

"Sons of the Sun!" Krysty's remaining one-hundred-man reserve chorused as they followed the flag into battle.

Krysty limboed beneath a sapling studded with nails. Jagged iron drew a pair of bloody furrows across her chest instead of smashing her skull. She snapped erect as the club passed, and slashed with her swords. The nightwalker howled as its hand came off at the wrist. It screamed as her second sword flashed and removed the lower section of its arm at the elbow. All it could do was gasp as she took the rest of the limb off at the shoulder. Krysty's killing blow was interrupted as two islanders screamed in and shoved their spears into the mortally wounded nightwalker's chest and stomach. The islanders crashed into the mob of nightwalkers like a wave upon the rocks. Their bones broke like kindling and their spears snapped like sticks, but the nightwalkers were beset on all sides. Every death they dealt out was rewarded by fire-hardened spear thrusts from all directions. Many had rocket arrows piercing their flesh already, and Krysty stalked among them.

The beach churned into a morass of red and purple blood.

Krysty killed and killed.

She left a sword in one body and broke the other deflecting the swing of another gigantic studded club. Krysty ducked in, leaving ten inches of broken sword blade under a nightwalker's sternum. Another nightwalker woman howled forward. Krysty skittered backward and snatched up the harpoon of the fallen nightwalker leader and rammed it between the nightwalker's breasts. Purple blood burst from its mouth and nose. Krysty ripped the cruel barb out of the she-creature's chest and shreds of its hooked heart came with it. She whirled and threw the harpoon like a thunderbolt at a nightwalker menacing Ago and the flag. The whaling weapon punched through its chest and burst out its back.

Suddenly there were almost no nightwalkers left.

One of the remaining charged her. It was pushing nine feet tall, and half a dozen spear shafts and rocket arrows protruded from its freakishly muscled body. It had no weapon and came at Krysty with its huge hands open to tear her limb from limb. Krysty ran forward and leaped into the giant's embrace. Its hands closed around Krysty's arms and raised her high, but she didn't care. She lashed one foot into the nightwalker's throat and it choked on broken chunks of its esophagus. Her legs scissored and her second kick drove the giant's septum into his brain.

Krysty dropped lightly to the sand as the titan fell, her body swathed in purple blood. The last living nightwalkers were on their backs being stabbed again and again. What remained of the sec men square was ankle deep in the surf and surrounded on three sides. They could retreat no farther because Jak had adjusted one of the cannons to maximum declination and had his hand on the lanyard.

They had won.

Krysty tottered as the power abruptly left her. The strength, speed and crystal clarity fell from her like water from a bucket that had burst its bottom, returning to the earth she had borrowed it from. All that remained of her was a bruised, empty and nearly broken vessel.

Ago caught her as she fell.

"WILL YOU YIELD?" Doc bellowed. He pointed his sword at the forlorn and collapsed sec men square standing in the cold surf as twilight fell. The surviving islanders gripped their spears with grim determination. Nearly half of the 750 who had marched out to the dunes beneath the banner lay dead in the sand. The toll on the invading sec men had been even more terrible. The wounded moaned among the mounds of the dead. The annihilation of the nightwalkers was total. Not one had been left alive. The islanders and the sec men stared at one another over their weapons. The sec men dared not raise their bayonets to reload for fear of another all-out charge. They awaited the cannon above to send its high-explosive shell into their huddled ranks. Nearly every man of each side bore a wound or mark. All were exhausted. No one wanted to start the final engagement.

J.B. leaned heavily on a spear. His blasters were empty, and he had been bayoneted through the leg when it had gone hand-to-hand. Doc looked over at him. J.B. shrugged.

"Will you yield?" Doc repeated.

He was surprised to see Sylvano Barat rise from among his men, though it took a pair of them to prop him up. His face was a mask of purple blood in the gloaming. "We yield."

Doc sheathed his blade and stepped into the no-man's-land between the lines. "Then come forth and let us parley."

Sylvano limped forward with his great sword once more across his shoulder and his hat upon his head. His men had washed his face with seawater, but purple blood still leaked down between his brows.

Doc bowed. "I am pleased you live, Senhor Barat, but I do wonder how."

Sylvano doffed his hat and tossed it to the sand. It thudded with far more weight than mere felt. "We feared there might be something of a hand-to-hand battle before the Sister Islanders broke. I wore a steel cap beneath my hat." He winced as he shook his head. "I will admit we did not expect massed slingers. What are your terms?"

"Simple." Doc leaned heavily on his cane. Exhaustion often exacerbated his mental illness and he struggled to focus. "You and your men will lay down all arms, powder and shot."

"I will not have my men tortured or humiliated."

"As you planned to do to the islanders?" Doc asked archly. He regretted it immediately as Sylvano stiffened.

"Be that as it may." Sylvano's voice was ragged with exhaustion, as well, but he spoke through clenched teeth. "My men are willing to die. You must also realize that though it will take time, my father will launch a second invasion, and beneath his banner there will be no mercy. Only I can stay his hand."

"Be that as it may, we will have your ships, your cannons and your rifled muskets. We will train the islanders in their use and with the steamer in our hands you will face the threat of counterinvasion."

Sylvano glanced at Doc's sword. "We could resume our duel."

"A battle between champions would save lives, and you and your men might honor it, but we both know your father never would. He would avenge your death no matter how honorable the circumstances, and these people will never willingly go back to being slaves."

"Then we are at an impasse."

"We are at nothing of the sort, Sylvano. You have fought with every honor in the name of your father the baron, but now, I pray you listen to the entreaty of humanity. Yield, and fear no reprisal. Simply lay down your arms, see to your wounded, and take three of the motorized boats to bring you and your brave soldiers home."

Sylvano gazed upon Doc warily. "And then?"

"And then a new relationship between these two islands will have to be negotiated in good faith." Doc shrugged. "Failing that, the slaughter of total war will still be available to you and yours, and ours."

Sylvano nodded. "I believe you are an honorable man, Dr. Tanner."

"By your lights I find honor in you, as well. I implore you to accept our terms."

Sylvano looked at J.B. "You agree?"

"Yeah," J.B. said. "Take your wounded. Leave your weapons. Go. Come back when you're willing to talk."

Sylvano saluted Doc with his sword and thrust it into the sand in surrender. "Very well, Dr. Tanner, I accept your terms and—"

"J.B.!" Jak shouted from the deck of the steamer. "Doc!" He pointed furiously out over the water. Night was falling. The sky had turned purple and across the strait the main island was little more than a dark mass. Except for the ville. It was lit by a yellow and orange glow. Black smoke lifted up into the night.

The ville was burning.

Doc looked to J.B. again. "Ryan?"

"No." Sylvano Barat pulled his sword from the sand. His eyes were terrible in the fading light. "Raul."

RYAN HAD AWOKEN to thunder, screaming and blaster-fire in the distance. He and Moni watched the ville burn. Ryan received word from refugees who had escaped the slaughter and up into the hills. Most were headed for the fortified farms. The mill foreman, Honore, and one of his men were among them. By all accounts the situation in the ville was grim. Honore said that at dusk explosions had rocked the ville proper. Long ago the men of the ville had walled off the preskydark sewer entrances, but the nightwalkers had been filching sulfur from the ville mine in the hills. Combined with potassium nitrate deposits scraped from their caves and the charcoal from their cook fires, they had been manufacturing their own very crude black powder for some time. They had blown the sewers open and emerged from the smoking holes like devils emerging from hell right in the middle of the ville. Baron Barat had left only a token force of sec men behind and they had been swiftly overwhelmed.

"The baron?" Ryan asked.

Honore sat on a stump. His ghostly, bald head was nearly black with bruising. His leather apron was caked with blood and a sledgehammer lay across his knees. "Raul crucified him, or so I am told. I know not whether he is alive or dead."

Ryan eased his arm out of its sling. He felt a sick ache in his elbow where the needle had been ripped free, but at the moment he wasn't bleeding through the bandage. "How many?"

"A hundred? Two hundred. It was hard to tell. They were everywhere at once. They took the sec station first. I heard the families of the shore battery crews were taken hostage. The artillerymen have run out the weapons and are manning them under duress in the eventuality of Sylvano or your friends returning. Though I hear many people are holed up in the church. Raul was a pious young man before he turned, and it seems so far he has been unwilling to blow it up."

"You're heading for the farms?"

"It is the only safe place left."

"Not safe at all. The nightwalkers have black powder. They'll isolate each farm, and then dig you out like ticks."

"You destroyed the powder mill!" Honore glared. "The remaining stocks in the ville are in the night-walkers' hands! What would you have us do?"

"Retake the ville," Ryan answered.

"Retake it?" The foreman shook his head. "You're mad."

"We take the med wag. Drive from farm to farm. Have the owners gear up for battle. Free the slaves."

"Free the slaves!" the foreman spluttered. "You would—"

"Give any man who isn't too old to swing it an ax, a pick, a shovel, anything heavy that comes to hand."

"I—"

"You come with me to convince the farm holders. Moni will talk to the slaves. Have your man here start rounding up refugees coming up the road and get them organized. You'll be safer in numbers." Ryan needed the foreman and decided to take a chance. He held out one of the auto-blasters he had taken from the clinic. "Here. Take this. We don't have much time."

Chapter Twenty-Five

The steamer chugged across the strait. J.B. examined their fighting force and thought about the battle to come. It wasn't good. Sylvano had thirty men left. His men were brave and well trained, but the mutated form of porphyria that afflicted them made most of them bleeders, and they didn't respond well to open wounds. Thirty was all the baron's son could muster that would not bleed out if they went back into action. The casualties had been horrific on both sides. The survivors had turned the church into a hospital ward, and the remaining pews were full of the wounded and dying. Mildred was swamped. Krysty could barely stand, but she was assisting as she could. J.B. ran a grim eye over Sylvano's thirty chosen men and their rifled muskets. The ville men were desperately low on gunpowder. Sylvano had told them of Ryan's escapades and the destruction of the powder mill and the clinic. J.B. looked at the Sister Isle contingent.

After the battle on the beach Doc had explained to the islanders that the ville was under attack and that he was going to save it from the nightwalkers. Most of the surviving Sons of the Sun had said let it burn, but Doc was walking with some pretty big medicine at the moment. He'd said he was going to ask for volunteers. Ago had raised the sun banner behind him. Fifty had agreed to follow Doc, Ago and the flag across the strait. They had appropriated powder and shot bags from fallen sec men and filled them with sling stones, and resharpened their spears.

Most of them were currently seasick and vomiting over the rail.

"How many nightwalkers?" J.B. asked.

Sylvano looked up from running a stone over the edge of his great blade. "An interesting question." He looked to his sister.

Zorime's eyes never left the approaching glow of the burning ville. They gleamed with unshed tears. "We keep a census of those who are driven out of the ville and into the caves. However, we have evidence that they often keep growing until even their mutant strength is not enough to let them walk or function. On the other hand, they breed among themselves down in the dark, as well as steal occasional slave women from the farms. How many turn into true nightwalkers? How many are stillborn or unsustainable freaks? It is hard to determine. I will tell you that five years ago my uncle made a demand for more food to be left by the cave entrances. That implies population growth."

"Yes." Sylvano sheathed his sword. "And while my uncle Raul is insane, he would not have made his move to take the ville if he did not believe he had the strength."

Jak shrugged. "Fifty less."

"Yes, and I cannot believe my uncle was willing to simply sacrifice them. He will expect that we routed your forces. I believe his plan was to have his brethren turn on us in the night."

"Then we might have surprise," J.B. said.

"Possibly," Sylvano mused. "But how to employ it?

If Raul holds the ville, then he has the harbor guns. He can run them out and blow us out of the water when we sail in."

"Caves," Jak said.

"The caves?" Sylvano dismissed the idea. "They are extensive. The island is riddled with them. We could wander them for days."

"Nightwalkers? Down there generations," Jak countered. "Plenty sign."

"He's right," Doc said. "Your people never go down in the caverns because that is where evil dwells, but that is the point. It dwells there, and has lived there for an age. The inhabited sections and paths will show evidence of long use."

"That may be the case," Sylvano said. "But I have proposed going down in the caves before, always with at least a hundred men, with all the modern blasters of the ville, powder charges and smoke of the Lotus. I fear what we might meet down there, and it is the brethren's territory. They will have every advantage."

"Sylvano." Zorime spoke quietly. "This is our uncle Raul's night of terror, his night of triumph. He won't have held back a reserve. For that matter, once the slaughter started in the ville, I doubt he could hold any of them back. They will be fully committed to their—" Zorime's tears spilled as she contemplated what had to be happening to her friends and kinsmen "—revelry."

"You are right. Very well, let us do as Senhor Jak says. We shall go through the caves and come out among them."

Doc cleared his throat. "I do not doubt our brave islanders' courage, but seeing as the nightwalkers are their very image of the devil, I am not sure they will follow us down into their subterranean lair. It is their hell. It may be too much to ask of them."

Everyone had to admit Doc had a point.

"And we need a diversion," J.B. said. "Something to make them look the other way."

"Very well." Sylvano rose to his full height. "I propose this. If we come, Raul will expect us to come in cannons and rockets blazing. I say we do. Senhor J.B., your leg is wounded. You will take command of the ship and the cannon. Sail into the harbor, then let yourself be driven back. That will draw their attention."

J.B. had been given better assignments. "You?"

"I will lead my men through the beach cave. I would like Dr. Tanner to accompany me. Should we emerge successfully I will fire a blue rocket. Once we are engaged, come in and attack again if you are still afloat."

J.B. looked at the islanders. "Them?"

"The slaves? I see little they can—"

"Not slaves!" Jak snarled.

"Veterans now," J.B. agreed. He looked at Sylvano coldly. "And every man a volunteer. You show some respect, or you can forget about your ville and we can finish our battle right here on the deck of this tub."

Zorime put a hand on her brother's shoulder. "Sylvano..."

Sylvano didn't need restraining. He looked over at the groaning, seasick men and sighed bleakly. "The Sons of the Sun," he corrected. "Very well. I agree with Dr. Tanner. They will most likely balk at the caverns and will serve no purpose on the ship. I propose they disembark with my forces, but approach the ville landward along the coast. Senhor Jak will lead them. At the signal they will attack inward from the seawall."

Jak shrugged.

J.B. pondered the three-pronged land, sea and subterranean attack. At night. With troops who hated each other. Sylvano seemed to read J.B.'s mind. He regarded the Armorer dryly. "What could possibly go wrong?"

Jak rolled his ruby-red eyes.

J.B. wished Ryan were here. "Kill the running lights. Head for the sea cave. We all attack on Sylvano's signal."

RYAN STOOD BEFORE his army. He had hoped for far more. Many of the farmers had refused to leave their families and their land. Others had flat-out refused to free their slaves, and Ryan didn't have the time or the manpower to try to force them. Two hundred and fifty men from among the islands farm holders had signed on. They were led by a young man named Balduino. He was too young and too inexperienced in Ryan's opinion, but apparently he was important and he was willing. Men came when he asked. His men were armed with single or double blasters. Most of those were scatterguns rather than longblasters, but at least they were loaded with lead instead of salt. Most of Balduino's men had swords and looked like they might know how to use them. Moni had managed to recruit five hundred slaves. They had been grudgingly promised their freedom, and return to Sister Isle, assuming there was anything left of it, if they fought. They limped behind their overlords uncertainly, fingering the farming implements that had been thrust into their hands.

Victory was far from certain, and Ryan suspected losses would be appalling regardless.

"Honore, tell Balduino he needs to creep as close as

he can to the ville. I'm going to take the med wag and ram the roadblock into the ville. When I'm in, they charge. He leads them."

"I will come with you."

Ryan stared down at the stout foreman. "Why?"

"Because I can drive a wag, and I am old and don't charge well anymore. I drive. You shoot."

"Fair enough," Ryan decided. "Ask for six volunteers with blasters to ride in back. We crash the roadblock and head straight for the sec station and try to take it. If we can't get to it, we head for the church. Either way that might be enough to distract them, and Balduino is inside before the nightwalkers know what happened. No mercy. We chill them all or go cold trying. Even if we fail and we hurt them bad enough, the rest of the farmsteads and Sister Islanders may have a shot of survival."

Honore stared up at Ryan. "Why would you do this?"

"If my friends are dead, I live or die with the ville. If they're alive, they need something to come back to besides nightwalkers and the shore blasters."

"You are a brave man."

"You just keep the wag on all four wheels when we crash the roadblock."

Every head turned as the seawall lit up with the flash and thud of cannon fire. Out in the harbor answering fire illuminated a ship. Even at this distance Ryan could tell that the shore blasters were far bigger, and there were more of them. Shells hit the seawall with little effect. The shore blasters found their range, and the second salvo was brutal. The steamer's crane tore from its moorings and fell across the deck, crushing crewmen. Two cannon balls punched into her side like explosive fists and ripped her belly open to the sea. The steamer got off two more badly aimed rounds that did little but dig craters in the beach. She limped toward the safety of the darkness beyond the harbor lights and the ranging buoys.

"So much for the sea assault," Ryan remarked.

Honore shook his head. "I do not believe Sylvano would give up so easily."

"Weight of shot. He's outgunned." Ryan shrugged. "Mebbe he's dead."

Honore grunted. "Perhaps."

Ryan strode to the med wag. "Pick your men, and let's hit them while they're celebrating."

DOC WALKED THROUGH Dante's Inferno. By torchlight the caverns of the nightwalkers were hell on earth. They stank of human waste, and the fire pits were full of human bones. In many of the chambers the embers of the fires were still glowing. The smell of roasted meat was fresh, and every man knew what kind of meat it was. The walls were painted with blood and charcoal and who knew what else. The artwork ranged from the abstract to childlike depictions of the horrific and the obscene.

The nursery was the worst.

Torches burned in crude sconces gouged out of the rock. Nearly two dozen infants and toddlers lay in cribs made of dried seaweed, feathers and scraps of cloth. Four filthy, brutally abused Sister Isle women in various states of pregnancy were bound on similar beds. The wet nurses were seven-foot mountains of bloated, swollen lactating flesh. They rolled forward ponderously, shrieking at the invaders and waving huge billets of driftwood. They fell beneath a fusillade of musket fire. The nightwalker offspring screamed and howled. Sylvano turned to his lieutenant in disgust. "Vasco, bayonets."

Doc was horrified. "Sylvano!"

Sylvano ignored him and nodded at Vasco. "Be swift."

"Baron Barat!" Doc shouted.

Sylvano froze. So did Vasco.

Doc pressed on. "If the ville is taken, then surely you are baron now, Sylvano. I implore you, as lord of the ville, do not do this."

"The nightmare ends here, Dr. Tanner. Tonight."

"You yourself have said the nightwalker gene does not always run true! And look beneath the filth! Are any of these children deformed? Indeed, do not some have the pink skin of Sister Isle blood? The populations of both islands have taken terrible losses this day. You will need these children! They are innocent, unknowing, and as human as you or I until if and when the change comes upon them in puberty. I implore you, Baron Barat, do not begin your reign with infanticide."

Sylvano stared into the middle distance wearily. "Very well, Vasco, stoke the fire to keep the children warm. We shall come back for them after the battle." His voice was bleak. "Or their parents will."

They continued through the twisting cavern system. They came to a chamber being used as a smokehouse and human limbs hung suspended over slow fires of driftwood and seaweed. Another cave was a storehouse containing hundreds of skulls. Doc's compass told him they were roughly paralleling the beach and he detected they were slowly moving downward. The passage ahead opened on a blackened hole of blasted brick that led into the ville's predark sewers. The sewers were a maze, but Sylvano seemed to know where he was going, and all they had to do was to follow the stench of burned powder and the muffled sounds of screaming above.

Doc clambered up the rusting ladder and arose from the underground like Orpheus ascending from Hades onto a side street.

The surface wasn't any better.

Half the ville was ablaze. Men, living and dead, were crucified on wagon wheels or hung from the eaves. Women were tied across barrels and sawhorses for whatever pleasure a passing nightwalker wished to take. Others turned on spits over cook fires. Nightwalkers tore charred flesh from human limbs like drumsticks, up-ended barrels of wine into their mouths and raped and killed. In the light of the bonfires and burning buildings they looked like the ogres, giants and trolls of Doc's childhood fairy tales. They wandered about the conquered ville like dogs drunk on slaughterhouse blood. Baron Xavier Barat hung nailed to a great *X* of timber in the middle of the ville square. What had been done to him beggared description. Yet he was still alive, and they had left him his eyes so that even out of the peeled-off mask of his face he might watch the rape and fall of the ville.

Without thought Doc drew his LeMat, put his front sight on the butchered baron's chest and fired. The baron's body sagged on the frame. Nightwalkers throughout the square looked up from their pleasures. Doc blinked and lowered his blaster. "Sylvano, I—"

"You saved me the sin of patricide." Baron Sylvano Barat barked out orders as his men came up onto the street. "Three ranks of ten! Vasco! Fire the rocket!" Vasco put punk to fuse and the signal rocket streaked up into the sky. It burst like a hard shimmering blue flower against the clear night. A dozen nightwalkers roared forward, waving war clubs. Sylvano barked out battle orders. “First rank, kneel!” The first rank knelt with their blasters leveled at the charging nightwalkers. The second rank took aim over the first. “First rank! Fire! Second rank! Fire!”

The rifled muskets rippled in volley fire and all but two of the pale giants toppled and fell. Sylvano put them down with a burst each from his auto-blaster. “Reload!” Two female nightwalkers came screaming from an alleyway waving stone-tipped spears. “Third rank!” Sylvano bellowed. “Fire!” The pair of she-things fell almost at Sylvano’s feet. “Reload!”

“First rank! Loaded!” Vasco called.

“Second rank! Lo—” A stone the size of a bowling ball crushed the skull of the second rank leader. A spear tore through another man’s back like the bolt from a siege engine.

“They are on the rooftops!” Doc shouted. He flicked the hammer on his LeMat and the blaster brutally recoiled as he fired the shotgun barrel. A nightwalker on the eaves above screamed and clutched its face as the cloud of buckshot shredded its skull.

“Fire at will! We make for the church!” Sylvano shouted. Doc followed the surge across the square. They lost two more men to stones and spears hurled out of the alleyways and from the rooftops. The nightwalkers faded back into the alleys and out of sight on the rooftops. Sylvano snarled as he fired bursts at shapes in the smoke. “Where is your friend Jak and the Sons of the Sun?”

“I do not know!” Doc started as a throw stick the size of a scythe whirled inches from his head and broke the neck of the man next to him. Doc fired at the thrower, but the nightwalker had already melted back into the night. “He is delayed!”

"Delayed..." Sylvano roared. "Chosen men! Form square!"

The remaining men formed a very small square and moved in good order with bayonets bristling across the ville main square.

Raul's voice boomed across the ville in mocking thunder. "You are too few, Nephew!"

Doc looked at the mutilated body of Xavier Barat in passing and then at the new baron of the ville. Sylvano's face was desperate.

"Your rate of fire too slow, Nephew!" Raul taunted.

They ran up the steps of the church, and Sylvano hammered the butt of his blaster on the massive door. "Open! I command you!"

The bars were thrown back and the chosen men spilled into the church. It was already packed to the rafters with refugees. Doc estimated over two hundred, most women and children. A young man with a scalp wound and wearing the robes of an acolyte greeted them as other men slammed the great door closed and barred it. "Sylvano! We—"

Sylvano's voice was iron. "Baron Barat."

The acolyte goggled. "Baron..."

"Where are the landowners and their men?"

"Barricaded, each in their own manses, Baron. Barricaded as we are. It is the only safe place."

"This church is not safe at all. The only reason the nightwalkers have not taken it already is because they do not wish to, and that keeping you bottled up here serves their purposes."

"What shall we do?"

The conversation was cut short by a deep, feminine voice calling out in singsong outside. "Oh, Sylvano, my dearest! I have a new lover now! Come out and meet him!"

"And whom is that?" Doc asked.

"Xadreque." Sylvano's long teeth ground. "The woman I loved." Sylvano raised his voice angrily. "Fight me, Uncle! Let this be between us!"

"Very well, Nephew! Let it be a duel. Let this battle be decided by champions!" Raul's voice boomed amiably. "Come out and let us see the man you've become!"

"You don't want to go out there," Doc advised.

"You are right. I do not." Sylvano unsheathed his great sword and handed his auto-blaster to Vasco. "If I slay my uncle, break out and charge. The nightwalkers may falter. If I fall, go out the back. Either way, make a fighting retreat of it to the beach and link up with the doctor's friend Jak. Take the pier if you can and get our people on boats."

"Baron?" Doc said. "I would come with you."

"Oh?"

"If this is a duel, then you will need a second."

Sylvano smiled bleakly. "Then I accept, Dr. Tanner. Come, let me introduce you to my uncle. Vasco, bolt the door behind us." The door was opened and Doc followed Sylvano down the steps onto the square. Doc gaped at a nightmare. Raul Barat strode out of the smoke with horrible casualness. Red-velvet drapes stolen from a house were belted about him with ropes in a toga of royalty. Laurels of woven branches crowned him in a twisted mockery of Roman splendor and the crucifixion. He carried a horrific, hafted blade with sickening ease in one hand. A woman well over six and half feet tall and similarly bedecked spooned into his side. She carried a net over her shoulder and a spear in her hand. Blood smeared both their mouths from feasting.

"Greetings, Nephew." Raul turned his ghoulish gaze up and down Doc. "Dr. Tanner, I presume." He looked at the huge sword in Sylvano's hands. "For me?"

"I had it forged specially." Sylvano nodded. "I named it Raulslayer."

Raul eyed the great blade. "Charming." He weighed the flensing blade in his hand. "You know the sad thing of it is, we have taken most of the ville's blasters, and yet our hands are too large to wield them." He plucked Xavier Barat's blaster out of his toga. "But my petite flower Xadreque has no such problems." He tossed the weapon to her.

The titaness caught it with a grin. "Goodbye, my love." Xadreque shot Sylvano through the head. The iron cap he wore beneath his hat could stop a stone but not a bullet and he fell dead to the ground.

"Foully done!" Doc shouted. His sword hissed from its cane. Instantly he knew he had made a mistake. He should have drawn his pistol and shot, but the shreds of his honor and the dark clouds of madness often fought within him. In this case they were in agreement. Xadreque pointed the blaster at Doc. He ignored her as he drew himself up and saluted his blade. "Raul Barat, I challenge you for the barony."

"I gave my dear brother the fate I had long planned for him. Sylvano died like the fool he was, but you, Dr. Tanner? My brother actually suggested a duel between you and I. Let us see what you can do." Raul's flensing blade hissed through the air like a razor-sharp meteor at Doc's head.

The duel was lopsided from the onset. Doc was a

scarecrow standing in front of a mountain. It was like a man with a toothpick battling a man armed with a shovel. Raul's reach was literally inhuman and his whale-breaking weapon threatened to shatter Doc's slender blade with every parry. All Doc could do was evade. Raul had every advantage Sylvano had had, but at twice his power level and even greater speed. Raul was as fearless as he was cruel, and he was insane. He played Doc like a cat with a mouse as Doc's strength flagged. The old man once more took refuge in the one thing he had faith in.

"Why do you smile, Dr. Tanner?" Raul enquired.

"Because I know something you do."

"Oh, and what is this mutual information we share that amuses you so?"

"That no matter what happens here, my friend Ryan will kill you."

Raul snarled and Doc hurled himself into a last desperate attack. At that moment explosion after explosion rocked the shore batteries and the call "Sons of the Sun!" rocked the seawall. Automatic blasterfire ripped into life on the inland edge of the ville followed by crashing and nightwalker screams. Raul disengaged and stepped back. All Doc could do was put his hands on his knees and wheeze in relief.

A twentieth-century ambulance came tearing down the main street of the ville with its lights flashing and siren blaring.

Chapter Twenty-Six

Ryan and Honore rammed the roadblock with the lights flashing and the siren wailing. The carts blocking the road came apart, and so did one of the nightwalkers behind them. The med wag's tires were from a carefully maintained stock of preskydark material, but the ancient rubber ripped off the steel belts as the wag fishtailed across the cobblestones from the impact. Honore struggled to keep the wag on course. Ryan leaned out of the passenger window, his blaster on full-auto. A nightwalker towered out from between two burning buildings, topping the roof of the wag by a head. Ryan shoved the submachine blaster out like a big pistol and held down the trigger. His burst walked up the giant from crotch to collar.

Behind them Balduino and his tiny army of landowners charged the broken roadblock. The new freemen of the main isle limped after them in a mob. The med wag caromed down the street toward the square. The men in the back shouted in alarm, and the wag swerved even more wildly as huge rocks and chunks of lumber struck the wag's sides. Honore hit the square and weaved through bonfires, barbecuing bodies, crucifixions and rape racks. Ryan's eye narrowed. Dead ahead Doc appeared to be in another fencing match. This time it was with Raul, and Doc appeared to be losing. "Step on it!"

Honore put the hammer down, and the med wag roared forward. Raul stepped away from Doc, and the old man collapsed. Ryan and Honore flinched as Xadreque emptied a blaster through the windshield. She hefted her spear and hurled it. The windshield of the wag proved no obstacle. Honore proved even less as the spear punched through his chest, his seat and a screaming ville man behind him. Ryan grabbed for the wheel and the windshield shattered completely as the wag hit Xadreque at forty miles per hour. The shredded tires lost their grip on the cobbles, and Ryan braced himself as the wag flipped. Ryan's world spun and became one of flying glass, screaming metal and brutal impact. The wag rolled three times, but it felt like a hundred. It came to rest on its roof like an overturned turtle.

A huge hand snaked through the empty windshield and bodily ripped Ryan out of the wag and hurled him to the cobbles. Ryan rolled and came up on one knee. Raul stood in front of him, limned in firelight like a colossus. "Good evening, Senhor Cawdor."

Ryan looked about him.

Doc was on his hands and knees throwing up. Things looked better elsewhere. There was a full-on battle raging on the seawall. Another was shaping up within the ville proper as Balduino and his men surged inside and engaged. Sec men were emerging from the church in good order with bayonets fixed. The ship Ryan had seen exchanging cannonades was back in the harbor. It was smoking, but still heading for the pier. "Looks like you lost, Raul."

Raul smiled. "You know? Your friend Dr. Tanner said that no matter what happened, you were going to kill me."

"Doc's right." Ryan considered a lunge for Doc's LeMat, but he knew he'd never make it. Sylvano lay closer. Ryan very slowly picked up the fallen blade Raulslayer where it lay beside Sylvano and rose to his feet. "I'm going to cut off your head."

Raul's hunting scream shook the sky as he attacked.

Ryan felt the damaged vein in his left elbow reopen as he flung the great blade underhanded like a harpoon. The six-foot sword was a clumsy missile, but it was heavy and it flew point-first, and Raul's insane blue eyes went wide at the unexpected danger. Raulslayer rang like a bell, and Raul's flensing blade bent as he batted the flying sword aside. Ryan closed the distance between them with his panga already in hand. The shaving-sharp blade whispered in. Purple ichor flew as Raul's arm opened from wrist to elbow. Raul roared and Ryan ducked. The return swing of the flensing blade literally clipped an inch off the top of Ryan's unruly black locks as Raul sought to open his opponent's skull from temple to temple.

Ryan was no swordsman, but he and Raul fought with chopping blades, and machete fighting was a science unto itself. It was a science that Ryan had assiduously mastered. He stayed within the giant's reach, dancing in the jaws of the serpent so that he could land his blows. Ryan cut and cut again. He relieved Raul of his left little finger. The panga passed across Raul's ribs, but the giant's bones and muscle were so thick it was impossible to make a killing cut. Raul was just as fast as Ryan but at a cubed power level. Like Doc, all Ryan had in his corner was experience. Raul had been trained as a swordsman in his youth, but now he wielded a flensing blade and he had spent the intervening decade terrorizing slaves in the night. Cuts weren't enough. Raul wasn't afraid of bleeding to death. Ryan's death consumed him, and his strength and stamina were far beyond human.

Raul accepted a cut across his collarbones that was meant for his throat and swung with all his might. Ryan had no room to dodge. All he could do was put his panga in the way. Sparks shrieked off the blade as the flensing knife shaved metal. It didn't stop the blow, but it was enough to turn it. Ryan took the flat in the chest rather than the edge.

Nevertheless it was like being slapped in the chest with a cast-iron pan by a man who was eight feet tall. Ryan's heart made a fist as he was flung backward. Instinct took over and he rolled as he hit the cobbles. Raul bore down with his blade held overhead in both hands for the killing blow.

Ryan threw his panga.

It revolved once and punched into Raul three inches below the rope belting his toga and sank to the hilt into his bladder. Raul screamed in real agony. Ryan tottered two steps and grabbed Doc's swordstick and drew the rapier. Raul put up his giant hands to protect himself, and Ryan lunged low. Raul screamed as Doc's blade entered his bowels beside the panga. Ryan staggered back as Raul fell to his knees, clutching at his belly with his viscera full of steel.

Ryan picked up Raulslayer.

The cutting edge had been brutally turned by Raul's parry, but the great sword had two of them. Blood spurted out of Ryan's left arm as he wearily bore the sword aloft in both hands. Ryan swung. Raul fell forward to hands and knees as the blade his nephew had forged to slay him bit into the bull-like muscles of his neck. Ryan swung the blade like a man chopping wood. With the third blow Raul's Frankensteinian skull left his shoulders and rolled across the cobblestones. His body collapsed, fountaining blood and fluids.

Ryan dropped to his knees and leaned on the great blade. It was the only thing holding him up.

Doc crawled over and shoved his kerchief against Ryan's elbow. He gasped as he spoke. "I am sorry…I tried…I tried as hard as I could…"

"I get the feeling you did real good today, Doc."

Doc was done. The Blood of the Lotus had left him. His strength was gone, and madness and exhaustion danced around his damaged mind, but a flicker of sanity surged at Ryan's rare praise. "You should have been there. The battle for the Sister Isle…" A smile cracked across Doc's fatigued face. "We were something to see."

"You can tell me about it late—"

Ryan stopped as Doc dropped face-first and twitching to the stones of the square. The one-eyed man eased Doc's LeMat out and leaned on the great sword like a crutch as half a dozen sec men ran forward. Blood stained their bayonets. Ryan cocked back the antique blaster's hammer. The sec men stared back and forth between Ryan, Raul, Doc and Sylvano. Their leader eyed Ryan uncertainly. "I am Vasco."

"Yeah?"

"I am Sylvano's second in command."

Ryan nodded at Sylvano's corpse. "Looks like you're first now."

Vasco started. "I…do not claim the barony."

Ryan regarded the blasters and bayonets that weren't quite pointed at him. "Neither do I."

"Then you want—"

"I want to get Doc off the ground and someplace safe."

Doc feebly shoved himself into a sitting position. "I am all right."

He wasn't, but at least he was lucid. Ryan and Vasco turned as a small army came marching up from the seawall. Jak led a band of spear- and sling-armed Sister Islanders. J.B. was limping alongside Zorime, and a small contingent of ville sailors and sec men from the boat. Zorime stood for long moments looking at the butchered, crucified thing that had been her father. Then she cried out and ran to her brother. Ryan looked at his friends. "Where's Krysty?"

"Back on Sister Isle," J.B. said. "She did her Gaia thing during the battle, but she's okay. She and Mildred are tending the wounded."

"Saw your sea battle."

"It was a diversion." J.B. shrugged. "Looks like it worked."

Ryan nodded. "Jak?"

Jak shrugged. "Snuck up. Blew shore battery powder stores. Took seawall."

Zorime looked up from her brother.

"You should know your brother died going forward," Doc said. "Sword in hand. I was with him."

Balduino and his force of landowners reached the square, followed by the limping mob of ex-slaves. They looked to have lost half their number. "My lady?"

"I am baron now. What is the situation?" Zorime asked.

"We killed at least fifty nightwalkers. The rest have fled the ville for the hills. I did not think pursuit wise.

My men are too few and the…freed men?" He sighed and looked at the hobbled left foot of an ex-slave. "Cannot give chase. I thought it best to secure the ville first and then mount a proper hunt in the morning."

Ryan scanned the rooftops. The surviving nightwalkers had pulled a fade. "Jak?"

"Killed least as many," Jak said. "More."

"We slew fifty more on the other island," Doc said.

"Then they are crushed and leaderless." Zorime rose from her brother's side. "And by the population rolls I would think there can be fewer than fifty functioning adults left. The survivors will head back to the caves. Some will undoubtedly go feral in the hills. All must be hunted down. Vasco, secure the ville. Balduino, take a heavily armed patrol and visit each farmstead. Tell them we have retaken the ville and to be armed and ready for the hunt at dawn."

Balduino gave Ryan a hard look. "Baron, you should know that this one destroyed both the clinic and the powder mill."

Zorime flinched as the mess she had inherited kept getting messier. "I suppose that was to be expected."

Balduino shook his head. "And what is to be done about this?"

The freed men and the men of the Sister Isle had begun mingling. Many fathers, uncles and sons were tearfully reuniting, and the younger generation was quickly swelling with anger as they saw how their elders had been hobbled and enslaved.

"First tend to the wounded, theirs and ours," Zorime ordered. "Then break out the festival caldrons and open the storehouses. Feeding them will be a first step."

"Baron." Doc rose shakily to his feet, and Ago rushed

over to support him. "Though it grieves me, there is something I must tell you."

"What more can you add to this night, Dr. Tanner?"

"Simply this. You told me the story of your people, and the refugee fleet who were the Sister Islander's ancestors. They know the story now, as well. I warn you, if it is your intention to drug these people at feast and then cull them like you did their forebears, they are forewarned. You should also take into consideration that you have scores of wounded back on Sister Isle, and sufferance of the islanders is at its limit. If you betray these men here, my friends Krysty and Mildred will not be able to stop the answering slaughter across the strait."

"I admit the idea did occur to me, Dr. Tanner." Zorime looked out across the burning ville. "However, we will need every man."

"Every slave goes free," Ryan said. "Or the battle begins again right here."

"You misunderstand me, Senhor Cawdor. Both islands have sustained terrible casualties, and nearly all of it among the able-bodied male populations. We are all going to have to start making babies very quickly, and if the curse of the nightwalkers, indeed the porphyric curse of my people is to end—" Zorime gave Ago and his oxlike physique a frank look of appraisal "—then a great deal more interbreeding will be required between our two islands."

Balduino and Vasco made appalled noises.

Zorime cut them off with an imperious glare. "I believe I gave you both orders." Ryan noted that Zorime wasn't having many problems assuming the mantle of the barony. "Take Dr. Tanner back to the manse and make him comfortable."

"I will not rest until my friend Ryan is attended to," Doc protested.

Zorime nodded. "I will see to it personally."

Chapter Twenty-Seven

"Lover!" Krysty jumped up from a wounded islander she was tending and ran to the church door and the man filling it. As she hurled herself into Ryan's arms, he winced. Krysty ran her hands over him and her beautiful face clouded with concern. She had seen Ryan in bad shape before, but he currently looked like a poorly dressed side of beef wearing boots. "What happened?"

Ryan touched his face, his arm and his side. "Shot, hooked, stabbed, bled, was in a wag wreck, some giant bitch tried to pull my balls off." Ryan shrugged. "I got salted. A lot. How's it here?"

Krysty sighed and looked at the blood on her hands and clothes. "Mildred did her best, but we lost a lot of the wounded. The ville people are bleeders, and the islanders charged massed blasterfire. They've got a couple of midwives and herbalists here, good enough for a fever or a broken leg, but they don't have anything for or any experience with bullet holes. It's been bad. Where're the rest of us?"

"J.B. did a deal with the new baron, Zorime. He's helping the blacksmith service the ville weapons and help get powder back in production again. In return they're going to fill our mags. Doc's resting up in the baron's manse drinking something called Madeira and reading books. Jak persuaded the Sister Isle detachment to stay and help with the hunt, but they've also been going from farm to farm to make sure the baron keeps her word and the slaves are really free. The farmholders aren't happy about it, but it's hard to argue with three hundred men at your door."

"So what're we going to do?" Krysty asked.

"The baron has given us permission to stay as long as we want on either island, and Ago doesn't want us to go ever. I figure mebbe we take them up on their hospitality. Lie up for a week before moving on. According to Zorime, the mat-trans should be on a fresh cycle now, and at the start no one gets left behind traveling from this end."

"Baron Zorime," Krysty mused. "She's very beautiful."

Ryan didn't mention that she had offered herself to him to open up the population drive while she tended his wounds, or that he had politely refused. He did relate what happened next. "She summoned Ago to her manse to 'negotiate' terms, and word is they haven't been out of her bedroom in twenty-four hours."

Krysty laughed. "She didn't waste much time."

"She doesn't have much time." Ryan looked around the makeshift hospital ward. "None of them do. Both islands are pretty much defenseless now, and both need to get their crops in. It's going to take a lot of negotiating both in and out of beds to make up the shortfall of manpower around here."

"Well, you know, lover?" Krysty ran her eyes up and down Ryan's battered frame speculatively. "I'm feeling a shortfall of manpower myself."

"Oh, yeah?"

"Yeah."

Ryan's scrotum still ached from the mauling

Xadreque had given it, but he figured there was a good chance Krysty could figure out something to make him feel better. Krysty was a skilled healer with talented hands, and pretty much a talented everything else. Ryan grinned lopsidedly at the best thing in his life. "I know a guy who might loan me a hut tonight."

"Mildred and I have been sharing Father Joao's cottage." Krysty grinned back. "It has a real bed."

"I know a guy who's gonna loan Mildred his hut tonight."

"Go have a nap. I'll be along."

Ryan limped off to Father Joao's cottage and flopped on a bed with blankets that smelled like Krysty's hair. He closed his eyes, and it wasn't long before he reopened them to find Krysty sitting on the bed naked beside him with a bucket of hot water and a cloth. She moved over his wounds with her hands, her lips, her breasts and hot water. Ryan wasn't surprised to find himself rising to the occasion.

Krysty Wroth was a resourceful girl.

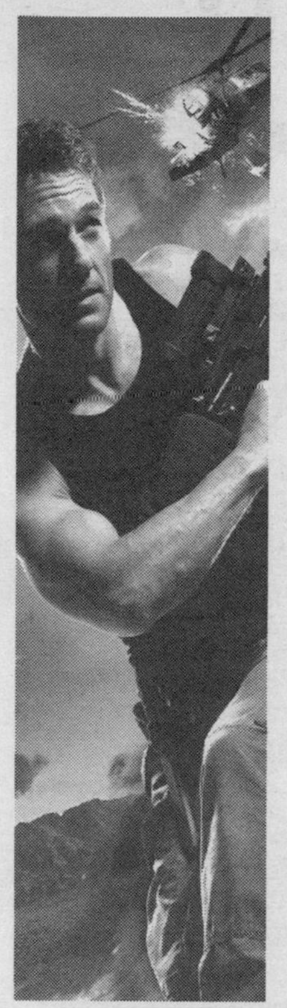

Sabotage

Someone is sabotaging the U.S. military...and The Executioner is taking it personally.

A series of assassinations of U.S. soldiers returning from the Iraq and Afghanistan wars is followed by horrific revelations in the media of atrocities supposedly committed by the American military. Stepping in to investigate, Bolan does not find a serial killer... but instead a "peace" activist looking to deliver the U.S. into the hands of the Communist Chinese!

Available in April wherever books are sold.

Or order your copy now by sending your name, address, zip or postal code, along with a check or money order (please do not send cash) for $6.99 for each book ordered ($7.99 in Canada), plus 75¢ postage and handling ($1.00 in Canada), payable to Gold Eagle Books, to:

In the U.S.
Gold Eagle Books
3010 Walden Avenue
P.O. Box 9077
Buffalo, NY 14269-9077

In Canada
Gold Eagle Books
P.O. Box 636
Fort Erie, Ontario
L2A 5X3

Please specify book title with your order.
Canadian residents add applicable federal and provincial taxes.

www.readgoldeagle.blogspot.com

GSB133